author of over 70 works and the
winner of a host of prizes including
the National Book Award and a
Guggenheim Fellowship. Oates
is Professor of the Humanities at
Princeton University.

Also by Joyce Carol Oates

The Barrens

Beasts

Rape: A Love Story

The Female of the Species: Tales of Mystery and Suspense

The Museum of Dr. Moses

A Fair Maiden

Give Me Your Heart: Tales of Mystery and Suspense

The Corn Maiden and Other Nightmares

Daddy Love

Evil Eye: Four Novellas of Love Gone Wrong

High Crime Area: Tales of Darkness and Dread

Jack of Spades: A Tale of Suspense

JOYCE CAROL OATES

THE DOLL-MASTER

AND OTHER TALES OF TERROR

A Mysterious Press Book
for Head of Zeus

First published in 2016 by Mysterious Press,
an imprint of Grove/Atlantic, New York.

This paperback edition first published in the UK in 2016 by Head of Zeus Ltd.

9 7 5 3 1 2 4 6 8

A catalogue record for this book is available from the British Library.

ISBN (PB): 9781784971038
ISBN (E): 9781784971007

Printed and bound by CPI Group (UK) Ltd, Croydon, CR0 4YY

MIX
Paper from
responsible sources
FSC® C020471

Head of Zeus Ltd,
Clerkenwell House
45-47 Clerkenwell Green,
London EC1R 0HT
WWW.HEADOFZEUS.COM

To Danel Olson

THE DOLL-MASTER

Contents

The Doll-Master   1

Soldier   33

Gun Accident: An Investigation   75

Equatorial   143

Big Momma   223

Mystery, Inc.   261

The Doll-Master

for Ellen Datlow

"You can hold her. But don't drop her."

Solemnly my little cousin Amy spoke. And solemnly Amy held out to me her beloved doll.

It was a baby-doll, in baby-clothes, a little top adorned with pink baby ducklings and on the tiny baby-doll-feet, little pink booties. And a baby-diaper, white, with a silver safety pin.

A soft fleshy baby-doll with a placid baby-face, malleable baby-fingers and fleshy little baby-arms and -legs that could be manipulated, to a degree. The baby-hair was fine and blond and curly and the baby-eyes were slate-blue marble, that opened and closed as you tilted the doll backward or forward. There is a scary ticklish sensation you feel when you see a baby close up because you think that the baby could be hurt and this is how I felt about Baby Emily though she was *only a doll* . . .

My cousin Amy was three years old which was younger than my age by eleven months. This is what we were told. A birthday is an important event in our family, our parents said.

Amy was the daughter of my mother's younger sister who was my Aunt Jill. So, Mommy explained, Amy was my *cousin*.

I was a little jealous sometimes. Amy could talk better than I could and adults liked to talk to her marveling at her "speech skills" which made me feel bad, for nobody marveled at mine.

Amy was a little girl, shorter than me. Smaller all over than me.

It was strange—friends of our mothers thought it was "darling"—to see such a small child as Amy clutching a baby doll. Fussing and fretting over Baby Emily as Amy's mother fussed and fretted over her.

Even pretending to "nurse" Baby Emily with a tiny baby bottle filled with milk. And "changing" Baby Emily's diaper.

Between her fleshy baby-legs, Baby Emily was smooth. There was no way for Baby Emily to soil her diaper.

I did not remember ever soiling my diaper. I do not remember now. I am inclined to think that, as a baby, I did not have to wear a diaper but that is probably inaccurate, and irrational. For I was a fully normal (boy) infant, I am sure. If there were "accidents" in the night especially, in my pj's as my mother called them, I do not remember.

I do not remember "nursing," either. I think that I was "nursed" from a bottle.

All this is a very long time ago. It's natural not to remember.

You can hold her. But don't drop her—these were Amy's words which I do remember. They were an echo of an adult mother's words which you often hear.

* * *

It was a terrible surprise in the family, when Amy *passed away*.

At first they said that Amy was "going to the clinic for tests." Then, they said that Amy would be "in the hospital for a few days." Then, they said that Amy would "not be coming home from the hospital."

In all this time, I was not taken to the hospital to see Amy. I was told that my cousin would be home, soon—"You can see her then, sweetie. That will be soon enough."

And, "Your cousin is very tired right now. Your cousin needs to sleep, and rest, and get strong again."

Afterward, I would learn that it was a rare blood sickness my cousin had. It was a kind of leukemia and very fast-acting in young children.

When they said that Amy would not be coming home, I did not say anything. I did not ask any questions. I did not cry. I was *stony faced*, I overhear my aunt saying to my mother. I wondered if to be *stony faced* was a bad thing, or a good thing. For then, people let you alone.

If you cried, they tried to comfort you. But if you were *stony faced* they let you alone.

It was around this time that I stole Baby Emily out of Amy's room. We were often at my aunt's house and while my mother and my aunt were crying together I went to Amy's room and lifted Baby Emily from my cousin's bed where the doll was lying with other, less interesting dolls and stuffed toys as if someone had flung them all down, and had not even made up the bed properly.

3

I did not think that my parents knew that I'd stolen Baby Emily inside my jacket, and brought her home with me. But later, I would realize that probably they knew, as my aunt knew, and did not say anything to me; they did not discipline me.

Talk was all of Amy, for a long time. If you entered a room and adults were speaking in lowered voices, they would cease at once. Bright adult faces turned toward you: "Hello, Robbie!"

I was too young to consider whether such a rare blood sickness might be "genetic"—that is, carried in the blood from one generation to the next.

When I was older I would research *leukemia* on the Internet. But still, I would not know.

When I was alone with Baby Emily we cried because we missed Amy. I did not cry because Amy was *dead* only because Amy was *gone*.

But I had Amy's baby-doll. I snuggled with Baby Emily in my bed and that made me feel better, a little.

When I was five years old, and going to preschool, Baby Emily disappeared from my room.

I was so surprised! I looked under the bed and in the closet and in each of my bureau drawers and then I looked in all these places again as well as beneath the covers at the foot of the bed but Baby Emily was gone.

I ran to my mother, crying. I asked my mother where Baby Emily was for there was no secret about my cousin's doll-baby now. My mother told me that my father "didn't think it was a good idea" for me to be playing with a doll at my age. Dolls are for girls, she said. Not boys. "Daddy just thought it might be better to take the doll away before you got 'too attached' . . ." Guiltily my mother spoke, and there was softness in her voice, but nothing I said could change her mind, no matter how I cried, or how angry I became, slapping and kicking at her and saying how I hated her, my mother did not change her mind because my father would not allow it. "He said he'd 'indulged' you long enough. And he blames me."

In place of Baby Emily who was so sweet and placid and smelled of foam-rubber my father had instructed my mother to buy me an "action toy"—one of the new-model expensive ones— a U.S. Navy SEAL robot-soldier that came fully armed, and could move forward across the room, empowered by a battery.

I would never forgive either of them, I thought. But particularly, I would never forgive *him*.

The first of the *found dolls* was Mariska.

"Take her. But don't drop her."

My Friend spoke quietly, urgently. Glancing about to see if anyone was watching. Many times I'd walked to school, and home from school, avoiding the school bus where there were older boys who taunted me. My family's house was at the top of Prospect Hill above the city and looking toward the river which was often wreathed in mist. The middle school was about a mile down the hill along a route I'd come to memorize. Often I took shortcuts through alleys and across backyards where I moved swiftly with the furtiveness of a wild creature. This street was

Catamount with a narrow lane that ran parallel behind it past six-foot wooden fences beginning to rot, trash cans and piles of debris.

My Friend said *Never make eye contact. That way they don't see you, either.*

No one ever saw me. For I moved quickly and furtively. And if they saw me at a distance they saw only a boy—a young boy with a blurred face.

My Friend was very tall. Taller than my father. I had never looked directly at my Friend (who forbade it) but I had a sense that my Friend had features sharp and cunning as a fox's and his natural way of moving was agile as a fox's and so I had to half-run to keep up with my Friend who was inclined to impatience.

"Take her! No one is watching."

Mariska was a beautiful ceramic doll very different from Baby Emily. Mariska had creamy ceramic-skin and on her cheeks two patches of rouge. She was dressed in the dirndl-costume of an Eastern European peasant—white blouse, full skirt and apron, white cotton stockings and boots. Her blond hair was braided into two plaits and she had a rosebud mouth and blue eyes with thick blond lashes. It was strange to touch Mariska's skin which was a hard and unyielding ceramic-skin except where it had been cracked and broken.

Mariska's arms were outspread in surprise, that such a prettily dressed blond girl with plaited hair and blue eyes could be allowed to topple from a porch railing into the mud, her hair soiled, her skirt soiled and torn and the white stockings filthy.

And her legs were at an odd angle to one another as if the left had been twisted at the hip.

Walking with my Friend along the lane behind Catamount Street and between the rotted boards of a fence we saw Mariska. My Friend gripped my hand tight so that the bones hurt.

She is our prize. She is the one we've been waiting for. Hurry! Take her! No one will see.

It was a thundery dark afternoon. I was shivering with cold or with excitement. For my Friend had appeared walking beside me with no warning. Often I did not see my Friend for days, or a week. Then, my Friend would appear. But I was forbidden to look at his face.

When my Friend came into my life, I am not certain. Mariska came into my life when I was in eighth grade and so it was earlier than that time.

Mariska's house was one of the ugly asphalt-sided houses down the hill. Not just one family lived in the house but several families for it was a *rental*, as my mother said.

These were people who lived *down the hill* as my mother said. They were not people who lived *on the hill* as we did.

Yet, children played here. Played and shouted and laughed here at the foot of Prospect Hill which was so very different from the crest of Prospect Hill where my family had lived for decades.

Because of the steep hill, a flight of wooden steps led down from the crude porch at the rear of Mariska's house to the rutted ground ten or fifteen feet below. But no one walked here much—the ground was covered in debris, even raw garbage.

Mariska had fallen from the porch railing where someone had carelessly set her. I thought this must have happened.

Unless Mariska had been tossed from the porch, by someone who had tired of her rouged cheeks, rosebud mouth, colorful peasant costume.

My Friend said eagerly *She is our prize. No one else can claim her now.*

My Friend said *Lift her! And put your hand over her mouth.*

My Friend said *Inside your jacket. Walk quickly. Don't run! Take the back way.*

Mariska was heavier than you would think. A ceramic doll is a heavy doll.

Mariska's arms and legs were awkwardly spread. By force, I managed to subdue them.

I could not hide Mariska in my room where she would be found by my mother or our housekeeper. I could not hide Mariska anywhere in the house though it was a large house with three stories and many of its rooms shut off. So I brought her to the "carriage house"—which was used as a garage for my parents' vehicles and as a place for storage and where I believed the beautiful ceramic doll would be safe, wrapped in canvas many times and placed in one of the horse stalls in the cobwebby shadow.

It had been proudly recounted to me: my father's grandfather had been mayor of the capital city six miles to the south which was now a *racially troubled city with a high crime rate*. After my father's grandfather was no longer mayor he'd moved his family to Prospect Hill in this suburb of mostly white people beside the Delaware River. In those days there'd been horses in the carriage house, in four stalls at the rear, and still you could smell the animals, a faint odor of dried manure, horse-sweat, hay. Here, I knew that Mariska would be safe. I would come to visit her when I wished. And Mariska would always, always be there, where I had left her, wrapped in canvas for safekeeping.

When my Friend did not come to me I was very lonely but if there had been horses in the stable, as there had been in my great-grandfather's time, I would not have been so lonely.

My parents had warned me not to "play" in the carriage house. The roof leaked badly and was partly rotted. There was a second floor that sagged in the middle as if the boards had become rubbery. Only the front part of the carriage house was used now for my parents' vehicles and the rest was filled with abandoned things—furniture, tires, an old broken tricycle of mine, a baby buggy, cardboard boxes. Nothing was of use any longer, but nothing was thrown away.

Hornets built their nests beneath the eaves. The buzzing was peaceful if the hornets were not disturbed.

No one had told me exactly but I knew: my father's family had been well-to-do until the early 1960s; then, the family business had gone into decline. Bitterly my father spoke of *overseas competition.*

Still, the house on Prospect Hill was one of the old, large houses envied by others. There were real estate investments that continued to yield income and my father was an accountant for a prosperous business of which he spoke with some pride. My father was not a distinguished man or in any way unusual except for living in one of the old, large houses on Prospect Hill which he had inherited from his father. I thought that my father might have loved me more, if he had been more successful.

"What a terrible thing! Now it's coming *here*."

The terrible thing was not a robbery or a burglary or an arson-set fire or a shooting-murder but a little girl missing here in our suburban town and not in the capital city six miles to the south. The news was in all the papers and on TV and radio. Such excitement, it was like dropping a lighted match into dried hay—you could not guess what would erupt from such a small act.

At our school we were ushered into assembly and announcements made by the principal and a police officer in a uniform. The little girl who was missing was in fourth grade and lived on Catamount Street and we were warned not to speak with strangers or go anywhere with strangers and if any stranger approached us, to run away as quickly as possible and notify our parents or our teachers or Mrs. Rickett who was our principal.

At the same time, it was suspected that the little girl who'd disappeared had been kidnapped by her own father who lived in New Brunswick. The father was arrested and questioned but claimed to know nothing about his daughter.

For days there was news of the missing girl. Then, news of the missing girl faded. Then, ceased.

Once a child is *gone*, she will not return. That was a truth we would learn in middle school.

Mariska was safe in her hiding place, in the farthest horse stall in the old stable at the rear of the carriage house behind our house where no one would ever look.

It was not my fault that my cousin Amy *went away* and left me.

All your life, you yearn to return to what has been. You yearn to return to those you have lost. You will do terrible things to return, which no one else can understand.

The second *found doll* was not until I was in ninth grade.

Annie was a pretty-faced girl-doll with skin like real skin to touch except some of the dye had begun to wear off and you could see the gray rubber beneath which was shivery and ugly.

Annie was a small doll, not so large and heavy as Mariska. She wore a cowgirl costume with a suede skirt, a shiny-buckled belt, a shirt with a little suede vest and a little black tie, and on her feet were cowboy boots. She had been partly broken, one of her arms was dislocated and turned too easily in its shoulder socket, and her red-orange curly hair had come out in patches to reveal the rubber scalp beneath.

What was pretty about Annie was her placid blue-violet marble eyes and the freckles on her face that made you want to smile. Her eyes, like Baby Emily's eyes, shut when you leaned her backward, and opened when you leaned her forward.

My Friend had seen Annie first, in the park near my house. Beyond the playground where children shouted and laughed swinging on the swings there was a little grove of picnic tables and beneath one of the tables in which initials had been carved and gouged the cowgirl-doll lay on the ground, on her back.

Here! Hurry.

My Friend shoved me forward. My Friend's hard hand on my back.

What was this, beneath the picnic table? I was very excited—I stooped to see.

A doll! A cowgirl-doll! Abandoned.

Picnic debris had been dumped onto the ground. Soda bottles, food-packages, stubs of cigarettes. It was very cruel that the cowgirl-doll with the freckled face and red-orange hair should be abandoned here.

Her arms were outstretched. Her legs were at odd angles to her body and to each other. Because she had been dropped on her back her eyes were partly closed but you could see the glassy-glisten beneath, of surprise and alarm.

Help me! Don't leave me.

Distinctly we heard this plea of Annie's, my Friend and me. Her voice was whispery and small, her chipped-scarlet lips scarcely moved.

Inside my hooded jacket, I bore Annie to safety.

My Friend guided me from the park by an obscure route.

My Friend preceded me, to see if the way was clear.

It was a quarter-mile to the carriage house and to the shadowy horse stall at the rear.

In this way in a trance of wonderment Cowgirl Annie the second *found doll* was brought home.

* * *

By this time the little fourth-grade girl who'd lived on Catamount Street was rarely spoken of. For she had *gone away*, and would not be returning.

And this new girl who'd "gone missing"—from Prospect Heights Park—when her older sister and brother who'd been supposed to be watching her at the swings had been distracted by friends—she too had *gone away*, and would not be returning.

Another time, much alarm was raised at our school. Though the missing girl was a third-grader, at another school. Though we had heard the warnings about strangers many times by now, by ninth grade. The uniformed police officer who spoke to us from the auditorium stage reassured us that "whoever took this child will be found" but these too were familiar words, some of us smiled to hear.

In the park that afternoon there'd been solitary men, always in a park near a playground there are solitary men, and some of these men have criminal records, and these were taken into custody by police, and questioned. But we knew, the little girl would never be found.

Now I was no longer taunted by the older boys on the school bus for I was not one of the younger children. In my eyes such hatred blazed for these boys, they had learned to avoid me.

I learned that to be respected you had to be steely-calm and still. Or, you had to be reckless. You could not show weakness. You could not be "nice"—you would be ground beneath the boots of the strong like a beetle.

But now the second of the *found dolls* had come into my life, I did not care what these boys thought of me, or anyone else except my Friend.

The second of the *found dolls*. When I was fourteen.

Not soon, for my Friend cautioned me against recklessness.

Not soon but within two years, the third of the *found dolls* entered my life.

Then, after eleven months, a fourth *found* doll.

These were not local dolls. These were dolls discovered miles from Prospect Hill, in other towns.

For now I had a driver's license. I had the use of my mother's car.

At school I was a quiet student, but my teachers seemed to like me and my grades were usually high. At home, I was quiet in a way that maddened my father for it seemed to him *sullen, rebellious*.

I had a habit of grunting instead of talking, or mumbling under my breath. I had a habit of not looking at any adult including my parents for it was easier that way. My Friend did not want me to look at *him*—my Friend understood the effort such looks require. You can look into a doll's eyes without fear of the doll seeing into your soul in a way hostile to you but you can't be so careless looking at anyone else. And this too maddened my father, that I would not meet his gaze: I was *disrespectful*.

My father said *I will send him into the army—not to college. They'll straighten him out there.*

My mother pleaded *Robbie should see a therapist, I've told you. Please let me take him to a therapist.*

So it happened, on the day of my eighteenth birthday I had an appointment with Dr. G., a (psycho) therapist whose specialty was *troubled adolescents.* I sat in a chair facing Dr. G. in a trance of fear and dislike not raising my eyes to hers, but staring resolutely at the floor at her feet.

Dr. G.'s office was sparely furnished. Dr. G. did not sit behind a desk but in a comfortable chair, so that I could see her legs, which were the legs of a stout middle-aged woman, and I thought how much preferable it was at school where our teachers sat behind desks so that you could see only the tops of their bodies mostly, and not their legs. It was easy to think of them as big ungainly dolls that way, whose jaw-hinges were always moving.

Dr. G. asked me to sit in a chair facing her, about five feet from her, and this too was a comfortable chair though I did not feel comfortable in it and knew that I must be vigilant.

"Robbie? Talk to me, please. Your mother has said that your grades are very good—you don't have trouble at school communicating, evidently—but, at home . . ." The more kindly the woman was, the less I trusted her. The more insistently she looked at my face, the less inclined I was to raise my eyes to hers. My Friend had cautioned *Don't trust! Not for an instant, you'll be finished.*

It was then I noticed a doll in a chair on the farther side of the room. Her head was large for her body and her face seemed to glow, or glare, with an arrogant sort of beauty. And her thick-lashed eyes were fixed upon *me.*

Dr. G.'s clients included young children, I'd been told. Teenagers, children. *Troubled*.

Though the office was sparely furnished yet there were a number of dolls of varying sizes and types, each distinctive and unusual, a collector's item: on shelves, on a windowsill, and in this white wicker rocking chair which was a child-sized chair. Barely I could hear the therapist's voice, which was warm, friendly, and kindly, so powerful was the doll's hold upon me.

"You're admiring my antique Dresden doll? It's dated 1841 and is in quite good condition. It's made of wood with a painted face, the colors have scarcely faded . . ." Dr. G. was clearly hoping that I would react to this information but I sat silent, frowning. I would not smile as others had smiled in my place nor would I ask some polite but silly question. As a boy, I could not be expected to care about dolls.

Staring at the doll who stared at me with marble eyes that reminded me of Baby Emily's eyes; and in those eyes, a subtle sign of recognition.

It was exciting, the Dresden doll did seem to "know" me. Because of the therapist's presence, however, the Dresden doll was not in the least frightened of me.

She was a beautiful doll though made of wood, and unlike any of my *found dolls*. At first you thought she had dark wavy hair then you saw that the hair was just wood, painted dark brown.

"Some of my very young clients prefer to talk to a doll than to me," Mrs. G. said. "But I don't suppose that's the case with you, Robbie?"

I shook my head *no*. It was not the case with Robbie.

Elsewhere in the therapist's office were smaller dolls. On a shelf was a gaily painted Russian doll which I knew had another, smaller doll inside it, and another, smaller doll within that doll. (I did not like these Russian dolls, that made me feel slightly sick. I thought of how a woman carries a baby inside her and how terrifying it would be if that baby carried another baby inside it.) There were rag dolls arranged on a shelf like puppets. There were little music boxes covered in seashells and mother-of-pearl and there were Japanese fans and animals carved of wood.

Though Dr. G. had furnished her office sparely, and the colors of the furniture and of the carpet on the floor were dull, dun-colors that could not excite any emotion, as Dr. G. wore dull, dun-colored and shapeless clothing that could not excite any emotion, yet these collectors' items suggested another, more complex and secret side to Dr. G.

"Tell me why you find it so difficult to talk to your parents, Robbie. Your mother has said . . ." In her quiet stubborn woman-voice Dr. G. spoke.

Because there is nothing to say. Because my real life is elsewhere, where no one can follow.

I did not like many people. Especially, I did not like adults who wanted to "help" me. But I think I liked Dr. G. I wanted to help Dr. G. establish a *diagnosis* of what was wrong with me so that my parents would be satisfied and leave me alone. Yet I could not think how to help her for I could not tell her the secrets closest to my heart.

Badly I wanted to examine the Dresden doll with the painted face. Badly I wanted to take the Dresden doll home with me.

In all, I would see Dr. G. approximately twelve times over the course of five or six months. I was not a good client, I think—I never "opened up" to Dr. G. as "troubled" people do to their therapists in movies and on TV.

Never during these visits did I reveal anything significant to Dr. G. But I was riveted by the Dresden doll who stared at me boldly through the full fifty-minute session.

The Dresden doll was not afraid of me because she was protected by Dr. G. who never left the office and never left us alone together.

You can't touch me—not me! I belong to her.

You didn't "find" me. I was always here. And I will be here when you are not.

Such a look came into my face, of longing, and anger, Dr. G. broke off whatever she was saying to exclaim, "Robbie! What are you thinking?—did something come into your mind, just now?"

Something *coming into my mind* like a maddened hornet? A paper airplane sailing? A nudge in the ribs?

Quietly I shook my head *no.*

Lowering my gaze, to stare at a spot on the carpet.

As my Friend had warned *Never make eye contact. You know better.*

This was so. I had made a mistake. But it was not a fatal mistake for no one knew except the Dresden doll.

She was only a doll, I thought. Something made of wood.

She could not be a *found doll*—for I could never touch her.

Never bring her to the carriage house for safekeeping among her sister dolls.

"Is something distracting you, Robbie? Is it something in this room?"

Shook my head *no*.

"Would you be more comfortable if we moved to another room?"

Shook my head *no*.

Then at our next meeting—(which would be our last meeting)—I was shocked to see that the Dresden doll had been removed from the white wicker rocking chair. In her place was an embroidered pillow.

I said nothing of course. My face locked into its frozen expression and would not betray me.

"I think you might be more comfortable now, Robbie?"

Dr. G. spoke gently, proddingly. I hated this homely graceless female now, that she'd sensed the hold of the Dresden doll over me; she alone, of all the world, might guess of my fascination with *found dolls*.

I hated her and I feared her; that suddenly I might lose control, I might begin to shout at her, demanding to see the Dresden doll again; or, I might burst into tears, confessing to her that I had stolen the *found dolls*, that were hidden in the carriage house.

It is a terrible thing to feel that you might break down, you might utter a confession that could not then be retrieved. And so, I did not speak at all. My throat shut tight. Dr. G. asked her usual picky little friendly-seeming questions to which I could not reply and after some minutes of awkward silence on my part, Dr. G. handed me a notebook and a pen and suggested that I write out my thoughts, if I could not speak to her; I took the notebook from her and with the smile of a shy-but-determined boy. I wrote *GOODBYE* and handed it back to her.

Already I was on my feet. Already I was *gone*.

After high school it was decided that I would "defer" college. My grades had been high, especially in physics and calculus, and at graduation my name had been asterisked in the commencement program to indicate *summa cum laude* but I had not gotten around to applying for any college or university. My teachers and the school guidance counselor were perplexed by this decision but my mother understood, to a degree. For my father had departed from the house on Prospect Hill and you might think that a concerned son would not leave his mother alone in such a large house, at such a time.

Only I knew, I could not leave my *found dolls*.

I could not risk strangers finding them. The possibility of the *found dolls* being discovered was too terrible to consider.

Often when I couldn't sleep, I took a flashlight and went out into the carriage house. By moonlight the carriage house seemed to float like a ghost ship on a dark sea and all was still except for the cries of nocturnal birds and, in summer, a raucous sound of nocturnal insects buzzing and humming like insidious thoughts.

The *found dolls* lay quiet in their makeshift cribs of plywood and hay. They had been placed side by side like sisters though each doll was quite distinct from the others and might have made a claim for being the most beautiful.

Mariska. Annie. Valerie. Evangeline. Barbie.

Barbie was one of that notorious breed—*Barbie Dolls.*

In this case, *Bride Barbie.* For the angelic blond girl-doll wore a white silk gown that shimmered and shook when you lifted her and on her flawless head a lace veil. Her figure was not a child's figure but that of a miniature but mature woman with pronounced breasts straining against the bodice of the wedding dress, a ridiculously narrow waist, and shapely hips.

My Friend had observed *One of these will do. We should give Barbie a chance.*

Barbie had given me the most difficulty, in fact. You would not think that a doll so small and weighing so little could scream so loud and that her fingernails, shaped and polished and very sharp, could inflict such damage on my bare forearms.

If she doesn't obey, you can chop her into pieces. Tell her she's on trial for her life.

In her makeshift crib of plywood and hay Barbie lay motionless as if in a trance of great surprise and great loathing. Not ever would Barbie cast a sidelong glance at her sister-doll beside her, a soft boneless cloth doll with a startlingly pale, pretty face and a little tiara on her platinum blond curls sparking with tiny rhinestones.

Evangeline had come from Juniper Court, a trailer-village on the outskirts of our town. Hardly protesting Evangeline had come with me at my Friend's suggestion for she was a doll lacking a substantial body; her head was made of some synthetic material like plastic, or a combination of plastic and ceramic, but her body was boneless, like a sock puppet. She could not put up much of a struggle and seemed almost to fall before me in a swoon of abnegation, as a sock puppet might do for whom the only possible life is generated by another's antic hand.

No one had searched for Evangeline. It was believed that Evangeline was a *runaway* like other children in her family and in Juniper Court.

When I left the dolls I covered them beneath a khaki-colored canvas, neatly.

This khaki-colored canvas was the cleanest covering I could find in the carriage house.

Many items of furniture and other abandoned and forgotten things in the carriage house were covered with pieces of canvas that were soiled and discolored, but the covering for the *found dolls* was reasonably clean.

I would have drawn quilts over them, to keep them warm, but I worried that someone would notice, and become suspicious.

No one ever came into this part of the carriage house. Not for years. But I had an irrational fear that someone might come into the carriage house and discover my *found dolls*.

My Friend said *They're happy here. They're at peace here. This is the best they've been treated in their short tragic lives.*

One night not long after I'd stopped seeing Dr. G., I heard a sound at the entrance to the stable, like a footfall, and shone my light there thinking in dismay *Mother! I will have to kill her . . .*

But there was no one there and when I returned to the house it was darkened as before.

I was relieved, I think. For it would not be an easy or pleasant matter to subdue, silence, and suffocate Mother, so much larger than any of the *found dolls*.

Most nights Mother slept deeply. I think Mother was heavily medicated. Sometimes I stood in the doorway of Mother's room seeing her motionless mannequin-figure by moonlight beneath the bedclothes of the large canopied bed and listening to her rhythmic breathing which sometimes shaded into a soft snoring that was a comfort to me. For when Mother was awake, and in my presence, always Mother was aware of me, and looking at me; always Mother was addressing me, or asking me a question, waiting then for me to reply when I had no reply for her.

Though I only murmured or grunted responses, and avoided looking Mother in the face, Mother was never discouraged and continued to chatter in my presence as if she were thinking aloud and yet at the same time addressing *me*.

My Friend laid a sympathetic hand on my shoulder. It was the first time that my Friend had appeared inside my house.

You know that it would be better, Robbie, if the woman were silenced. But this is not a task for the lily-livered.

* * *

(How strange this was: *lily-livered* was not a phrase my Friend had ever spoken before. But *lily-livered* was a phrase that my father had sometimes used in a voice of mockery.)

There was a sixth *found doll*—as it turned out, a disappointing one. But I could not have guessed so, beforehand.

Still, I kept Trixie with the others. Though sometimes I didn't remove the canvas from her crib, for her sour curdled-milk pug-face and reproachful green marble eyes were discomforting to me; and her cheap sleazy silly costume, a low-cut sequined top that showed the cleavage of her breasts and a frilly frothy ballerina-skirt in matching turquoise, and spike-heeled little shoes, were frankly embarrassing.

No more of Trixie!

I will draw the khaki-covered canvas over Trixie—*Voilà!* As my Friend says.

And the seventh *found doll*—a boy doll.

His name was an exotic name—Bharata.

He had taffy-colored skin of the finest rubber that so re-sembled human flesh, you shivered as your fingertips caressed his face and felt a semblance of warmth, as of capillaries close beneath the surface of the skin. And his eyes were not glassy-brown but a warm chocolate-brown.

And thick-lashed. Beautiful as any girl's eyes.

Bharata wore chino shorts, a sky-blue T-shirt, blue sneakers on his small feet and no socks. His legs were well-formed with a look of small sinewy muscle, more defined than his sister-dolls' legs.

The palms of his hands were lighter-colored than the rest of his body. I was fascinated by this—did "people of color" normally have palms lighter than the rest of their body? I had not ever known any "people of color"—no one in our family did.

My Friend said, *You see, Robbie? You were prejudiced against boys but now, you have a surprise in store.*

Bharata was one of the larger dolls, with a sweetly pretty boy-face and very black curly hair; his black eyelashes swept against his cheeks, which appeared to be lightly rouged. You could not have told if Bharata's mouth was a boy-mouth, or a girl's.

Bharata was the only doll who tried to speak in actual words, not merely soft squeaking sounds. Bharata's mouth moved and I leaned to him, to listen, but heard only what sounded like *Where—where is—who are you—I don't want to be—don't want to be h-here* . . .

The other *found dolls* might have exhibited some jealousy, or envy, of my taffy-skinned *found-boy-doll*. But they disguised their emotions well for they knew their place and did not wish to offend me who was their *Doll-Master*.

It was my Friend who had told me, one day *Robbie, you are the Doll-Master. You must never surrender your authority.*

Mother said, "We have no choice, really. The house is so large, most of the rooms are shut off, and unheated. A house of this size was meant for a large family and now there is only us."

Only us was hurtful to me, to hear. As if *only us* were an admission of such shameful defeat, it had to be murmured, near-inaudibly.

"So what do you mean, Mother? Do you want to—sell the house?"

A clanging in my ears had begun, as of a fire alarm. I could barely hear my mother's reasonable voice asking me if I would call a Realtor, if I would oversee the selling of the house.

"It's a profound decision. It's a profound step in our lives. But I think we have no choice, the property taxes alone are . . ."

It was so: property taxes were rising. Taxes of all sorts were rising in New Jersey.

"Now there's no one in our family going to public school, it seems a shame to pay for 'public education.' My sister was showing me brochures of condominiums on the river, two- and three-bedroom, very modern and stylish . . ."

Mother chattered nervously, excitedly. Mother would not expect me to react to her suggestion in any emphatic way, for that was not Robbie's nature.

Father had not only departed the sprawling old Victorian house on Prospect Hill but also had dissociated himself from it entirely: in the divorce settlement he'd signed over the property to my mother. There were to be no alimony payments for my mother had a small income from investments she'd inherited. Mother sometimes wept but more often expressed relief—*Your father has gone.*

Since the separation several years before, Father and I rarely saw each other. Father did not like to return to our suburban town—it was an effort for him, as he made clear, to attend my high school graduation and to resolutely avoid my mother and her relatives—and I did not like to leave our suburban town and so we exchanged emails occasionally and, less frequently, spoke on the phone. *It is the easiest tie to break*—my Friend consoled me—*the tie that was badly frayed to begin with.*

You could say that Mother and I were "close"—in the way of two actors on a TV show who have been together on the set for many seasons, reciting prepared scripts, uncertain of the direction in which their narrative was moving, what would be the fate of their "characters"—yet not anxious, not quite yet.

I was twenty years old. Soon then it seemed, I was twenty-two years old. No more than one *found doll* a year seemed necessary, or prudent. At the time Mother wanted me to sell our house, I was twenty-three years old. I had not attended college after all. In an alternative life, I would have majored in science and math at a good university—perhaps Princeton. In an alternative life I would be a graduate student now at Cal Tech perhaps, or MIT. I might be engaged, or even married.

No, probably not: not engaged, and not married.

Quickly time passes if you don't keep up with your generation of high school graduates. Where time seemed to have virtually stopped for my mother, who continued to see a small circle of women friends, several of them widows, and older female relatives, over the years, time moved rapidly for me. I was not unhappy, though you would have to call me reclusive. I did not consider myself a dropout from society, or a failure, in the way that my father considered himself a failure, and that had poisoned his life; my relationships with the world were primarily through the Internet, where I'd established a website under the name *The Doll-Master*, through which I'd made many acquaintances; here I posted shadowy, oblique, and "poetic" photographs of the *found dolls*, images too dark and irresolute to be identified, though visitors to the site found them "haunting"—"eerie"— "makes me want to see more!" My website visitors have become faithful correspondents and my emails take up a large part of my life for it is thrilling for me, as I believe it has to be for them, and some of these females—(I think)—that we skirt the edges of our essential subject, and seek metaphors and poetic turns of speech to express our (forbidden) desires. For it has been revealed to me as a fact, that where the dull-essential nature of our lives is eliminated, such as age, identity, education, employment, place of residence, family ties, daily routine, etc., the thrilling-essential is revealed.

Mother believes that I have contacted a real estate agent in town, and have met with her; Mother believes that the house is listed tastefully, with no ugly sign at the foot of our lawn, and only "serious home-seekers who can afford the property" considered; but Mother does not ply me with questions about the house sale, for Mother would rather not think of where we would live if the house were really sold, and what our circumstances would be. And I am comforting to Mother by saying, with a smile: "One step at a time, Mother. The real estate market is 'flat' now—we might not have any serious interest until spring."

* * *

Yet, that domestic comfort has come to an abrupt end.

My Friend has abandoned me, I think. For my Friend has no advice to give me now.

It was the occasion of a new *found doll*. I had not brought a *found doll* back to the carriage house for thirteen months which I believed was a sign of fortitude and character; for I could not be called impulsive, or reckless; rather, over-scrupulous, I think. For when I brought my new *found doll* to the carriage house, and lay her in her little crib beside the others, I lingered too long, in a state of infatuation; I lost track of the time, as dusk shaded into night, and I gazed at *Little Farmer-Girl* in the beam of my flashlight, and marveled at her uniqueness. Of all my dolls, with the possible exception of the rag doll Evangeline who lacked a substantial body, this doll was soft, will-less, hardly more than fabric with a hard doll-head, yet strangely appealing; not beautiful, not even pretty, but *winning*; for when I washed away the grime on Little Farmer-Girl's face, she was revealed as a sweet homely cousin-sort-of-girl, with stiff pigtails, a funny mouth, wide unblinking marble eyes of an amber hue; her body was made of cloth, from which some of the stuffing had leaked out; she wore denim bib-overalls and a red plaid shirt beneath, and on her spindly legs red tights, and on her tiny feet boots. Her costume was dirty but yet colorful—for she had not been discarded for long, it seemed.

I'd pulled Little Farmer-Girl out of the trash behind our suburban train station where there is an old, unused railroad yard with a fence around it, long fallen into disrepair; no one comes here, though passengers awaiting the train are gathered on the platform only a quarter-mile away, except children, sometimes, or "runaways"—it was plausible to think that Little Farmer-Girl was a "runaway" whose difficult life had brought her to this place and to my discovery of her in the peaceful interregnum between trains when the depot is virtually deserted. It was a game of kidnap, I decided, since Little Farmer-Girl was so soft-bodied there was no effort involved in lifting her, folding her, and carrying her beneath my hooded jacket; when she struggled, I tied her wrists and ankles and stuffed a rag in her mouth so that her cries were muffled and could not be heard by anyone farther than six feet away.

No effort then to place Little Farmer-Girl in the trunk of the station wagon and to drive slowly back home to the top of Prospect Hill.

Why Little Farmer-Girl exerted such a spell over me is a mystery but I suppose, as my Friend would say, with a laugh— *Robbie, you're so funny! Each of your dolls was enthralling to you, initially.*

I thought, too, that I would begin taking pictures of Little Farmer-Girl that very night, to record more conscientiously than I had the others, before the inevitable incursions of time, decomposition, and decay intervened; my experience was that flash-photos were particularly effective, in these circumstances, as more "poetic" and "artistic" than photographs taken by day, even in the shadowy interior of the stall.

"Robbie? Is that you? Why are you here, Robbie?—what are you doing?"

So absorbed had I been squatting over Little Farmer-Girl, I hadn't heard Mother approach the rear of the carriage house; too late, I saw the groping beam of her flashlight, moving upon me, and upon the row of *found dolls* on the floor of the stall, that occupied now most of the stall.

"Robbie! What is . . ."

In the crude light of Mother's flashlight the *found dolls* were revealed as small skeletons with rags of clothing and wisps of hair on their battered skulls; their faces were skull-faces, with mirthless grins and eyeless sockets; their bone-arms were spread, as for an embrace.

This was Mother's crude light, not the light of the *Doll-Master*.

Quickly I took the flashlight from Mother's shaking hand. Quickly I comforted her, telling her that these were sculptures that I'd done, but had not wanted to show anyone.

"S-Sculptures? Here . . . ?"

I would explain to her, I said. But first, I would shut the outer door.

Soldier

They have advised me *Do not open your mail.*

They have advised me *It could be a fatal mistake, to open your mail.*

And yet, I am not a coward. I am insulted that anyone should think that I am a coward, to be protected from the mail that comes addressed to *Brandon Schrank.*

Therefore, the mail accumulates. It has not been decided by my "legal team" (as they are called) what exactly to do with the avalanche of mail that has been forwarded to me. I would like to open some of the letters, I think. For I am eager for friends. I am not afraid of my enemies.

Uncle T. has told me—*You are a hero to your race. There's some will want you to be a martyr but fuck that.*

Most of the mail comes to *Brendan Schrank c/o Glassboro County Courthouse* but of course *Schrank* is spelled all kind of illiterate ways and *Brendan* is half the time *Branden* or *Brennen.*

There are many more emails of course—(so I am told)—but they do not come to me because I do not have an email account any longer. I do not have a Facebook account any longer. When you are in police custody you are not allowed the use of a computer even your own laptop is forbidden to you. So this censorship began in early April when I was first arrested. Then when I was released on bail my court-appointed lawyer advised against anything to do with "social media" for the time being.

"This will not be forever, Brandon. But it is wisest, for now."

And she said, "There are many sick people out there, Brandon. We must keep our distance from them."

At first before the trial there was a trickle of mail addressed to *Brandon Schrank* which the lawyer did not show to me. Then through the weeks of the trial there began to be more mail each day as TV and online coverage called national attention to the prosecution of a man who had shot and killed to defend his own life who had no prior record of lawbreaking as an adult and so by the end of the trial there had accumulated by the estimate of the lawyer more than 1,000 articles of mail in her custody, carried in cardboard boxes from the courthouse to a "safe house" in the country to be sorted through by the lawyer's assistants from the Public Defenders Office.

In fact the trial would be a "mistrial"—for after twenty-two days of testimonies and three days of jury deliberation the foreman of the jury reported to the judge that they were "hopelessly deadlocked." And so, Brendon Schrank was released to freedom that is a great relief and yet an ordeal of waiting for the prosecutor has declared that there will be a second trial and again I will be held captive in the Glassboro County Men's Detention for the duration of the trial and made to endure the humiliation of being charged a *rabid racist murderer*.

It was a sign of the race hatred stirred against me, in the Men's Detention before the trial I was kept in the segregated unit with men like myself (white). I did not have a cell mate. Not even black or Hispanic guards were assigned to me for fear that they would do injury to me or harass me.

It was my court-appointed lawyer who insisted upon this for there had been many death threats made against me. (And also against her for defending me.) I was not so happy that the lawyer insisted too that Brendon Schrank be placed on suicide watch for this meant that the lights in my cell could never be turned off but only dimmed and that not only would a guard observe me every ten minutes through a peephole in the door but a TV surveillance monitor was turned upon me every moment I was in that cell.

I tried to protest, I did not want radioactive rays weakening my bones! I did not want cancer cells to be activated in my blood, by the TV monitor that could not be turned off and from which I could not ever hide.

Dear Branden Schwank,

You are despicible. It was most disgusting how you sat in the court with hands folded like in "prayr" so the jury would see you & think you are a Christian person & not a despicible murderer of an unarmed Black boy.

God have mercy on your evil soul, you will not live long it is promised.

Quickly I thrust away this letter which was written as an angry child might write in ballpoint ink. A hot flush came into my face and there was a ringing in my ears.

This was a letter that had come to me early in May before the trial before the "legal team" made a decision to keep such letters from me.

It was self-defense against five of them. I was in fear of my life.

How many times I have sworn this simple fact. How many times I have made this statement. Immediately to the police officers who were summoned to the scene and again at the police station and again to my court-appointed lawyer and to the officers at the courthouse and many times since then so that in the night I am pleading in my sleep *It was self-defense against five of them. I was in fear of my life.*

They were not boys nor were they men but in-between though taller than I am, and harsh in their speech and faces contorted in hatred of me—of the whiteness of my skin.

White fag. White fag-fuck.

See what we gon do with you, white fag-fuck? We gon make you squeal.

Of course they ran when I fired the first shot—all of them ran except the one who was on top of me attacking me. And it was too late for him.

Not what I caused to happen but which happened to me.

Crossing through the empty lot behind the Glassboro Post Office where the old Sears used to be now mostly rubble and rusted iron and broken glass and they came at me from behind there were five of them—they were taunting me saying what they would do to me if I didn't give them my wallet—one of them had an iron rod he'd picked up swinging-like at my head so I was trying to protect my head and that made them laugh harder like they were drunk or high and the thought came to me—They will kill me, there is only eleven dollars in my wallet—because it has happened, people have been killed for not having enough money to give to muggers. I did not think of the color of their skin for I was so frightened, I could not see clearly—I did not think that they were "boys" for they looked and behaved older and they were taller than me and there were five of them and I was alone—I was in fear of my life—one of them was the loudest and angriest calling me white fuck—*rushing at me swinging the iron rod closer and closer to my head like he intended to knock out my brains and I was praying to God to help me and somehow then it happened, I reached inside my jacket, they would think I was reaching for my wallet but it was the gun—my uncle Trevor's .45 caliber police service revolver . . .*

How many times I shot him I don't know. Just kept pulling the trigger until he dropped the iron rod and—whatever happened after that, it was God's will.

At such times you give yourself over to His will. There is no opposition to God, there is only surrender.

The judge set the bail at $110,000 which meant eleven thousand bail bond which was far too high for my family of course. We are not rich people.

The prosecutor had argued for no bail. Saying that Brendon Schrank had shot an unarmed minor for reasons of racism at no provocation and was a flight risk. Saying that Brendon Schrank had demonstrated "depraved indifference to human life" and could be considered dangerous in the community. My lawyer had argued to the judge that Brendon Schrank had lived all of his twenty-nine years in Glassboro, New Jersey, and had close ties to his mother, his uncle (Lieutenant Trevor Schrank, Glassboro PD, retired), as well as other relatives in southern Jersey; though not working at the present due to the recession he had been employed by Toms River Contracting for seven years and his employer there indicated faith in him as a "reliable and responsible" citizen as did the minister of the Glassboro Church of Christ to which he and his mother belonged. Especially, the lawyer argued that Brandon Schrank was not a flight risk for he was "devoted" to his mother who owned property in Glassboro and was currently undergoing chemotherapy at Ocean County Memorial Hospital and so, the son would never flee Glassboro County and leave his mother.

It is not possible to know what a judge is thinking. But following my lawyer's argument the judge granted bail against the prosecutor's wishes, of $110,000; and following this, there began to be donations sent to me in care of my lawyer and the Public Defender's Office my *defense fund*—which was a total surprise to me.

These were small-denomination bills, that came with some of the letters. And there were citizens in Glassboro who came forward to donate money including some prominent citizens (who wished to remain anonymous). And members of our church group gathered donations. Until at last eleven thousand dollars was collected and I was released from Detention where I'd been made to feel like a common criminal.

They are saying that I *shot and killed an unarmed black boy for no reason except race hatred.* God knows the truth, that I did not know he was a boy or black and there were others with him shouting and threatening me and I was in fear of my life.

It is told to me that each day there are more threats against my life. Calls come to the Glassboro courthouse as well as to relatives of mine and to others in south Jersey who share my name or a name resembling it. Both my mother and my Uncle T. (who is Mother's brother-in-law) have disconnected their land phones and have only cell phones now.

There are lawyers at the Public Defenders Office who receive death-threats calls who have nothing to do with my case!

Since my release from Detention, I have lived in several different places through the arrangements of my "legal team." My whereabouts are a secret to the media but must be known at all times to the Glassboro County prosecutor's office.

Of course, I no longer live with my mother on Eagle Street, Glassboro, or in any residence belonging to any relatives. This has been announced repeatedly in the media to protect my family.

I did not always get along so well with my relatives. On my father's side of the family, after my father died. But the Schranks are supporting me now. They are all supporting me and some of them (like Uncle T.) have said publicly that they are "God-damned" proud of me.

It is true, one of the charges filed against me is that I did not/ do not have a permit to carry a handgun for that is a *concealed weapon* illegal in the State of New Jersey. And it is true, the gun was not/is not registered in my name but in my uncle T.'s name. And it is true, Uncle T. did not know that I'd taken his gun from the house until he received a telephone call that night from the Glassboro PD informing him that his nephew had been arrested and that he, in whose name the gun was registered, was requested to come to police headquarters immediately.

Poor Uncle T.! Having to drive to the precinct where he'd been a police officer for thirty-seven years and where many officers knew him!

When Uncle T. retired from the PD for medical reasons at age fifty-nine he was required to surrender his .45 caliber police service revolver to his precinct captain, which he did. But Uncle T. had other firearms, and among these was a privately purchased .45 caliber police service revolver for which Uncle

T. had a homeowner's permit. In his house Uncle T. has also a short-range deer rifle and a double-barreled shotgun from the time when he used to hunt and would take me and my cousins with him.

Along the Chautauqua River on this side of the river was Uncle T.'s favorite place for hunting. My father was not so interested as he was not interested in fishing either. And so, my father's older brother we called Uncle T. who had no children of his own took us hunting and fishing and all those years we were growing up none of us would ever have thought that our uncle would lose interest in such things like we'd never have thought he would retire from the PD.

For years my Uncle T's .45 caliber revolver was not touched. I am pretty sure that this is so. I don't even think that Uncle T. cleaned it anymore—which is surprising since (Uncle T. used to say) cleaning a gun is your duty to your firearm, and your responsibility. Cleaning his gun was something Uncle T. would do at the kitchen table in his house, Saturday mornings. And he'd let us kids help him, which we liked doing. And he'd say to me, you can pick it up, Brandon—but don't ever aim it at anyone even if it's not loaded like it is now.

And so, the smell of the gun oil and the weight of the gun in my hand was something I would always remember, with a shiver. And just the feel of the gun—the smooth nickel finish in my hands . . .

If you are sweating there's a smell of the gun on the palms of your hands. It is a smell hard to describe but unmistakable.

(The smell is on my hands now. I have washed and washed my hands but the smell never goes away. In my sleep I smell it.)

Where Uncle T. kept the .45 caliber revolver was in a drawer in the kitchen of his house where he lived alone after my aunt Maude passed away. Not a drawer that was used often where you'd find loose nails, thumbtacks, old rolls of tape, old grocery coupons, Caesar's last dog-tag (Caesar was Uncle T.'s boxer, he'd loved like crazy who'd died ten years ago) and other junk. Like Uncle T. had just shoved the gun in the back of the drawer and forgot it, never opened the drawer so he never saw the gun to remind him of when he'd been a police officer all those years until he got into some trouble and it ended fast—his Captain turning against him, and no friends in the PD he'd thought he had had. Plus medical problems, that would get worse every year. Which made us feel bad for there've been times Uncle T. has forgotten other things, once left his car at the garage to be serviced but forgot and thought somebody'd stolen it from the driveway, called 911 to report a car theft, and a recent time he'd started a fire in his kitchen when a dish towel caught fire on the gas stove and Uncle T. ran out into the street in underwear in freezing snow and scariest of all he has confused me with my father who has been deceased twelve years.

Uncle T. was not happy with me, that I had taken his gun from his kitchen drawer without his knowledge or permission. A stream of pretty nasty swear-words came out of Uncle T.'s mouth when the opportunity arose but since then Uncle T. has said he is "one hundred percent" behind me.

It is true about the gun, and I have pleaded guilty to that charge. Concealed hand weapon, unlawful possession of weapon, bringing of weapon onto U.S. federal property (post office). These charges, I have pleaded guilty following my lawyer's advice.

My lawyer is determined that I will be acquitted of the charge of *second-degree murder*. Then, she is sure that the judge will give me a suspended sentence for the gun charges.

My lawyer tells me how fortunate we are, the prosecution can't argue for a change of venue which would mean that the trial might be held in a city with a sizable black and Hispanic population, like Trenton or New Brunswick. Or Newark. "In Glassboro, you're a hero. The jurors will reflect that sentiment. And we only need one."

Do not seek out your name online. Do not engage in any online communication. This could be very dangerous, Brandon—there are many people who hate you.

In Detention it was not allowed that any of the inmates could use a computer as we had no personal use of cell phones or iPads. But now that I am living in a "safe house"—(a farmhouse owned by a relative of my lawyer in Pine Barren which is eighteen miles south of Glassboro)—and when my lawyer is not here, and there is no one to observe, I can log on to the computer here and type *Brandon Schrank* into Google. And there are 17,433 results!

It is like when you are little and you spin around and around and become very dizzy. And when you stop spinning, you open your eyes wide and see that things keep spinning around you. It is scary but makes you want to laugh—*Jesus! I am famous.*

But it is not so good, to see what has been posted about *Brandon Schrank.*

A helpless feeling, to see the pictures of me, that I had not ever seen before. Pictures of my face that somebody took with a camera or an iPhone without my knowing or giving permission.

Racist. Murderer.

Guilty verdict expected & deserved.

Too bad there is no capital punishment in N.J. In Texas or Florida this racist-murderer would get lethal injection.

My heart is beating hard, there is the ringing in my ears that comes with dizziness. I know that I should not be seeing such things, it is what my lawyer has warned against.

"It was not that way. I did not 'murder' anyone. I was in fear of my life and had no choice"—these words of protest come to my lips, I have uttered many times.

In the upstairs room, I shouted and shouted. My throat was raw with shouting, and my eyes brimmed with tears of hurt and indignation.

"The only one who knows is—*him.* The one who attacked me and wanted to kill me and instead—the gun went off, and I killed *him.*"

Sometimes I am so agitated, I feel faint and sick and have to sit on the floor. Sometimes so weak, I lie flat on my back on the floor, as the room spins.

When my lawyer's brother-in-law (who is a social worker in Pine Barren County) returns home he finds me on the floor upstairs, in a corner of the room where I have crawled. Managed to sit up with my legs spread like a rag doll that has been tossed down. He checks the computer screen with a little whistle and he understands what has happened.

"If you go fishing in a cesspool you will get shit on your hands, Brandon. Leave that to us, OK? We're pros."

It is like a nightmare. It is like a room of bright blinding lights where whenever you open the door the same words are being uttered over and over.

Did you see the face of the boy you shot, Bran-don?

You claim that he was not a boy but a man, Bran-don—did you know Nelson Herrara was sixteen years old?

You told police officers at the scene that there were five men who attacked you—but why has no one else ever seen the other four?

You claim that you did not recognize that Nelson Herrara was black, Bran-don? You expect us to believe that?

You claim that you did not see "any color of any skin," Bran-don? You expect us to believe such bullshit?

Of six shots fired all but two were fired downward into the boy's body at a sharp angle yet you claim, Nelson Herrara was taller than you and "standing over" you swinging an iron rod—how is that possible, Bran-don?

This iron rod—why are there no fingerprints on it, Bran-don? Why weren't you hit with it even once, if you were in fear of your life?

People who knew you at Glassboro High, Bran-don, said how some of the black students harassed you, and chased you, scared the shit out of you—d'you remember, Bran-don? No?

Well maybe it was a long time ago—like, twelve years—is that it, Bran-don? Maybe you just forgot.

And all I can say is what I have said. And what I will say to the last day of my life.

God guided my hand, except for God I would be dead now.

My head would be broken, my brains and blood splattered on the concrete rubble in the old Sears lot. And they would've run away, and nobody would know who had killed me. And nobody in their neighborhood who knew them would talk for fear they would kill them for that part of Glassboro, the east side, is their territory. And after a while, nobody would care except my mother and a few others that I had died.

Except God guided my hand, and my hand went into my pocket and there was Uncle T.'s gun, it was like Uncle T. was an instrument of God to save me. And so my life was saved.

Yes this is my sworn testimony. Yes so help me God.

For here is the injustice: only if you are killed, are you "innocent." If you fight for your life, you are "guilty."

Dear Brandon,

Believe me there are many of us are sick to heart, you are unjustly persecuted. You are not a Murderer but in defense of your life. I have seen your face on TV, your face is not the face

of a Murderer. You are a young boy like my own son who gave
his life in Iraq. We are praying for you for you are Innocent
in defense of your life. God bless you & set you free as you
deserve.

In this envelope, which I am not supposed to see, but have
found in the lawyer's station wagon, there are three twenty-
dollar bills!

And in another envelope with a postmark from Barnegat, New
Jersey, I am shocked to see—a hundred-dollar bill!

It is the first time that I have seen and touched a hundred-
dollar bill with the face of *Benjamin Franklin* on it—I think he
is one of the U.S. presidents of a long time ago.

Each day, the defense fund is growing. Since news of the trial
was released nationally more than fourteen thousand dollars has
accumulated some of it in small bills and some in large bills and
some in checks.

The largest donations are checks.

In the night when there is no one to observe I type *Brandon
Schrank* into the search engine and see that there are now 42,676
results!

Uncle T. has told me *This country is at war. But it is not a war
that is declared and so we can't protect ourselves against our enemies.*

Sunday morning I accompany Mother to church. Our Glassboro Church of Christ is located on the Barren Pike Road

just outside town. I am aware of excited eyes moving on us as I walk beside Mother and she leans on my arm, breathing quickly and quietly as she does, in that way of hers like a small animal panting. Since April Mother's life has been a nightmare as she says, yet it is thrilling to her, that she is the mother of Brandon Schrank who is a hero in many eyes. Yet, Mother must have chemotherapy every two weeks in the aftermath of breast cancer surgery at the Ocean County Hospital, and I am no longer able to drive her.

Inside the church more eyes fix upon us. They are friendly eyes—I believe. This is our congregation, Mother is well-liked here and there are no black faces here, no one to judge harshly and unfairly.

My "legal team" would not approve of my attending Sunday services here, and so I have not told them.

In the fifth pew, near the center aisle of the church, Mother and I take our places. It has been a while since I have been here but Mother comes most Sundays if there is someone to bring her. Those weeks I was in Detention many of the members of the congregation came to her, she said, and took her hand to comfort her—*Mrs. Schrank, it is so unjust, to arrest a man for defending his own life!*

And—*We are praying for your son. We have faith God will set him free.*

At the pulpit Reverend Baumann reads from the Bible to us, and speaks of the meek that shall inherit the earth, and our Savior who brings not peace but a sword. He speaks of the many "trials and tribulations" that are the lot of humankind, that we must bear without complaint for it is the will of God. And if there is a "global warming" it is a sign that God is displeased with humankind, for there is growing atheism, and hatred of Christ, and our political leaders have forsaken us in pursuing the ways of Satan.

I am hoping that Reverend Baumann will not call attention to my presence in the congregation as he has sometimes called attention to the presence of war veterans of whom some have been seriously injured—I am hoping that he will not speak of "hero"—"heroism"—for this would be embarrassing to me, though I know that Mother would be thrilled.

I am feeling very strange. My skin is prickling. I am thinking— *No, please. No.*

As he is about to leave the pulpit Reverend Baumann glances in my direction, and a flicker of approval comes over his face, a small smile of welcome, and support. It is very fast—fleeting. And I smile just a little and nod my head in acknowledgment of this recognition that is so subtle, many in the congregation will not notice. But Mother has noticed, and others in the pews close about us.

We are all so proud of you son!

Then, a sudden burst of sound—an explosion of organ music—for a moment I am cringing hunched in the pew thinking that there is some sort of attack on the church, aimed at Brandon Schrank; but it is just the (female) organist playing a hymn, one of those I've been hearing all my life without listening to the words—*Rock of Ages, cleft for me. Let me hide myself in Thee.*

The congregation sings. The congregation sings loudly, and happily. It is a happy time—singing hymns. Even Mother sings, though her voice is very weak. And my heart is beating hard and I am thinking—*He will take me in and hide me. The cleft will open for me.*

For it was like that when God guided my hand inside my jacket. *Thy rod and thy staff shall comfort me, all the days of my life.*

After the service there is a feeling of uplift and exhilaration. The organist is playing loudly as the congregation leaves the church—"Onward Christian Soldiers."

Mother looks forward to such times when she can linger with her church-women friends who are women like herself older and widowed. Several of these are accompanied by their (unmarried) sons.

I am not so comfortable now. I would like to wait for Mother in the car but do not want to seem unfriendly, or rude to Mother.

"Are you Brandon Schrank? Wow."

He is a son like me but he is older than I am by fifteen or twenty years. He is a schoolteacher bald and fat-faced and wears eyeglasses that give his eyes a thick suety look that fastens onto me and makes me feel weak and sick.

His voice is hoarse, adenoidal: "Momma? Y'know who this is—*Brandon Schrank*?"

But the midget-sized white-haired mother is deaf, and only just smiles and blinks baffledly at me.

I am trying not to smell the fat-faced son's hair oil, and I am trying not to meet his suety gaze. I feel a spurt of rage like a burst artery, and have to turn away wincing like something has hit me in the gut.

White-fuck fag. You gon squeal, fag.

To B. Schwank

You think you are a Hero to kill an inocent dark-skin boy but you are scum. It is fitting that your initials are "B.S."— you are utter shit. You do not deserve to live. One day you will find yourself in the wrong place where I will be waiting. You will hear your name and turn to see and that is the last you will hear for I have a shotgun for you, both barrows. You will not live through the year when Nelson died shot down like a dog, that is my promise.

This letter which is typed on a single sheet of plain paper I crumple in my fist and throw into the trash. I am grateful that no one can see the look in my face and I am thinking—*All of you will die, just wait long enough. You will see who has the shotguns.*

It is revealed to me that there was a "bomb scare" at the Public Defenders Office which is at the rear of the Glassboro County Courthouse so the entire building had to be evacuated and did not open until the following morning. These threats do not scare me much any longer for such people are cowards who (probably) lack the guts to actually build a bomb, let alone bring it to a public place.

By the time this news is conveyed to me, I have seen on local TV news how a heavily uniformed bomb squad came to take away the package where it had been wedged beneath a stone step by the entrance to the Public Defenders Office. The package which contained no address label was wrapped in brown paper and weighed eight pounds and was treated with great caution though, as it would be revealed, it contained nothing except several two-pound bags of flour that had to be carefully analyzed for fear of anthrax.

Always there is a mild air of humor, on TV, when a "bomb scare" turns out to be harmless. As if there is disappointment that there has been no bomb, and no explosion; and the TV news broadcasters are made to feel foolish, that they have disappointed TV viewers.

I have noticed how law enforcement officers look at me, when I am at the courthouse. For all of them know me—of course. Some of them stare at me as you might look at a relative of yours who has done something to call attention to himself of which you don't approve exactly but you would not pass harsh judgment on him. But all of the officers are professionals and never smile at me, still less do they exchange any words with me.

Already it is August. And then it is September. Since April, I have been moved four times.

My life is so confusing to me now, I could not describe any of the places in which I have stayed except my parents' house where I lived when I was a young boy, that seems long ago now.

There is a kind of amnesia that sets in, when you are moved so much. It would be like being the child of a career army officer—you would move from place to place and register in school after school. You would see many faces but recall none of them, and feel no emotion for any of them. Once, I wakened in the night with a sensation in my guts of utter sickness and despair not having any idea where I was, or when this was, or who I was, or was supposed to be.

There was the boy Nelson Herrara. In moonlight I could not see his skin except that it was in shadow like my own. I was trying to explain to him something complicated that had to do with nobody understanding what had happened except us—that it had *happened to*.

But the words did not come for I am not a smooth talker and often when I am questioned, my throat is so dry the sound comes out hoarse and cracked.

Often when I am questioned by the young assistant prosecutors, a look passes among them like—*He is not right in the head—is he? He is retarded, he is crazy. He is pathetic*.

It is true, I am very tired sometimes. It is like I am carrying a bag of cement over my shoulder. I am being made to *march*—for I am a Soldier of the Lord.

They do not jeer at me, outright. It is just a look that passes among them like a Ping-Pong ball. The older prosecutors look at me differently for I am work to them, I suppose. Preparing for my trial(s) is their work for which they are paid and at the end of the day they go home grateful to forget me.

The public defender staff moves me by night for safety's sake. Often in a vehicle I am hunched in the rear seat and turn to look out the window and it is shocking to me—*There is no one there*.

Of course, the Glassboro authorities know where I am at all times, as my mother and Uncle T. do not. And what a shock it was to me to overhear two of the young public defenders entrusted with driving me saying

That racist punk. Jesus! All the money he costs.

Half our fucking budget. We should drop him off in Trenton.

Until now I had thought the public defenders were my friends! Except for the black lawyers, that is. Female mostly, they are polite in my presence but look like there is a bad smell in the air.

It was some kind of joke at the courthouse when bail was set. When they asked me to "surrender" my passport it was a comical moment for my lawyer said smiling, "Your Honor, my client doesn't have a passport. I don't believe that my client has ever traveled out of Glassboro County."

This is not true of course. Many times I have traveled to Atlantic City which is in Ocean County, New Jersey.

Now, I am in the Cassells's house on Bear Tavern Road, Muhlenberg. They are a friendly older couple, the man wears his coarse gray hair in a straggly ponytail and the woman has smiled so hard and so often there are sharp crow's-feet beside her eyes.

It is not clear to me if the Cassells are lawyers like my lawyer or some other kind of lawyer but they question me as my lawyer and the police had done though I have given these answers many times. They are saying that they will record my testimony and my life story and that I should "hold nothing back" for my story will be sold to TV for a high sum. Which cable channel, they have not yet decided. And there are interview programs and newspapers that will pay for my interview.

None of this can be acknowledged before I am tried and acquitted, I am told. The Cassells estimate this could be some time in the fall and until then, I may not receive and cash any check for my story. But the Cassells are preparing me, every night we talk together at dinner. Mrs. Cassells makes our meals. Mr. Cassells does household chores as he calls them. The windows of their cedar wood "ranch house" are covered in plastic that lets in some light but you can't see through, so that no one can spy on us. Tied outside in the yard are three Doberman pinschers who set up a terrible barking and yowling if any stranger turns in to the driveway.

Will you sign this agreement, please Brandon?

I'm asking what it is, and they say *It is an agreement of restriction. That we are your exclusive agents for TV one-time or serial adaptation, book, newspaper and magazine rights to your life story ("Live Free or Die—The True Story of Brandon Schrank") and that you will sign no other agreements with any other agents.*

I'm asking what I will be paid for this, and they say *We will demand a minimum of $150,000 for exclusive rights but that is only a minimum. When two or more parties are in a bidding war—"The sky's the limit!"*

It has been arranged that I will accompany Reverend Baumann's wife to the Toms River Haven Home each Thursday. This is a nursing home for the elderly associated with the Glassboro Church of Christ. Here I move among the residents (many of whom are in wheelchairs) who smile at me as if hoping to recognize me, but they never do. Mrs. Baumann says not to worry, the residents of Toms River Haven Home never read newspapers and never watch TV news, they have no interest in "news" except what is happening in their families, or in the Home.

Mrs. Baumann has a joyous rising voice—"Hello! Hel-*lo*! Here is Brandon who has come to visit you! And you know me—Meg!"

We have brought a bag of clementines from Safeway to the elderly residents. It is not good for them to have sweet things, so we are to bring them fruit. We help them peel the clementines, if they have trouble.

We read from the Bible to the ailing and elderly residents of Toms River Haven who listen eagerly at first as if we have brought news to them of their own lives, it is crucial for them to know. And there are some whose eyesight is so poor, they can no longer read their own Bibles. Mrs. Baumann talks happily about Jesus to the residents—"Jesus is an old friend of yours—you've known Him a lot longer than I have, I'm sure!" She has a high-pitched laugh and a habit of clutching at my arm as if she is in pain but it is a happy pain.

Soon, the residents begin to be sleepy. Especially those in wheelchairs begin to doze off as Mrs. Baumann and I alternate readings from the Gospels, the Book of Esther, Psalms—

"'O sing unto the Lord a new song: for He hath done marvelous things: His right hand, and His holy arm, hath gotten Him the victory. The Lord has made known His salvation: His righteousness hath He openly shewed in the sight of the heathen . . ."

My voice wavers but is strong. And Meg Baumann reaches out to take my hand in her warm dry fingers, to lend support.

Often I return to the Toms River Haven Home. None of the ailing and elderly residents recognize me, there is a comfort in this.

What a nice young man. A nice polite young man.

An elderly woman takes my hand and whispers to me—"Have you come to take me home? You are Harvey—are you? Please?"

The nursing staff knows me of course—"Hello, Brandon!"

My life would be a happy life, I think, if I were on the staff of the nursing home. It is good to bring happiness to strangers. Sometimes I eat lunch there, at a table with the residents. There is a music hour, one of the residents plays the piano with heavy chords like an organ and we sing together, Christian hymns. I have spoken with Reverend Baumann who advises me to return to school when the second trial is over and my name is cleared; I will enroll in Glassboro Community College where I will pursue a major that would allow me to work in a nursing facility like Tom River Haven Home—not as an attendant or a nurse's aide but as a health care administrator or assistant.

The staff is friendly to me. Most of the staff is friendly to me.

I have become acquainted with some of the nurses. One of the nurses is Irma who is my age or a little older, a big-boned woman with short curly blond hair and a nice smile, and one day Irma says to me when we're alone and no one else can hear, "I just want to say, Brandon, what a courageous thing you did! You stood up to those punks, it was just you against five of them, and they learned they better not push us around . . . There's been black men followed me, and said things to me, if I'd had a gun maybe I'd have stood up to them better than I did."

Irma asks me to sign a notepad for her, my autograph.

Brandon Schrank

Uncle T. has told me *The war that will undo this country is the race war. It is not acknowledged by the Government, that is in collusion with the immigrants and nigras that vote for the welfare state.*

One evening, the Cassells introduce me to Mr. Jorgenson who is a vice president of American Ace Firearms, Inc. with headquarters in Wilmington, Delaware. Mr. Jorgenson shakes my hand and is very friendly. He surprises me by right-away saying that his company is willing to help pay for my new trial, or possibly pay entirely for a new trial, if I will agree to a private lawyer of their choice—"One who is skilled in 'self-defense' law."

I am excited by this offer but feel guilty at the thought of firing my court-appointed lawyer. After some time discussing the situation with Mr. Jorgenson and with the Cassells, as it is pointed out to me that no public defender really has time and resources to present a defense like a private lawyer, and that the lawyer who would be hired by American Ace Firearms is one of the five top defense lawyers in the U.S., I say yes, and agree to switch to a new, private lawyer; and the Cassells tell me what a wise decision this is.

Mr. Jorgenson calls me "son." He pats my shoulder, squeezes my hand hard, calls me a hero.

"In our way of looking at this tragedy, which should be presented to the jury and to the U.S. public in a more forceful way than your attorney has done, you are being crucified for defending your own life. Except for the liberal media making a stink for political reasons, there is not a person living who would blame you or in your place would behave differently."

Later this week a photographer hired by American Ace Firearms arrives at the Cassells's house to take pictures of me though I have tried to explain to them, I hate to have my picture taken . . . (This goes back to high school when my senior yearbook picture was so fucking ugly, I would've liked to tear it out of every copy of the yearbook I could get my hands on.)

American Ace wants a "boyish"—"sensitive"—portrait of me, not with any firearm—of course!—to offset the ugly images of Brandon Schrank that have been circulating since April. It is important (they say) that my posture is "perfect"—that my head is held high and that in my face there is a look of "pride."

It is astonishing to me how many pictures the photographer takes, through much of an afternoon, and how fussy he is about lighting. For when we see a picture of a person we think—"This is how he *is*."

A website has been established for BRANDON SCHRANK and here, the new photos are posted. At first I hardly recognize myself—the portraits have been "Photoshopped" to remove blemishes on my forehead, shadows beneath my eyes—but gradually I am not so embarrassed, and come to see that I am actually kind of good-looking when my face is smiling and not so dour.

There is a T-shirt you can purchase for a donation of any sum beyond twenty-five dollars. In XL, L, M, S, XS sizes, in white, stamped front and back with my picture and LIVE FREE OR DIE BRANDON SCHRANK.

Response to the website is amazing. Letters and donations pour in each day. Many requests for the T-shirt. The Cassells do not keep me from seeing many of these, that are passed on to me by their assistants—

You are our hero Brandon Schwrank. We are praying for you.

We are enclosing a donation to help seccure Justice for you Brandon. And we are praying for you.

Soon, more than fifty thousand dollars has been received for the defense fund. And with each day, more donations arrive.

There is a race war. There is a war of atheism against the Christian people. The country is at war, the Government is the enemy. The president is guilty of treason. Brandon Schrank you are a soldier in this war, you must not give up hope. The second trial will end with AQUITTAL—this is a prediction!!!

My new lawyer Mr. Perrine calls with good news: the second trial has been postponed!

It is set now for Monday, October 6.

It is always to the advantage of the defendant, Mr. Perrine says, when trials are postponed. Witnesses can change their minds over time, in some cases witnesses can disappear. The second trial lawyer profits from the mistakes of the first lawyer and he is not surprised by the prosecution's case.

"We will throw a bomb at them, son—we will put you on the stand to testify on your own behalf."

This is a surprise! The public-defender lawyer said no no no never, we would never put you on the stand Brandon, to be eviscerated by the prosecution. And I had to wonder about that, for if I am innocent—if I am *not guilty*—it would seem strange to the jurors that I am not willing to testify.

"Don't worry, we will rehearse your every word. You will be a fledgling whose every wing-tremor will be rehearsed. The radiance of truth will shine in your face, son. All who look upon you will be blinded."

Mr. Perrine talked like that. Like Reverend Baumann when he was worked up. There was a flamey sensation you felt if you stood too near Mr. Perrine, a fear but an excitement too that you would catch flame. His wide mouth gleamed with silvery spittle.

America Unite! has joined American Ace Firearms to take on expenses of the trial. The Cassells explain to me that America Unite! is an organization of several million members dedicated to the preservation and protection of the English language, the Second Amendment, and the right of states to administer capital punishment, among other campaigns. Photographs of Brandon

Schrank are posted on America Unite!'s website to be many times replicated online.

It is very exciting. It is so exciting, I am not able to sleep except with sleeping pills the Cassells provide for me. And then, when I sleep, I do not dream. It is like switching off the TV—just blank, black.

In our dealings with them we should always hold the line. We should never move the line—not a foot, not an inch! And we should never show our weakness, and never give in.

I am holding the revolver in both hands. My finger is on the trigger. From a faraway star the thought comes to me dazzling my head—*This is the start of the new life.*

Irma asks me, what was it like? When did you *know* . . . ?

(I think Irma means: When did I know that I would shoot to kill.)

But even at such a time, when we are alone together in the darkness of Irma's bedroom, and there is no one to see my face, or record my words, I will never speak of the shooting.

It is not just that I have been warned not to speak of the shooting. Not just that I have been warned not to speak of that day in my life, the decision I made, or presumably made, when I entered my uncle's kitchen and took away his .45 caliber police service revolver without telling him, and concealed it in my waterproof polyester jacket; when I carried the gun against my heart for how many hours, how many minutes of mounting excitement, as one might feel carrying a bomb strapped around his waist that is set to explode at an unknown time. Not just that I have been warned not to speak of these minutes of which many are lost to me, like water that has plunged into water in a deafening cascade, many tributaries that flow into a single rushing river, but that I don't know how to speak of what happened—what happened *to me*—not *what I did*.

And when Irma asks me what am I thinking when I am so quiet, what am I feeling, the way women will ask that is like picking at a scab to see if the scab will come off and blood will ooze out below and they will then be upset and repelled by what they see—I am very quiet trying not to be visibly angry, that this person would wish to pry into my life, get beneath my skin when my skin is all that I have, to protect me.

I am safe at the Toms River Haven Home, and I am safe at church, and I am safe here (in the Cassells's house where I have a room at the back that had once belonged to the Cassells's son who'd been shipped to Afghanistan and had not returned except in a body bag to be buried in the Muhlenberg cemetery), but I am not safe in many places including my mother's house and my uncle T.'s house and my relatives' houses; I am not safe *in public*. My life has been threatened many times—(hundreds? thousands?)—but I am mostly unaware of these threats that are online, on the Internet, on Twitter, the name *Brandon Schrank* is everywhere.

In the Cassells's son's old room there is a water stain on the ceiling that you might think, if you stare at it long enough, lying on the bed with your eyes open and unblinking, is a widened and lidless eye staring back at you.

I was armed not because I wished to harm others but I wished to protect others.

On a bus for instance if there is a gang of "youths"—if they are threatening to women or older persons—(who might be persons of color themselves, as well as white people)—I would think that I might intervene. I was not looking to be heroic but to make a difference in life.

I am not sure what the wrong thing was, that I did that day. Taking my uncle's gun without asking him—that was the start of it. Yet, if I had not been armed, I might not be alive now. And so it was a decision that, though "wrong" at the time, would seem to be "right" now.

Yes. I have discussed this issue many times with my minister.

Yes. I have discussed this issue many times with my therapist.

I have given much thought to this issue for it is like one of those plastic games like a remote control where you have to push the little colored squares around, to make a pattern. You try, and you try, and you try to make a pattern, which is to "win" the game, but you can't, though you know it can be done and that by accident, at least once, you have done it yourself.

Yes. I believe that God has forgiven me. I know that many people are outraged at me for saying this simple fact but I never believed that God had been angry with me that He would need to "forgive" me. I never believed that God would wish to deny me my life since God gave me my life thirty years ago this November 2.

Leaving the old red-brick post office building on Main Street with so many stone steps. Where I'd gone to talk to my cousin who works there, not at the counter but back in the sorting area, so it was a hassle to get him, and I was feeling pissed, and Andy wasn't in a great mood, and it is no one's business the transaction between us—(that I needed to borrow money from Andy for repairs to my car). And behind the post office, down a hill, is the old Sears site now rubble and trash, but there's a cleared-away space for people to park their vehicles and not pay money at a meter. And there are these kids hanging out there, not all the time but sometimes, harassing people, or just looking at them in a way that is like a threat like if you were a (white) woman, for instance; or a (white) man. These kids hanging out in the lot are not always black-skinned, actually. There's white kids you see there sometimes, or older guys, any-color-skin, drug dealers could be, they are thugs—"gangstas"—and you walk past them quickly not meeting their eyes. And they laugh saying *Fag! Faggot!* Not always but sometimes, this has happened sometimes, and I am thinking how I will be prepared, as I was not prepared in high school, I would be prepared and I would take the gun out of my jacket, and lift and aim and pull the trigger as Uncle T. had taught me as a kid—you don't jerk the trigger, and you don't pull the trigger—you *press the trigger*. And the smirking faces turn to looks of astonishment and horror as the fucking thugs protest *No! Hey no man—don't shoot . . .*

When I pray on my knees the congregation of the Church of Christ is praying with me. Reverend Baumann has said *What is done to the least of you, is done to me. Always remember—Jesus said to the good thief, today you will be with me in paradise.*

It is never clear to me, what the Bible means to say; or what ministers draw from the Bible, to convey to us. It is mostly like a foreign language you hear somebody speaking in which now and then—(maybe it's mistakenly)—you hear something that makes sense.

Jesus in your heart. His love will bear you through the Valley of the Shadow of the Death not once but many times Amen.

Not a great day, last April. No work again this week and my damn fucking car needs an overhaul. Dropped by Uncle T.'s to ask for a few dollars' loan but can't get the words out, Uncle T. would give me the money (probably) but I already owe him—how much, can't remember—God damn embarrassing, at my age and with my skills. And Uncle T. goes down the hall to use the bathroom (and I'm seeing the old guy unsteady on his feet, having to press a hand against the wall so's to keep his balance which is painful to observe)—and there I am opening the drawer and have the gun in my hand, inside my jacket pocket thinking this .45 caliber police service revolver just *kept there* in the God-damn

drawer with kitchen crap. And at the back of the door is Uncle
T.'s gun like some damn forgotten toy. And I'm not thinking a
thing—nobody will believe me maybe but I am *not thinking a
thing not premeditating or planning* just—suddenly the gun is in
my hand, and that feels right.

Like solving the plastic puzzle, pushing the right colored
square in just the right place. And you know—*it's a fit.*

And I'm out of there, and Uncle T. blinks at me in surprise—
had just one beer with him, and he'd been expecting a session
of serious drinking.

Driving aimlessly into town, and on the pedestrian bridge by
the railroad track there's a tall skinny black kid leaning on the
railing so I park a half-block away and return and there's a bulge
in this kid's pocket for sure—(knife? gun?)—but there's other
kids, schoolkids just getting out yelling and tossing stones down
into the river and the black kid changes his mind about hanging
out there, and leaves walking fast. And later, by the high school,
the drive-through parking lot at the back and there's black kids
looking a lot older and meaner than they'd looked when I was a
student there. And later I'm on foot behind the Market Basket
there's this older black kid maybe nineteen, just kind of standing
there and he's looking at me kind of funny—(I think)—and his
mouth working like he's talking to himself—and my heart starts
beating fast before I am even thinking—*We are alone and there is
no one to see. If I turn my back, he could jump me.* But then two
things happen, to interfere: a (white) man opens the rear door,
calls to the black kid, and the kid comes over and disappears

inside then emerges with a case of something heavy and takes it to a pickup truck and he's delivering groceries or something like that so I'm thinking kind of mocking to myself—*Fuck this, asshole. Just go home, you're fucked.*

But then after the post office and talking to Andy there, and I'm not in a great mood, feeling really shitty, and there's some kids in the alley, loudmouths like rappers, and pants hanging half down their asses like gangstas, and I'm thinking how in the winter there's a problem in the parking lot here with kids throwing snowballs, harassing customers from the post office and my car was struck by a damn snowball last winter. It's mostly black kids, a certain kind of black kid, not all black kids but the majority, it's like they are interchangeable like some race thing how they hang together and look at you, and you can see how they're like hyenas or something that'd want to tear out your throat with their God-damn teeth that for all we know they sharpen like razors, like some savages in Africa sharpen their teeth.

First off, there was some black kids at the edge of the parking lot, five or six of them coming home from school, yelling and laughing like hyenas, and this other boy, who wasn't with them, and had to be older, and he's crossing through the lot like he has some destination and I'm standing there in his path so he has to look up at me kind of surprised, and he decides he will go around me but without looking at me now, and his head bowed, like he is not even aware of me and how I am looking at him; and I'm standing in front of him again, and he's thinking what the hell, I see a flash of his eyes and it's then that I see there are no witnesses right now, and this is my chance.

God has sent you a sign out of your entire life. You would be a shameful coward to run from it.

So I say to this fuckface black kid what's he want with me? Why's he following me? And he right-away says he is not following me which is what any of them would say, who intend to mug you or beat your head in with a rock. And I'm not excited, my voice is not raised, like on TV I am calmly telling this kid to get out of my way, better get out of my fucking way, and he's scared as hell I can see, and looking around to see if anybody's watching, and ready to run so I tell him stay where he is, I have the gun in my hand but held low, against my leg held in such a way that if anyone saw us from (for instance) the alley beside the post office they wouldn't see what is in my hand. And I tell him get onto his knees. I am still calm-seeming telling this punk to get onto his knees and pray and if he prays for his life the right way, so that God hears him, he will not be hurt.

It is a surprise to me, a good surprise, to see how scared this kid is, though taller than I am, and I see that he is (maybe) younger than I'd thought he was. Skinny kid like the other one at the pedestrian bridge, almost I'm embarrassed to have caught this one like catching an undersized fish or hunting and shooting an undersized buck, or a doe or fawn. And yet, God has sent this one to me. I tell him he isn't praying hard enough—"God havin trouble hearin you, man."

(It's funny, in black jive-talk dialect. Except the kid is too scared to appreciate the humor.)

I am not frightened but I am excited and my hand holding the gun is shaking and so I steady it with my other hand so the shaking is less. And I am swallowing hard for my throat is very dry. It is a joke to be doing this—(isn't it?)—for I do not intend to shoot this kid, or any kid of any-skin color only just to scare him a little, teach the motherfucker respect.

He is on his knees in the rubble. He is not praying but he is begging *me*.

He is saying *Don't shoot me, please don't shoot me*—he is begging *me*.

Yet somehow, the gun goes off. I did not press the trigger but somehow, the trigger is pressed, and the gun goes off. The explosion is deafening to me but not very real. *This is not happening*— this thought came to me as from a distant star, as I pull at the trigger another time, and another, it is as if the gun is firing itself, once it has started.

The boy is face-first on the ground in the rubble. Like in a movie there is blood so fast, but it is not like a movie how I am standing here with the gun not knowing what to do now, next; and the gun is quiet now, all the bullets are gone. And I am thinking how lonely I am, I am all alone here. There is no one here now but me.

The defense fund is more than $120,000 and it is only September first!

Yet, of all the people who are my friends and who have sent money and prayed for me, still I am alone. And I am thinking that the only person who I could talk to, who would understand something of what this is, is "Nelson Herrara"—who I'd never known, when we were alive.

Leaving to visit Irma, who lives in a duplex across town with her two little daughters. Irma is making dinner for us so we are like a family the four of us at the table in her kitchen and with two little girls there is always chatter and something to talk about so the conversation does not depend upon *me*.

Irma is shivery-thrilled to be with me. Sometimes I see her eyes on me like a cat's eyes reflecting the light. And it is exciting to her, she has told just a few friends and relatives. When I drive to her house, I park at the back, so that from the street you can't see my car. And though there have been no incidents, and no particular threats associated with her, Irma has put up blinds on all the windows of her house that hadn't had blinds, upstairs and down.

On my way out of the Cassells's house I see that there is a package on the front porch. How it got there without the dogs barking like crazy is not clear.

This package does not seem to have been sent through the U.S. mail. Mail addressed to BRANDON SCHRANK does not come to this address but to a P.O. Box where there are provisions for large quantities of mail placed in bins.

I am thinking—Is it a present? Is it a bomb?

At such times, you can't predict which times, I can become very excited. That is, my heartbeat is quickened and the palms of my hands are cold so I know that I am excited though in my thoughts I am calm. I am thinking how, if you did a brain X-ray of me, you would see how my "brain waves" are slow and measured like a quiet surf. In a way I am calm as if whatever will happen has already happened long ago and it is all over. And *Nelson Herrara* and *Brandon Schrank* are granite gravestones side by side in some quiet place unknown to the public.

And I wonder for a minute if this is so?—if the second trial began and ended like the first, in a "mistrial." And if this is the case, will there be a third trial? Mr. Perrine has said *There will always be one holdout juror on our side. That is an incontestable fact.*

And so, the trial is yet to come. And guilt/acquittal yet to come.

Back in April already it was made clear to me, I am never supposed to touch such packages. Let alone lift them, or shake them, or try to open them. Of course—I know this! It makes me laugh to think of the Cassells and Mr. Jorgenson and Mr. Perrine and all the others on my side, who are counting on me to prevail, frowning at me now. Like they can scold *me.*

And Irma is waiting for me. And Irma has asked, are we engaged? Am I your fiancée, Brandon?

I am trying to gauge God's feeling here. Sometimes it is very clear what God feels, and sometimes not. One thing is clear: in my heart I am not a murderer. God understands for He sees into every heart. And so, it would be likely that the package, which is carefully wrapped in brown paper, will be some "gift" for me which could be home-baked cookies or my own picture taken from the website which someone has transferred onto a piece of colored plastic.

It is strange how I watch myself. Sometimes I think, I am in a cartoon like the *Simpsons* in which funny things happen nonstop and people are hurt sometimes but recover swiftly as Homer Simpson recovers every indignity. I am seeing myself behave strangely. I am seeing myself stoop to pick up the package— and bring the package into the house—and into the Cassells's kitchen. It is good that there is no one to observe for they would not approve. Mr. Cassell is gone from the house, and Mrs. Cassell is with some volunteer worker in the big room where my mail is being sorted, envelopes opened and donations retrieved. I am in the kitchen, and I have set the package on the kitchen table. There is some flashback to entering Uncle T.'s kitchen and opening the drawer to find the revolver—(that I knew absolutely was there)—as I pull open the drawer here to locate a pair of scissors. And I am thinking, the way I have come to think slow thoughts like lying on my back on Vernon Cassells's former bed staring up at the eye in the ceiling staring down at me—*If this is where I have been sent, it is right to be here. There is no other place for me, for now.* The package is a cardboard box measuring approximately eighteen inches by twelve inches and it is somewhat heavy—maybe ten pounds. I lower my head to listen, to see if it is ticking. (This is a joke of course. It is *not ticking.*) After rummaging around in the drawer, I have found it—a pair of scissors. I will cut the string and I will use the sharp point of the scissors like a knife, to open the package addressed in large black-inked letters

MR BRANTON SCHWANK

Gun Accident

An Investigation

1.

Do you recall the sequence of events? They asked me.

But I could not reply coherently. Because I could not remember coherently. *The gun was fired close beside my head. The explosion was so loud I could not hear and I could not see and when I realized where I was, the right side of my head had struck the hardwood floor just beyond the rug and that was where I was lying but I could not move. On the floor it came to me that I was shot, and (maybe) I was dead because I did not feel anything or hear anything.*

For a long time then I did not move for (maybe) I was dead. It was a thought a clever child would have—if I did not try to move, and did not fail to move, then I would not know (maybe) if I was dead or if I was still alive.

2.

I am begging him *No! Go away.*

It is still the time when he is alive. Before the bullet enters his chest, and his heart explodes.

Travis is alive and he is on his feet but he does not hear me. He is alive but he is laughing at me and so he does not hear me. And I realize that my throat is shut up tight and the words are trapped inside my head. *Go away go away! Please go away!*—I am begging him.

It is that time he cannot realize—he is still alive. He is laughing and his face is bright-glaring with happiness because he is alive and cannot imagine any time when he will be *not-alive* for (it is said) no animal can comprehend its own death.

There is Travis, and there is the other who is older than Travis. Instinctively I know that I must not look at his face. I must not lift my eyes to his face. I must not give him any reason to believe that I might identify him.

It is inborn, such cunning. It is as natural as trying to shield your face with your arms, doubling over to protect your belly and groin. It is purely instinct, this desperation to be spared harm.

And so, I do not look at the other. *The other* is the one at whom I do not look. It is my cousin Travis from whom I cannot turn away because it is my cousin Travis who has grabbed hold of me and it is my cousin Travis who has the gun.

3.

In dreams sometimes it is like this. I am lying very still, my arms and legs are numb or paralyzed. There is a medical term—*peripheral neuropathy*. A tingling sensation in fingers and toes that moves upward bringing with it a loss of feeling, a spreading numbness, a kind of amnesia of the body.

No I do not "believe" in dreams and would not bore or exasperate anyone with the idiocy of most dreams but this is not a dream exactly—for I am not asleep though I am paralyzed as in sleep.

There is an explanation for why we are "paralyzed" in sleep: a part of the brain shuts down so that when we dream of running, for instance, we don't actually run—we are prevented from moving our muscles, and waking ourselves.

Except of course sleepwalkers do "walk"—and remain asleep.

At such times I am very frightened and yet calm-seeming for it is crucial never to show fear. If there are witnesses who might laugh at you, or bring harm to you. As I knew my cousin Travis Reidl and the boy or young man who'd been with him—(whose face I never saw but whose voice I heard, and it was not a voice I recognized)—would laugh at me, and hurt me. And I was thinking *If I don't move I will not have to know if I am alive or not-alive. It is better not to move.*

It is a delicious paralysis like floating in water so icy-cold, there is no sensation at all.

Until one of the children wakes me, pulling at my shoulder.

"Mom-my! Mom-*my*!"—for children do not like to see their mother lying beneath bedcovers tense and tight as a clenched fist.

"Mom, *wake up*"—my daughter Ellen cries in her sharp furious child-voice that pierces the deepest sleep.

And so within seconds I am awake, and I am sitting up, and I am Mommy again. And I laugh at the children who appear frightened, to assure them that yes of course, Mommy is fine.

It is the morning of our yearly trip to visit the children's grandparents in Sparta, 350 miles away in upstate New York in the foothills of the Adirondack Mountains.

4.

Do you recall the gun, I was asked.

And the answer was *No—not the gun but the deafening gunshot, I recall.*

Not the gun (which I never saw clearly, my eyes were blinded with tears) but the consequences of the gunshot.

In the *Sparta Journal* the handgun would be identified as a double-action .38 caliber Colt revolver. It was the property of Gordon McClelland of 46 Drumlin Avenue, Sparta, who'd had a homeowner's permit for it issued several years before, in 1958.

A homeowner's permit means that the gun owner must keep his gun on the premises. It is not legal to remove the gun from the house, to carry it in a pocket or in a vehicle as a "concealed weapon."

Mr. McClelland also owned hunting guns—two deer rifles, a shotgun. These were locked in a cabinet in his home office that my cousin and his accomplice-friend could not open.

When the gun went off close beside my head I could not think.

I did not know what had happened—I did not know if I had been hit. I did not know if my cousin had knocked me down onto the floor—I'd been pushed, or shot.

I did not know if anyone had been shot. I did not know if the shot had been deliberate or an accident.

Twenty-six years later! No one asks me any longer but the truth is, I still do not know.

5.

Here is a surprise: the McClelland house is still standing at 46 Drumlin Avenue as if it were an ordinary house in which no one had died.

This is not a pleasant surprise. It is a surprise that grips me each time I return to Sparta, like a claw.

If I am with others, for instance my children, in this car, I never indicate that I am upset, or even distracted—usually I continue driving past 46 Drumlin without another glance.

For why have I come here, when there is no need? *Why?*—my fourteen-year-old self might shout at me.

"That house—an old teacher of mine used to live here . . ."

I hear myself speak in a faltering voice more to myself than to my daughter in the passenger's seat beside me, and to my son in the backseat.

How strange, and how misleading. To refer to Mrs. McClelland as *an old teacher*. In fact, I remember Gladys McClelland as anything but *old*.

Yet *former* seems too deliberate, too formal. In speaking to my children I speak an unadorned language which is the language of maternal affection. I don't want to impress my children, or even to teach them vocabulary words—I want them to trust me.

So they will think that their mother is someone like them, an adult but essentially a friend, whom they can trust as they can't trust other adults.

For I remember vividly, when I was a little girl, understanding that the loyalty of adults is to other adults, not to children. You dare not tell a parent your innermost thoughts. You dare not betray *secrets*.

My daughter Ellen asks what kind of teacher was Mrs. McClelland.

For a moment I am struck by *was*. I know that the McClellands moved away from Sparta a long time ago but I have no idea if they are still living—probably yes, since they were only just middle-aged in 1961.

"'What kind of teacher'?—a very good teacher. An excellent teacher. We all loved Mrs. McClelland . . ."

"What did she *teach*, Mom?"

"Mrs. McClelland taught social studies. And she was my ninth-grade homeroom teacher also."

Was. Impossible to avoid *was*.

You might expect Ellen to ask something more—why did I love my ninth-grade teacher, what was so special about Mrs.

McClelland, and what became of Mrs. McClelland—but she has lost interest; it is an effort for even a courteous eleven-year-old to care about a mother's memory of an old teacher. In the backseat, eight-year-old Lanny is peering out the window at something that intrigues him, in the opposite direction, as indifferent to his mother's chatter as if it were the droning of a radio voice.

"She was—Mrs. McClelland—someone special. In my life . . ."

I am gripping the steering wheel with both hands. I am staring at the dignified old Colonial with its soft-red aged brick looking just slightly weatherworn, and dark green shutters in need of repainting, and steep shingled roof with an antique weather vane at one of the peaks, the figure of a leaping deer. Has anything changed? *Is* this really the house? Each time I visit Sparta, each time I drive past this house, my senses are aroused as if with a whiplash to my bare back.

Only you, Hanna. No one else.

I don't think that I need to tell you—do not bring anyone else to this house. Do not let anyone else inside.

Of course strangers live at 46 Drumlin Avenue now. If I were to ask my mother who lives here, which I would never do, she would likely stare at me, and say, with a hurt, defensive little laugh, "Who lives there? I have no idea."

Within a few months of the shooting the McClellands moved out. At school it was known that Gladys McClelland could not bear to live in a house in which a "young person" had died.

Do you promise, Hanna?

Yes. I promise.

At my parents' house on Quarry Street in a very different neighborhood of smaller houses and smaller lots I turn my car into the familiar driveway with a flood of relief. But then the flood keeps coming, a rising pressure inside my head.

The children rush from the car, eager to run into their grandparents' house after the tedium of the long drive. But I am feeling too weak to move—leaning against the steering wheel weak-armed, dazed. Waiting for the pressure in my brain to subside. Waiting for the sensation of terrifying fullness to subside.

It had to be, what happened. There was no choice.

"Hanna? Dear, is something wrong?"

Someone has opened the car door, and is shaking me. My mother, leaning over me. Her anxious face is too near, like an unmoored sun. And behind her, my father looking grayer-haired than I recall.

My parents are concerned that I'd turned into the driveway—braked the car—the children ran inside the house—but that I'd remained in the car.

They'd hurried outside to see where I was and found me at the wheel—"Looking like you were asleep, but with your eyes open."

But I am all right now, I tell them. I am out of the car, and hugging my parents, and it is true, I am fully recovered from whatever it was that had gripped me fleetingly but terribly.

"Hanna, so good to see you! Welcome home."

6.

Helping out. Both my mother and I were proud of the fact that, during her husband's hospitalization in Syracuse, I'd been asked to *help out* my teacher Mrs. McClelland.

My responsibilities were to drop by the McClelland house once a day after school to bring in the mail and newspaper, to feed Mrs. McClelland's cat and to water her plants as needed—"Of course I will pay you, Hanna."

When Mrs. McClelland told me what she would pay for each hour I spent in her house, I was stunned—nearly twice as much as babysitting rates.

It was an emergency situation. The McClellands had not known that Mr. McClelland would require surgery so suddenly, and Mrs. McClelland would be away from Sparta for several days at least, staying in a hotel in Syracuse, near the University Medical Center fifty miles away. A substitute teacher would take her place. And Mrs. McClelland was hoping that I could *help out*.

It was April 1961. I was fourteen years old and in ninth grade and in love with my homeroom and social studies teacher Mrs. McClelland who seemed often to favor me—at least, I was one of a number of students whom Mrs. McClelland seemed to particularly like.

Gladys McClelland was a strikingly attractive woman of an indeterminate age—she might have been in her early forties but she seemed to us much younger, of a generation distinct from our mothers' generation, as her clothing, hairstyle, intelligence and zestful personality set her apart from other teachers at our school. She wore her shoulder-length blond hair in a "pageboy" — wavy, shiny, turned under; her face was glamorously made up, like a face on a fashion magazine cover; her shoes were high-heeled, and her stockings were sheer, often dark-tinted. Her girl students had memorized most of her clothing—cashmere sweaters, pleated skirts, tight-cinched belts; we knew her rings, jewelry; we knew several coats of which the most elegant was dark wool that fell nearly to her ankles, with a collar that might have been mink. Her figure wasn't what one would call slender but rather "shapely"—hips, breasts. She reminded some of us of the Hollywood actress Jeanne Crain—a beautiful woman who was yet *nice*.

It was known that Mrs. McClelland lived with her husband in a large, attractive house in Sparta's most prestigious residential neighborhood. It was known that Mrs. McClelland's husband was someone important—a World War II war hero, a retired army officer. He was a businessman, or a professional man— lawyer, banker. As Gladys McClelland resembled Jeanne Crain, Mr. McClelland resembled darkly handsome Robert Taylor.

Why did we love Mrs. McClelland? She wasn't an easy grader—she made us work—but she was sympathetic with us, and patient. She was often very funny. Her teaching manner was a combination of wit, humor, and seriousness; we laughed a good deal in Mrs. McClelland's classes, though what we laughed at was difficult to explain or to repeat to others. Mrs. McClelland had a way—almost, it was flirtatious; certainly, it was affectionate—of calling upon students who were reluctant to volunteer answers, and initiating with even the shyest or most awkward a kind of dialogue; one day, I would learn that this was the Socratic method—questions following questions in rapid-fire succession.

Mrs. McClelland's philosophy was: we all knew much more than we knew that we knew. The teacher's job was to draw such knowledge out of us—"Like poking through a grating with a big pronged fork, seeing what's there and hauling it up." (Was this one of Mrs. McClelland's clever remarks? We laughed to hear it.)

Boys were mesmerized by Mrs. McClelland, we knew. Some boys.

Others, sulky older boys who disliked school and shrugged off poor grades, biding time until at the age of sixteen they could quit school forever, said things about Mrs. McClelland that were not so nice, we knew.

By ninth grade a girl has been made to know that she is, in the eyes of (most) boys, her body. *Tits, ass.* And nastier words, some of us tried never to hear.

(It was rumored that sometimes, these words were scrawled on Mrs. McClelland's car in whitewash, or spray paint. And that as a consequence Mrs. McClelland was allowed to park her new-model yellow Buick in the area of the administrators' parking places, visible from the office windows.)

In Mrs. McClelland's warmly musical voice our names acquired a special distinction. I would remember the morning in our homeroom when Mrs. McClelland lightly touched my shoulder saying, "Hanna, may I speak with you?"—indicating that I should follow her out into the corridor.

I felt my face heat with blood, at this unexpected request. I felt the keenness with which my friends observed me, hurrying after Mrs. McClelland in high-heeled black leather shoes rimmed with ornamental red stitching.

There was no more alarming prospect, being asked to speak with a teacher in the corridor out of earshot of classmates. Like hearing your name over the loudspeaker, the dreaded commandment *Come at once to the main office.*

In such ways were hapless students informed of family emergencies, sudden deaths. Rarely such interruptions of routine brought good news.

It was not like Mrs. McClelland to betray unease or edginess. Even now though she was clearly anxious she smiled at me, and spoke calmly to me; she knew that I felt uncomfortable being singled out for attention. She told me about the sudden "family emergency"—her husband had to have surgery in Syracuse the next morning.

"It isn't major surgery," Mrs. McClelland said carefully. "Gordon will be all right. It's just that—we weren't prepared for—so suddenly—tomorrow morning at seven o'clock . . ."

Could I *help her out?*—Mrs. McClelland was asking.

Of course, I said *Yes.* I was touched that Gladys McClelland would select me for such a responsible task. Often in homeroom I assisted her in various small ways, passing out papers to classmates, watering and trimming her houseplants which grew profusely on the windowsills—spider plants, philodendron, cacti. When Mrs. McClelland sprained her ankle in a skiing accident, and came to school hobbling on crutches, I was one of those who helped her get around, carried things for her which she couldn't easily carry for herself. *Girls! Thanks so much. What would I do without you . . .*

Mrs. McClelland had swiped at her eyes, she'd been so moved. Some of us had brought her flowers for her homeroom desk: roses, carnations, and a *Get Well* card in the shape of a fluffy white cat.

I knew that my mother would not disapprove of my "helping out" my teacher in her emergency. My mother was often jealous on my behalf when other people's daughters seemed to be surpassing her daughter, and she was always eager to hear about my teachers' interest in me as if such interest reflected well upon herself, who'd been born in rural Beechum County in a ramshackle farmhouse, and had dropped out of school in ninth grade.

The McClellands lived only a few blocks from our house which was on a narrow street literally below Drumlin Avenue, winding along the edge of an ancient glacial hill. Often I babysat for neighbors, but I did not think that the McClellands had children.

I was a quiet, diminutive girl for my age, who wore her sand-colored hair in a way that partly covered the left side of my face, to hide a birthmark on my cheek. The birthmark was of the size and hue of a small strawberry and had something of a strawberry's texture—slightly raised, distinctive to the touch. To me, nothing was more defacing or ugly than this birthmark. As a young child I'd been tormented over the birthmark, mercilessly; even my friends had never let me entirely forget it. And even at fourteen I was sometimes singled out for mockery by crude boys. In any mirror my gaze moved involuntarily *there*—to check if the strawberry birthmark still existed, or had disappeared miraculously.

Is it a sign from God? But—why?

In my dreams even now, decades later, when the erasure of the old birthmark would make not the slightest difference in my life, still I find myself anxious to check my mirror reflection, staring into a cloudy glass as if my very life were at stake. Often in such dreams I am being harassed. Someone is shouting at me in derision, and laughing. But I am not able to see even my face in the dream mirror, let alone the little birthmark. Helplessly I think—*How foolish is vanity. How futile.*

I remember myself as a plain girl of no particular distinction, except for the birthmark. Yet, photographs of me taken at this time show a moderately attractive girl—when smiling, I might have been called pretty. I'd felt unpopular, friendless—though in fact I had many friends in school, among them several of the most popular girls in my class. I'd been elected vice president of our eighth-grade class and would be again elected vice president of our junior class in high school. I was involved in numerous "activities" and was always an honors student—but high grades seemed to me a kind of embarrassment, the consequence of hard work as hard work seemed but the consequence of desperation.

Nothing that I'd accomplished seemed of particular significance, since it had been accomplished by *me*.

And so it was wonderful, that Mrs. McClelland liked me enough to entrust me with visiting her house while she was away. This was enormously thrilling to me, I could have wept with gratitude.

When I returned to my homeroom desk several girls asked me what Mrs. McClelland had wanted with me?—but I couldn't tell them, just yet. My heart was filled to bursting with a secret so delicious, just to impart it too quickly was to risk diluting its wonder.

After school that day Mrs. McClelland walked me through the rooms of the large Colonial house on Drumlin Avenue which previously I had only seen from the street.

The McClellands' house was one of a number of handsome old houses on Drumlin Avenue with which residents of Sparta were all familiar. Dreamily you bicycled past such houses in which important citizens lived. In other neighborhoods in the small city (population 12,000) people were often viewed in their driveways, on front walks and front lawns; often, they were viewed working on their lawns. But never the residents of Drumlin Avenue, who hired others to do their lawn work. And if they appeared out of doors it was at the rear of their large houses, hidden from view.

Even in adulthood you would go out of your way to drive past such distinguished old residences, wondering at the secret lives within even as, with the shrinkage of time, you are apt to know that happiness does not require such houses, and that inhabiting such houses guarantees nothing.

How strange to me, at fourteen, to be so suddenly—so *easily* —inside this Drumlin Avenue house! And how strange, to be alone with my teacher Mrs. McClelland, in this private place.

It was rare for me to be alone with any adult not my parents or a close relative.

And Mrs. McClelland was not quite the same person whom I knew from school. On the eve of her husband's surgery she was visibly agitated. The witty, composed and self-assured teacher had vanished and in her place was a distracted woman of my mother's age, not much taller than I was. Though she was wearing her teacher's clothing of that day—red wool jacket with brass buttons, pleated red-plaid skirt, dark-hued stockings and black leather shoes—she did not exude an air of glamour. Her hair was brushed back behind her ears and her lipstick was worn off. Her usually lustrous, playful-alert eyes were red-rimmed and damp with worry. In a brave voice Mrs. McClelland told me that her husband had been brought by a private car to Syracuse that afternoon, to check into the hospital attached to the medical school; she would make the drive early the next morning, hoping to arrive at the hospital at about the time her husband's surgery was scheduled to begin. She explained that he was having "minor surgery"—"nothing to worry about"—adding then, with a breathless little laugh, "except of course any sort of surgery requiring anesthetic is not *minor*."

And several times she insisted: "It's important, Hanna— don't let anyone else in the house while you're here. Only your mother, if she wants to come with you, but—no one else. Do you promise?"

Gravely I promised *Yes*.

Soon after our conversation that morning in school Mrs. McClelland telephoned my mother. It had not occurred to me that she might telephone my mother at all. It would not have occurred to me that my teacher would require permission from my mother to hire me for this task of "helping out"—but of course Mrs. McClelland had acted properly, and graciously.

Mrs. McClelland was telling me that the upstairs rooms would all be shut: "No need to go upstairs at all. And my husband's home office—at the end of the hall, here—will be locked. When you bring in mail for 'Gordon McClelland' just put it with the other mail, on the dining room table."

Mrs. McClelland spoke quickly, with an air of distraction, leading me through the downstairs rooms of the beautifully furnished house. I had never seen such interesting furniture—a large, sinuously shaped coffee table seemingly made of a single piece of smoothed and polished red-brown wood, like the interior of a tree; a miniature piano, made of some sort of white wood—was this a harpsichord? I did not dare ask for I was too shy, and I sensed that Mrs. McClelland would be impatient with idle questions. Her instructions for helping out were more elaborate than I would have expected: I was to take care of the cat, and tend to the plants; bring in the mail and newspaper and anything that might be tossed onto the front steps; switch on lights in several rooms, raise and lower the blinds each evening in a different way, turn on the TV—to suggest that someone was in the house. "Try to spend at least an hour here, if you can. So that Sasha doesn't feel totally abandoned. You could do homework, on the sofa here. You could watch TV. You are welcome to eat anything you find in the refrigerator or the freezer but—of course—just *you*. No one else."

Mrs. McClelland spoke rapidly without uttering my name as if in the exigency of the moment, her eyes darting about, the fingers of one hand nervously turning her gold wristwatch around her wrist, she'd forgotten who I was.

One end of the elegant dining room had been extended into a sunroom with ceiling-to-floor plate-glass windows and a skylight and in this space were potted plants of various sizes and shapes. Some were spectacularly beautiful—a large Boston fern, in a hanging basket; a row of African violets in clay pots; a five-foot Chinese evergreen. These plants required a far more complicated care than the relatively simple plants Mrs. McClelland kept in her homeroom which were mostly cacti and jade plants, that could go without watering for long periods; fortunately I'd brought along my notebook, so that like the good-girl student I was, I could take notes.

Mrs. McClelland instructed me to water the ferns sparingly— "Enough to moisten the soil. You can judge how dry the soil is by touching it. *Don't overwater.*" No water for the "snake plant"—an ugly, tough-looking plant with tall spear-like leaves; no water for the enormous jade plant, which looked like a living creature with myriad, twisted arms; no water for the orchids, which looked impossibly exotic and fragile. There were English ivy and grape ivy, philodendron with flowing leaves, "spider plants," and "peperomia"—all of which would require watering/spraying in two or three days. Several African violet plants with small delicate petals required the most complicated care.

"If a leaf turns yellow, pinch it off. And don't move any of the plants, of course, each is in its optimum position for sunshine. Remember to test with your finger, to see if the soil is dry. And remember—*don't overwater*. Any more than you would want to drown, no plant wants to be drowned."

It was the sort of offhanded, wry remark Mrs. McClelland might make in school, with a smile that indicated she meant to be funny, and so we might laugh; but here in her house Mrs. McClelland did not smile, and so I knew she did not mean to be funny, and I was not meant to laugh.

She would leave the sprayer and the green enamel watering can on the floor by the plants, she said. There would be water in both, at room temperature; when I replenished the water, I should make sure that it was not too cold, or too hot.

All this while, a sleekly beautiful silver-blue Siamese cat was observing us at a distance, following us from room to room but never crossing a threshold. The cat's eyes were a startling blue. Her ears were much larger and more angular-shaped than the ears of an ordinary cat and her chocolate-tipped tail was switching with obvious unease or annoyance. I had never seen such a striking animal up close. Mrs. McClelland said that she hoped I might "make friends" with Sasha, but the prospect did not seem likely; the cat continued to keep her distance from us, even as Mrs. McClelland tried to entice her with a cat treat that resembled a handful of cereal.

"Sasha! Sasha, come here. Kit-*ty*."

Each day I was to open a fresh can of cat food for Sasha, Mrs. McClelland said, as well as provide her with dry food and fresh water. Sasha would be upset at being left alone, and so possibly she wouldn't eat—at first; but even if she hadn't finished her food from the previous day, I was to wash out the bowl and dry it with a paper towel and open a new can. I was to "vary" the cans—tuna fish, salmon, chicken, beef—in that order; each day I was to change the water bowl. Mrs. McClelland showed me Sasha's litter box which was kept in a corner of a large utility room off the kitchen, and this litter box was to be changed at least every other day—"Before it gets seriously dirty, or Sasha will refuse to use it."

Refuse! I had to smile thinking of our family cats who were forcibly put outside if they balked in freezing weather and who had not the privilege of any sort of refusal.

"Sasha, come here and meet your new friend! No one will hurt you."

The silver-blue Siamese kept a wary distance. Her icy eyes betrayed no more recognition of the devoted mistress who called to her in a cajoling voice than of her "new friend."

"You must not let Sasha slip outside—she may try to, when you open the door. She can be devious! But a Siamese is strictly an indoor cat and could not long survive outdoors."

Could not long survive outdoors. I wondered if this strangely phrased statement could be true. If the purebred Siamese would not soon adapt to a new environment, like any cat, and become a feral creature.

I assured Mrs. McClelland that I would not let Sasha slip outside.

At this moment the phone rang. Mrs. McClelland gave a little cry of pure fright and for a moment looked terrified. I was embarrassed to see my teacher fumbling for the phone, and looked away as Mrs. McClelland murmured evasively, "Yes, thank you! I'm fine. I will be driving to the hospital tomorrow. I've asked one of my very dependable ninth-grade girls to look in on the house while I'm away . . . Yes, of course I trust her!" Mrs. McClelland shot me a squinting smile as if to reassure me.

As Mrs. McClelland spoke on the phone to this person to whom she clearly did not wish to speak at this time, I drifted away so that I wouldn't overhear. Dropping to my knees, whispering, "Sasha! Kit-ty!"—trying without success to entice the sleekly beautiful Siamese to approach me.

It was disconcerting—it was shocking—to see our admired teacher in this state and to realize that this was the true Gladys McClelland, emotionally dependent upon a man, a husband; not so very different from my mother and my female relatives. The other, our glamorous teacher at Sparta Middle School, was a performer of a kind, who'd captivated our attention but who was not *real.*

Not until years later when I was a young married woman would I understand why Mrs. McClelland was so frightened. I would understand the blunt, terrible truth—*A career is not a life. Only a family is a life.*

Before we left the house Mrs. McClelland had me practice opening the door with her key—not the front door but the kitchen door, which was the door she wanted me to use; she gave me a typed list of instructions and telephone numbers; and she gave me several twenty-dollar bills—"In case you need emergency money."

Sixty dollars? I could barely speak. This was more than I might have fantasized earning if I'd helped out Mrs. McClelland for weeks.

Though I told Mrs. McClelland that I was perfectly able to walk the short distance home, she insisted upon driving me. I understood—(this was evident from Mrs. McClelland's classroom personality as well)—that once Mrs. McClelland had made a decision, she would not change it; she knew what should be done, and would do it.

"It's dark. It's cold. Of course I'm not going to let you walk home, Hanna."

Hanna. The sound of my name in Mrs. McClelland's voice suffused me with warmth.

In the November twilight, that comes early, and darkens to night by 6:00 P.M., I was grateful that my parents' small asphalt-sided house on narrow Quarry Street wasn't clearly defined and I was grateful that my mother had no idea that Gladys McClelland had pulled up to the curb in front of the house in her canary-yellow Buick—as in a teenager's nightmare, my mother might well have run outside to invite her in.

That evening my mother interrogated me about the visit. What sort of house the McClellands lived in, what my duties would be. My mother was pleased and excited for me—(she'd already begun to boast about my *helping out* my teacher to relatives)—but she was apprehensive too: if something happened to the McClellands' house, would her daughter be blamed?

Mrs. McClelland had told my mother how much she intended to pay me but my mother could have no idea that Mrs. McClelland had already paid me, several times more than the sum she'd promised. I considered whether to tell my mother about the sixty dollars, and when—but not just yet.

I felt a stab of rebellion, resentment. My mother would take most of the money from me, if she knew. But she didn't have to know how much money there was.

It's my money. I am earning it.

Like most of the adults of my acquaintance, my mother was not given to extravagant praise. Generosity of spirit was not typical of either of my parents' families who'd grown up on small, unprosperous farms in the area, adults who'd lived through what came to be called the Great Depression. If my mother and her female relatives spoke well of anyone, however it might be deserved, there was invariably a pause in their conversation, and a qualifying rejoinder—*Of course, look where she came from. That family.*

And so when my mother spoke positively of Mrs. McClelland—"gracious"—"kind"—"a real lady"—I waited to hear what she would add; but all she could think to say was, thoughtfully, "They don't have children, her and her husband. I wonder whose fault it was."

7.

"Hello? Hello . . ."

So nervous and excited the following afternoon when I first entered the McClelland house I couldn't resist calling out in this way as if I half expected someone to be home.

But the house was empty of course. Except for a murmurous sound, a muted cry, a rapid scurrying of cat-claws on a hardwood floor—the silver-blue Siamese fled from view as soon she realized a stranger had arrived.

"Sasha! Kit-*ty*."

I saw that a few things were not as I'd expected. Mrs. McClelland hadn't left the sprayer and the watering can on the dining room floor; these were in the kitchen. In the sink, breakfast dishes were soaking as if she'd departed hastily. On a kitchen counter, scattered pages of the previous day's *Sparta Journal*. A hall closet with door ajar, and a bare lightbulb burning inside.

I remembered how distracted Mrs. McClelland had been the previous afternoon. How frightened she'd been when the phone rang—as if she'd feared the worst.

We are sorry to say—bad news . . . Your husband has died.

Later, I would discover that several of the upstairs rooms hadn't been closed as Mrs. McClelland had planned—that is, their doors hadn't been shut. After some anguished deliberation I would close these doors, reasoning that if Mrs. McClelland believed she'd closed the doors, to discover them open would be a shock; naturally she would think that I'd been prowling in a part of the house forbidden to me.

Thinking *It might a test, how honest I am.*

But this was not likely: Mrs. McClelland already trusted me. Mrs. McClelland liked me. *Mrs. McClelland is my friend.*

I'd brought in mail and newspapers and left these on the dining room table where Mrs. McClelland had indicated. There were several letters for *Mr. Gordon C. McClelland* that appeared to be business letters or bills and just one letter for *Mrs. Gordon C. McClelland* that did not look especially interesting.

All this while I'd been calling for Sasha in a light airy voice. To my disappointment Sasha ignored me.

Deftly I removed yesterday's (partly eaten) cat food from the cat's plastic bowl, and opened a new can—tuna. The pungent odor of tuna fish filled the kitchen. Fresh dry food, and fresh water. It did look as if the lonely cat had eaten something, and when I checked her litter box in the storage room, that too had been used, if sparingly.

But where was Sasha? Keeping her distance.

Back in the kitchen, I washed and dried the dishes in the sink. Here too I was concerned that when Mrs. McClelland returned she might think that her student helper had left the dishes soaking, and not her.

I thought—*Mrs. McClelland will see how clean the house is! Mrs. McClelland will be impressed.*

With the same fastidious care I dealt with the houseplants. I was determined not to make any blunders, and disappoint my teacher who had such faith in me.

At close range I examined the orchids—so fragile, and so beautiful! These were native to Mexico and South America, Mrs. McClelland had said. Their flowers were so subtly colored, I could not have described them: silvery pink, pearly lavender. And the petals were so finely marked, like Japanese or Chinese calligraphy I'd seen reproduced in books.

I thought—*Someday I will have orchids like these. A house like this.*

I'd intended to examine some of the many books in the Mc-Clellands' bookshelves which had been built floor-to-ceiling in a library-like room adjacent to the living room—but I didn't feel at ease in this room; nor did I feel at ease turning on the McClellands' floor-model television, which was so much larger and more beautiful than my parents' small, black-and-white television. For what if something happened to the television set, when I turned it on? I had a dread of being blamed.

Next to the TV room was Mr. McClelland's "home office"— which Mrs. McClelland had locked, she'd said. I did not try this door for I could imagine Mrs. McClelland observing me, frowning.

Somewhere behind me—or upstairs—there came a sound, like harsh breathing. My heart leapt in my chest like a frightened little toad.

"Hello? Hello . . ."

There was no one—of course. (Was there? No one?)

This house was so much larger than my parents' house! I had not even any idea, how many rooms.

Suddenly, I had to leave. Had to get out of this house.

Though I had not been here for twenty minutes and had not executed all of the tasks Mrs. McClelland expected of me. Though the lonely Sasha must have been waiting for me to approach her, and plead with her to eat.

Hurriedly I switched off lights, and fled to Quarry Street to my own house. Not a thing had happened—and yet I felt shaken, and exhausted.

Seeing that I seemed distraught my mother questioned me about the visit. Had something gone wrong?

No! Not a thing had gone wrong.

"But is the house all right? Is the house as Mrs. McClelland left it?"

This was an odd question. All I could stammer was, "I think—it is. Everything is all right."

"She called me today. From Syracuse."

"Called you? Mrs. McClelland?"—this was confusing to me, I wasn't sure that I had heard correctly. "What—what did she say?"

"Gladys called to ask about the house, and you. I don't think she cares to talk about her husband, whatever it is that's wrong with him. She's a very private person and I can understand that—I'm exactly the same way. 'Minor surgery'—could be anything." My mother spoke casually yet with an air of pride. "It's like we're old friends, Gladys McClelland and me—over this emergency. I mean, the way she called upon you to help her out. She said you are a 'very thoughtful'—'very trustworthy'—girl. I guess she doesn't remember, but we've met once or twice, in town. I didn't try to remind her because it might have embarrassed her not to remember me."

This report of my mother's was astonishing to me. Mrs. Mc-Clelland and my mother, talking on the phone!—talking, at least in part, about *me*.

It was disconcerting to imagine Mrs. McClelland befriending my mother, for the "friendship" would be very one-sided. I dreaded the prospect of hearing my mother innocently boasting of her friendship with a woman who lived on Drumlin Avenue, and the relatives listening resentfully, and mocking my mother behind her back.

Who does she think she is! Making herself ridiculous.

My mother volunteered to accompany me to the McClellands' house, next time I went. Quickly I said no for Mrs. McClelland had expressly told me not to bring anyone with me.

"I don't think that Mrs. McClelland would mind, if you brought me," my mother said, hurt; and I said, "But I promised. I can't break my promise."

The second evening at the house I was determined to do everything Mrs. McClelland had requested. Mail, newspaper. Fresh cat food, water and litter box. Houseplants.

This time the lonely Siamese cat appeared in the kitchen doorway staring at me with icy blue eyes.

I spoke to Sasha in a gentle, cajoling voice as Mrs. McClelland had, but Sasha made no response as if I were invisible. Unless I was imagining it, the cat seemed to have lost weight already; I had never seen so sinewy-thin an animal, with such stark, staring eyes.

When I tried to approach her, submissively on my heels, Sasha crouched against the floor as if about to bolt, her chocolate-tipped tail switching violently. A low, strangulated growl issued from her throat. She hissed, and then she mewed plaintively. She could neither come forward to be petted, nor could she run away to hide.

Futile to plead with a cat, yet I heard myself pleading.

"Sasha! I'm your friend. You can trust *me*."

But Sasha would not trust me. With the cunning of the feral animal who has been only partly domesticated, she kept her distance.

It was nearing dark. And then it was dark. Again I wanted badly to flee to the comfort of my home.

I felt foolish lowering blinds in certain of the downstairs rooms—then, a little later, raising them again. (Or was I supposed to keep the blinds lowered overnight, and raise them the following night? I couldn't recall.) I'd switched on lights in all the rooms, too many lights?—while I tried to do math homework sitting on Mrs. McClelland's leather couch, that wasn't very comfortable, as the floor lamp behind my head cast shadows that made it difficult to read.

Yet, since Mrs. McClelland had gestured toward the leather sofa for me to use while doing homework, I felt obliged to sit there; I might have sat in another chair in the living room, or at the kitchen table beneath a brighter light, but somehow could not force myself.

Also, I could not seem to read coherently. I was distracted by my surroundings. The house that was so beautifully furnished seemed hostile and cold to me, like the interior of an expensive store; the living room was so large, it seemed to me that the farther walls dissolved in shadow. Cars passing on Drumlin Avenue cast the glare of their headlights against the walls and ceiling, though the house was set back a considerable distance from the street. From time to time somewhere in the house the lonely Siamese cat erupted in a high-pitched, piteous yowl, a cry of utter desolation and misery that chilled my blood, as if I had been torturing her, and was to blame for her suffering.

At last, to demonstrate to myself that I was not afraid and that I could behave as a normal teenager might in such circumstances, I switched on the television set. The screen glared with softly bright colors. Voices shouted at me out of an advertisement for detergent. Close up, the screen was too large for my eyes to focus on and when I tried to switch channels, the same advertisement, or one near-identical to it, appeared.

It was 7:15 P.M. when the phone rang. I was terrified, for a moment I could scarcely breathe. Then, I staggered to pick up the receiver, and a woman's voice was saying *Hello? Hello? Hello?*—it was Mrs. McClelland, sounding very unlike herself.

"Yes? Hello? This is . . ."

"Hanna! How are you? How is the house?"

"The house is—all right. I've done everything you told me . . ."

"And how is poor Sasha?"

"Sasha has been eating. She is still a little scared of me but—I think she will be making friends with me soon . . ."

Mrs. McClelland asked again about the house. She seemed anxious to know about the mail, and if the phone had rung while I'd been there. (This was in an era before voice mail. A phone simply rang and rang in an empty house, with no way of recording a lost call.) She asked about "my substitute" at school and seemed gratified to hear that the substitute wasn't at all sharp-witted or much fun, and didn't seem to be comfortable in the classroom—"We all miss you, Mrs. McClelland. Everyone is asking when you will be back."

"Soon! Next week, I'm sure I will be back."

I asked about Mr. McClelland and Mrs. McClelland said in a bright brave voice that he was doing well—though there were "complications" following surgery—"fever"—"infection."

I did not know what to say to this. Awkwardly I repeated that Mrs. McClelland's students all missed her and hoped she would be back soon.

"Thank you!"—Mrs. McClelland may have intended to add something witty and reassuring but her voice simply ended, as if a switch had been thrown.

Soon after this painful telephone call I switched off the lights and fled home.

8.

"Hanna. Han-*na*!"

The voice was singsong, just slightly mocking. At a little distance you would mistake it for playful.

That was what I thought—a playful voice. A friend of mine who'd learned somehow that I was inside the McClelland house, and had come to visit me.

It was 6:20 P.M. The evening of my third—and final—visit.

This time, I was resolved to spend at least an hour in the house, as Mrs. McClelland had requested. This time, the lonely cat seemed to be waiting for me in the kitchen, and fled only after she saw that I was not Mrs. McClelland.

As I cleaned out the cat's dishes, and set out fresh food, I saw that Sasha had returned, tentatively.

Though Sasha still distrusted me, and would have bolted if I'd made any move toward her, she began to rub her lean, sinuous silvery-blue body against the doorframe; she was mewing, not as an ordinary cat mews, but in the hoarse, throaty, interrogative way of the Siamese, that sounds almost human. It was touching to see the beautiful cat behaving in this way, desperate to show affection but not daring to come closer to me, or to allow me to approach her.

This was very encouraging! I would have something to report to Mrs. McClelland.

Unfortunately then, the doorbell rang. In the silent house the sound was jarringly loud.

Was someone at the front door? At first I was too startled to comprehend what the sound meant.

Immediately, Sasha panicked and fled.

My instinct was to hide—to pretend that I wasn't in the house—for only my parents knew that I was here, at this time.

Thinking *It must be someone who knows the McClellands. It would not be anyone who knows me.*

Not a delivery, at this time of evening. No one whom Mrs. McClelland would have expected.

If friends of the McClellands had planned to visit, they'd have called beforehand. Houses on Drumlin Avenue were not the sort of houses you dropped in upon casually, happening to be in the neighborhood.

Whoever was ringing the bell would reason that no one was home and give up after a few minutes, I thought.

Except: several of the downstairs rooms were lighted, as Mrs. McClelland had instructed.

And now I realized what a bad idea it had been, to switch on lights in the house! For whoever saw so many lighted rooms in any house would naturally suppose that someone was home.

In the living room, which was a long room with a row of windows facing the street, the blinds were drawn so that no one could look in. That, at least, was a good thing.

Yet, the individual at the front door rang the bell again. And again. And so I knew, this was not-natural. This was something else.

I was in the hallway by this time, looking toward the front door. Though the hall was darkened, the adjacent living room was lighted with a single chandelier—I'd switched on when I had entered the house.

By the way the bell was being made to ring-ring-ring several times in rapid and rude succession, I knew that this was no friend of the McClellands.

"Hanna. Han-*na*!"—it was a male voice, singsong.

At first, I wanted to think that the voice was playful. A voice out of my childhood past—*Hanna! Come out and play.*

Quickly I calculated who this might be. Must be.

My cousin Travis Reidl. It could be no one else.

But how could Travis know that I was here? I had told no one except my parents.

And then it came to me—my mother must have told one of the relatives, boasting about my *helping out* my teacher this week—and this person told my aunt Louise Reidl, an older half-sister from whom my mother was estranged, who lived nine miles north of Sparta in rural Beechum County. And Louise Reidl was the mother of my cousin Travis.

It was a shock to me. It was exciting, and it was a shock. My cousin Travis Reidl whom I had not seen in possibly a year. At the McClelland house, of all inappropriate places.

How like Travis, to show up where he wasn't wanted. Where he did not belong. Pressing his finger insolently against the doorbell, peering through the glass panel into the foyer which must have seemed to him absurdly elegant, like a foyer in an expensive hotel—in mock-playful tones calling, "Han-na! We know you're in there, baby-girl. C'mon! It's cold out here."

As if Travis had roughly tickled me, I began to laugh. But then, I began to tremble. How awful this was! I felt a stab of sheer dismay—shame—if Mrs. McClelland should learn of this . . .

"Han-*na!* Trick or treat!"

Travis began to strike the door with its knocker as if he wanted to break it.

"Open this fuckin door, Hanna, or we're gonna break it down."

We. I could see more clearly, there was a second person with Travis standing on the front stoop. Both were wearing hoods to obscure their faces.

My cousin Travis was my "rogue" cousin—so I thought of him, though I had never told him of course; Travis would have been flattered at first, then offended. All of the Reidls were quick to take offense if they suspected you were being condescending to them, or critical.

It was sobering to think that Travis must now be seventeen—when we were children, that would have seemed *old*. As a boy he'd been a sort of artist, or cartoonist—he'd drawn crude, funny, colorful pictures in emulation of comic strips and comic books; he'd wanted to be a musician, and acquired a secondhand guitar when he was twelve, which he taught himself to play surprisingly well. (Eventually, the guitar was broken or stolen. Travis had been devastated.) Now Travis had become a high school dropout who'd been arrested (as my mother had told me) on suspicion of vandalism, break-ins, and theft, with another, older boy named Weitzel who also lived in rural Beechum County; they'd received only suspended sentences and probation, not incarceration (as my mother believed they deserved).

My parents spoke disapprovingly of the Reidls—a large sprawling family to whom my mother was related through her half sister Louise. These were relatives who lived in the country, in old farmhouses, or in trailers, on what remained of farmland property, sold off over the decades. Rural Beechum County was surpassingly beautiful, in the steep glacial hills of the Adirondacks, but I would not have wanted to live there— everyone seemed to be poor, and being poor had hardened their hearts.

My aunt Louise had been married and divorced at least twice—three times?—and had had at least five children who'd "given her trouble" and of whom Travis was the youngest, and had once been the most promising.

Yet, I was Travis's "special" cousin. I know that he thought of me in that way, as I thought of him.

When I'd been a little girl and my mother had still been on friendly terms with her half sister Louise, she'd often brought me with her to visit my aunt who'd lived in a ramshackle old farmhouse near the Black Snake River. Though I was three years younger than Travis, my mother left me to play with him. My favorite times were when we drew pictures together with Crayolas on strips of paper. My drawings were of chickens and cats while Travis's were likely to be Viking warriors on horseback wielding swords and decapitating their enemies. At the age of eleven Travis created his own comic book—a vampire saga with white-skinned, bloody-mouthed creatures whose dark thick-lashed eyes bore an uncanny resemblance to his own. When he was older, Travis created a remarkable series of comic books relating the bloody apocalyptic adventures of "Black Snake Avenger"—a white-skinned Samurai warrior with a magical sword who inhabited a fairy-tale American city.

At unpredictable times Travis would suddenly lose interest in what he was doing and turn on me, teasing and bullying me as his older brothers teased and bullied him. He was easily excitable, moody and quick-tempered. Only when I began to cry he relented—"Hanna, hey! Don't cry. I don't mean it."

So suddenly it would seem, my cousin Travis was begging me not to cry, and speaking tenderly to me. Once we'd been running together and I'd tripped and fallen—(in fact, Travis might've tripped me)—and when my skinned knee began to bleed Travis washed the wound and found a Band-Aid to put on it. He told me not to tell my mother—"She won't let us play together if you do." Of course, I didn't tell my mother.

As we got older, Travis became moodier. His older brothers were brutal with him, and his mother's men friends treated him badly. Exactly when my mother stopped visiting my aunt, I don't know; it seemed to have happened abruptly, but may have been gradual. As the change in Travis must have been gradual.

Still, at the thought of Travis I felt a complex, pained emotion —a kind of love, but laced with apprehension.

I did not truly believe that my cousin would hurt *me*. But I did not trust him not to hurt others, or not to damage property or get in trouble with the law.

In the past several years we'd only seen each other a few times, by accident in town or at the mall. At a little distance Travis would wave at me, even blow a kiss—meaning to be funny. "Hiya there, Hanna! How's my sweetie!"—but he was with his friends and had no time for his young girl-cousin. He was in trouble for underage drinking, and for drugs. Though his grades at Sparta High were B's and C's he quit school at the age of sixteen after being suspended from school for fighting in the parking lot. (Though it was known that Travis had been defending himself against older boys, everyone involved in the fight was punished equally.)

I'd thought that my cousin had been treated unfairly by school authorities. Adults seemed fearful of him since he'd grown tall, and did not trust him. He'd cut classes, and was a "disruptive" presence in certain of his classes—male teachers were particularly threatened by him.

I remembered how he'd frightened me once with an elaborate fantasy about "committing a massacre"—his classmates and teachers at school, strangers at the mall, his own family.

He would wear a mask, he said—"No one would know it was *me*."

The perfect crime was murdering his own family in their sleep, Travis said. He would kill them one by one, with a knife; he would wash the knife thoroughly; he would return the knife where it belonged. He would take all the money he could find and hide it in his special hiding-place in the old hay barn. Then, he would break a window on the first floor of the house so that glass fell inside—cops always checked for break-ins. He would tell the police that he'd run away into the woods when the killing started, and that he had not seen who the killers were. He spoke with an air of childish glee, seeing how his fantasy discomforted me.

"Why would you want to kill your family? Your *mom*?"

Travis grinned and shrugged. Why not?

By the age of seventeen Travis had grown nearly six feet tall. He was whippet-thin. His eyebrows were heavy, coarse. His eyes were light-colored and sly. Often he blinked as if he had a twitch or a tic—you thought of fish moving erratically in dark water. Often his jaws were covered in stubble. His wavy-dark hair was parted in the center of his head, shoulder-length and straggly. He wore headbands, baseball caps, hoodies. He wore a black leather jacket, jeans and boots. His forearms were tattooed with eagles, screaming skulls. The back of each finger was tattooed with a miniature dagger. He worked at minimum-wage jobs—fast-food restaurants, loading dock at Wal-Mart. County road maintenance and snow-removal, tree-service crew. He quit these jobs, or was fired. He smoked dope. He dealt drugs. He was suspected of breaking into houses. He no longer lived at home and none of the relatives seemed to know where he lived, or with whom. The last time my mother spoke with Aunt Louise, who'd called her to ask bluntly why my mother seemed to be avoiding her, my aunt complained of Travis that he was "out of control" and there were times she was "scared as hell of him" and thinking of getting a court injunction so he couldn't step foot on the property—"Except if I do, I'd be afraid how he'd react. Travis might really get violent, then."

Louise had laughed, and her laughter became a fit of coughing. My mother was shocked and had no idea how to reply.

I knew that there were girls in the high school, and girls who'd graduated, who were attracted to my cousin Travis despite his bad reputation, and I felt a stab of jealousy. Thinking—*Travis will be mean to them. They will be sorry.*

"Hanna? Hey, Hanna? C'mon, be a good girl. Let us in."

Travis was striking the door with the iron knocker, pleading and braying. I had the idea that he was drunk, or high on drugs—I hoped it wasn't amphetamines, which I knew to be dangerous. I didn't dare come to the door to shout at him to go away—that would only provoke him.

I reasoned that Travis couldn't know that I was in the house. He could not actually know that anyone was inside. I told myself—*They will go away in a few minutes. They will not hurt anything. If I don't provoke them.*

9.

After what seemed like a long time, but may have been only five or six minutes, the loud rude knocking at the front door ceased. The ringing of the doorbell ceased. And my cousin's mocking singsong *Han-na!* ceased.

They'd given up and gone away. I thought.

Cautiously I approached the front door. There appeared to be no one on the front stoop, or on the sidewalk. In the living room I peered out a window where I saw nothing, no one—the Mc-Clellands' front lawn, the five-foot wrought-iron fence indistinct in light from Drumlin Avenue.

I was faint with relief. I didn't truly think that Travis wanted to harass or harm me. Nor would he want to steal from the Mc-Clellands—he'd be too readily caught. He liked me, he wouldn't want me to get into trouble—unless he resented me, as the Reidls resented my family.

Yet, I loved my cousin Travis. I did not want to see him— especially not tonight, in the McClellands' house—but I loved him, at a distance.

Thinking of how, after a storm, electric wires lay on the ground, lethal if you touch or step on them. Sometimes the wires are literally crackling with electricity, throwing off sparks.

Live wire. Travis Reidl was one of these—lethal if you come too close.

* * *

Seeing that Travis and his companion were gone, I was eager to be gone from the McClelland house myself.

There was no romance in lingering here. The glamour of the house had faded, now I felt so vulnerable. I would switch off lights, raise blinds. Quickly I watered and sprayed the plants—concerned that several of the African violet leaves were looking yellow. Badly I regretted that poor Sasha had been frightened by the doorbell ringing and had run away to hide somewhere—very likely in her cat-brain, she was blaming me.

I returned to the kitchen, which was brightly lit. I was preparing to leave when I heard voices and muffled laughter at the kitchen door.

"Han-na! Got you, girl."

To my horror the doorknob was being roughly turned—but the door had locked automatically when I'd shut it. Travis's face appeared at the window, livid with anger and mouthing ugly words: "*Let me in! Let—me—fuckin—IN.*" Before I could scream for him to stop, Travis struck the window with his fist, broke the glass pane which flew into the kitchen and shattered on the floor like sleet.

Now, Travis reached inside to turn the doorknob and open the door. Must've cut himself on jagged glass since there would be blood-splotches on the door, and on the linoleum floor, but he seemed scarcely to notice.

Outside, Travis's friend balked at following him into the kitchen. It seemed he hadn't expected Travis to behave so recklessly. "What the hell? What're you doing?"—I could hear him cursing Travis, as Travis was cursing him. If this was Weitzel, he was a stocky, heavy-jawed young man of about twenty with a fattish face, partly obscured by a gray jersey hood drawn tight over his head.

He and Travis were arguing. Then, he walked away. Travis called furiously after him, "Go to hell, asshole! Fuck you."

While the young men were arguing just outside the kitchen door I might have run through the house, and out the front door, screaming for help. I might have run into the street, to stop a passing vehicle—or across the street, to a neighbor's house. But I did not do this—(I would try to explain afterward, faltering and shamed)—instead I stood vague and blinking as if my legs had turned to lead; standing in broken glass wanting to think that my cousin Travis was just being playful, and had not meant to actually break a window, and force his way into the McClelland house. *Travis would not do anything bad to me! Travis is my friend.*

No matter that the window had been shattered, Travis shut the door behind him, hard.

Travis seized me, and shook me like a rag doll.

"Why didn't you let us in? God-damn Hanna this's all your fault."

I tried to push Travis away but his grip on my arm was tight, and painful. I could smell his breath which was fierce with fumes like gasoline. And I could see his eyes, blackly dilated. Travis was "high"—crazed. Travis was in the most excitable mood I'd ever seen him in, and had to be dangerous. Yet still I wanted to believe that my cousin would not hurt me.

I begged Travis to leave. I tried to explain that my home-room teacher lived in this house and that I was *helping her out* while her husband was in the hospital—except I didn't say that he was in Syracuse, hoping that Travis wouldn't have this information; possibly, Travis could be led to believe that Mr. McClelland was in the small Sparta hospital, and not thirty miles away.

"Don't worry, Han-han, nobody's going to hurt this fuckin millionaire house. And nobody's going to hurt you. Except—don't you try to call the cops, or make a run for it. Try anything like that, girl, you will regret it."

Was Travis joking? In our games as children, he'd sometimes talk like this—threatening, mean-sounding. If I gave in im-mediately, he would not usually continue; he would not shove me around, or hit me; if I cried, he would relent at once and say he'd just been kidding. But now, though tears shone in my eyes, and Travis could see that I was frightened and upset, he was not placated.

He was laughing, though he was angry. He was angry, though laughing. He had not expected that his friend would abandon him and several times looked out the window as if he might see him outside—"Damn asshole. *Coward.*"

When I dared to pull at Travis's arm, and pleaded for him to go away, he shoved me with the palm of his hand flat against my chest—"Don't fuck with me, Hanna. I'll go when I'm finished here."

"Neighbors might have heard you break in, Travis. Somebody might have called the police . . ."

"Fuck anybody heard anything! These millionaire houses, built so far apart, nobody hears anything and doesn't give a fuck anyway."

Travis was exploring the kitchen, which was certainly the largest kitchen he'd ever seen. With cries of mock admiration he flung open cupboard doors, yanked out drawers, snatched up a silver ladle to strike shining copper pans that were hanging from an overhead beam like a manic drummer striking drums—"This is like—what? 'Kettle drums'?" I was terrified that Travis would smash crystal glasses and expensive china out of sheer meanness. I was terrified that Travis would grab items out of the refrigerator—milk, fruit juices, jams, leftovers in plastic containers—and toss them about randomly. But his attention was drawn to a glass breakfront cabinet where he discovered a lavish store of wine and liquor bottles—here, he seized a bottle of Scotch whiskey with a hoot of triumph. He was very warm, feverish. He was laughing, muttering to himself, cursing under his breath. Suddenly feeling hot, he yanked down the hood of his cheap jacket, then struggled to free himself of the jacket, and flung it onto the floor. Beneath, he was wearing a black T-shirt cut at the shoulders, soiled work pants without a belt. It was shocking to see that Travis's hair, that had once been so wavy, and beautiful, was matted and stiff with dirt now, as if he hadn't washed it in weeks. Shocking to see that his skin was sallow, and blemished. There was something vulture-like about him, his narrow face, skinny and slightly concave torso, jerky motions—I would realize afterward that my cousin was a drug addict, a "junkie"—this is what junkies look like.

"Time for a drink! Celebrate!—gettin together again. Ain't you been missin me, Han-na? Ain't I your 'favorite' cousin?"

Travis poured whiskey into two glasses, and insisted that I drink with him. I told him no, I could not—but Travis forced the glass against my mouth, and forced my teeth apart, so that some of the liquid ran down my chin but a little remained in my mouth, so that I had to swallow; the liquor burned and stung with a medicinal pungency, and caused me to cough. Travis laughed at me, and pulled me after him into the hallway, and down the hallway to the first room, which was the TV room; here, Travis whistled through his teeth seeing the console-model television, which was surely the largest and most expensive television set he had ever seen. He switched it on, and switched through the channels so roughly I thought the knob might come off in his hand.

The TV screen glared bright-colored. Travis was too restless to watch anything for more than a few seconds. The volume was high, and so I thought—(but it could not have been a serious thought)—that neighbors might hear the unusual sound in the McClellands' house, and come to investigate; better yet, call for help. But this was my desperation, and not my common sense.

Travis muttered that he'd be coming back to take this TV— he'd need a damn truck to haul it. Music blared up from the

TV, the buoyant and brainless music of advertising, and Travis took hold of me in a pretense of dancing, clumsy, panting, laughing at the look in my face that must have been a mixture of horror, dread, embarrassment, shame—"What's the matter, Han-na, think you're too good for me? Your cousin from Black Snake River you're too good for?" He was belligerent, bemused.

Travis insisted that I swallow another mouthful of whiskey. Another time much of it dribbled onto my clothing, and some of it down my throat. Travis was gripping my hand at the wrist, hard. He joked how he could snap my "sparrow arm" anytime he wanted.

I was beginning to feel sickish, light-headed.

"All your family, you think you're too good for the Reidls. But I have news for you."

Travis drank more whiskey. To force me to drink, he slid his arm around the nape of my neck, held me tight, and pressed the glass against my mouth. I struggled, but he was too strong.

Thinking desperately—*He will stop, soon. He will go away. He does not want to hurt me . . .*

It was uncomfortable, the way Travis held me. He'd hardly looked at me before—his eyes had leapt about, blinking—but now he was looking at me, close up. I could see his blemished skin, the fine broken capillaries in his eyes. I could smell his breath, and the odor of his body.

"What're you afraid of, girl? You lookin like you don't know me."

I tried to ease away, laughing. I did manage to ease away from Travis's tight grip but dared not run from him, for I knew this would be insulting to him.

He said, as if thoughtfully, recalling something amusing, "You know, you're an 'accident'—just like me."

"I am not."

"You are! My mother says so. Your mother told my mother, she says 'Hanna is our accident.' And my mother said, 'Travis is *my* accident. I think you got the good deal, Esther.'"

I was stunned by this. The offhandedness of the remark. But knowing it could not be true, for my mother would never say anything like that. Especially, never to her half sister Louise.

I thought—*He's just teasing. Travis likes to tease.*

I hated Travis suddenly. I wished that Travis was away somewhere—in the juvenile facility at Carthage, or farther away—like one of his older brothers who'd joined the U.S. Army.

I did not wish that Travis was dead, though. I would never wish that Travis was dead, I would miss him so.

Though I continued to beg him to leave, Travis dragged me with him into the dining room. Here he mock-marveled at the "fancy glass chandelier" and the "plant jungle." He had nothing but scorn for the many potted and hanging plants. "What's this? Fuckin *orchids*?" He seemed both offended and amused by the beautiful flowers. He stooped to sniff at the odorless orchids and African violets. As I looked on in horror, he broke off a purple striated orchid flower, which he tried to stick behind his ear, but it fell to the floor.

"Travis! Please stop. Please just go away."

"Go away *where*? This is where I am."

Next Travis tormented me by threatening to urinate into one of the potted plants. And then, to my horror, that was what he did—unzipped his pants, and urinated into the jade plant.

Seeing what he was doing, I backed away hiding my eyes.

Heard myself laughing. A high-pitched shriek of a laugh, like one who has been tickled hard. Like one who has been killed.

"That's how we do in Black River. Nothin to surprise *you*."

Travis was enjoying this, tormenting his good-girl cousin. Wanting me to laugh with him. Almost, I felt a longing to join him in his bad, childish behavior in this house beautiful as a house in a magazine—except this was Mrs. McClelland's house, and I would never do anything to hurt or upset my teacher.

The whiskey was making me dizzy, light-headed. I had swallowed only a small amount, but it had gone to my head.

There was the watering can. I picked it up, and poured water into the jade plant, thinking to dilute the toxic urine. Belatedly I remembered, Mrs. McClelland had said *No water for the jade plant*.

This was very funny, for some reason. I began laughing, and then I was choking, and vomiting—spitting up hot liquid, as Travis laughed at me.

Wanting to go to the kitchen, or into a bathroom, to rinse my mouth. Nothing so disgusting as the taste of bile. But Travis forbade me to leave his side—he didn't trust me not to run away.

Travis was helping himself to fistfuls of silverware out of a breakfront cabinet. Seeing the look in my face he sneered. "All this fancy shit they got here, nobody's going to miss. Some folks got too much, and some folks too little."

So careless, some of the silverware fell to the floor. Travis gave it a kick.

"Travis, please go home. I won't tell anyone if—if you go home now . . ."

"Damn right you're not going to tell anyone, sweetheart. If you do, your whole face is going to look like that 'birthmark'—real red, and real ugly."

This hurt. This was malicious. I could not believe that Travis meant to say anything so cruel to me, knowing how I felt about the birthmark.

I stammered saying when the McClellands returned, and saw that things were missing, I would have to tell them who'd taken them; and Travis said coldly, without his simpering grin, "I doubt you will do that, Hanna. You will regret it if you do."

I knew that this was so. I would not tell anyone what happened here—what was happening, that I was helpless to prevent—what Travis did, or said. I would have to invent a story—as a frightened and guilty child invents a story stammered to adults who will wish to believe her, no matter how preposterous her words.

For I remember vividly, many years after I left the small city of my childhood to live hundreds of miles away, how I'd rarely confided in my mother, still more rarely in my father, as a girl. So many secrets, that had seemed shameful to me then but were surely trivial, commonplace—the secrets of early adolescence. What drifted through my head like sinuous undulating water snakes in Wolf's Head Lake, in the rushes where we'd catch sight of them sometimes, screaming with exaggerated horror.

Though I can remember crying and being comforted by both my parents, mostly I remember shielding from them, or keeping to myself, those things that must not be told to anyone.

10.

I did not see the face of the other person. He was wearing a hoodie like Travis but he did not lower the hood. But I could tell he was older than Travis—he was not someone I knew. I did not recognize his voice.

There was no time. From the moment they broke into the house and began taking things until they went into Mr. McClelland's home office and found his gun and the gun went off—everything happened too fast.

Because he was older than Travis, I think. Because they were both "high." Because Travis wanted to impress him. Because Travis had always had that weakness—teasing younger children, because he had been teased himself by older boys. And wanting to impress the older boys.

And so Travis did the hurtful things with the gun, to me. To make his friend laugh. Except his friend stopped laughing. His friend said for Travis to stop. And Travis would not stop. So his friend shoved Travis, and tried to pull the gun away, and the gun went off, beside my head. And Travis fell down. And I was on the floor, and I could not move in terror that I had died. And I could

*not think, for the ringing in my ears. And a black pit opened,
and I fell inside.*

11.

Begging my cousin Travis to leave the McClellands' house but
he will not leave. His face glows like a bulb. Like a deranged
sun/comet. Like the white face of a Samurai as the warrior lifts
his sword to swing and decapitate in a single terrible motion.

Dragging me with him through the rooms. Laughing at my
misery. Opening the door to Mr. McClelland's "home office"—
which had not been locked, as Mrs. McClelland said it would be.

And this too is a betrayal—*Mrs. McClelland had said she would
lock this door.*

Boldly Travis Reidl steps inside this room. Because there is
nothing and no one to prevent him.

Travis whistles through his teeth, impressed by the floor-
to-ceiling mahogany bookshelves filled with books. Fireplace,
enormous antique desk. "So many fuckin books! Nobody ever
read so many books." It is the resentment of one who might
once have wished to read such books, but knows himself lost
to them now.

Jeering Travis examines the items on Mr. McClelland's desk.
Ledger-sized appointment book, black fountain pen, silver lead
pencil. Silver! Travis shoves this into a pocket. There is a calendar
inset in a leather frame—"Lookit this fuckin thing!"—that seems
particularly to enrage him.

Grunting, Travis pulls out drawers in the large mahogany desk. Most are filled with files. I am grateful that he isn't yanking the drawers out of the desk and spilling their contents on the floor. In the lowermost drawer, he has discovered something—he whistles through his teeth. It is a gun. He lifts the gun in his hand, and his eyes narrow with excitement.

"Jesus! Just what I need."

I am very frightened. I did not know there was a gun in the house. I had no way of knowing. Why did Mrs. McClelland forget to lock the door!

I want to run away, to run out into the street and call for help, but I know that my cousin Travis will punish me terribly if I try. He will shoot at me—he will shoot one of my legs, to bring me down. And he will laugh at me on the floor screaming in agony. *Didn't I warn you, Han-na! You disobeyed.*

Somberly Travis examines the gun, turning the chambers. Is the gun loaded? Travis asks me if I know what Russian roulette is.

No. I tell Travis no.

I do not know what Russian roulette is. (Of course I know what Russian roulette is.)

I am trying not to cry. Still I am thinking *Travis likes me! He will not hurt me.*

It is like prayers in church. *Heavenly Father who gives us all blessings. All blessings are from You.* Begging God to be good to you because your terror is that God will not be good to you. And so I am begging my cousin Travis though I do not dare beg aloud.

Remembering how Travis had said in a dreamy voice he'd have liked to bring a gun to school. Remembering the "massacre" comics. There were no guns in his mother's house, for an older brother had fired an air rifle at Travis when he'd been a little boy, hitting him in the back, and his mother had taken the gun away from the brother, and threw it in the Black Snake River. And Travis had not been allowed to have a gun. He'd said, When I'm old enough I can buy my own guns. I won't be living here. I don't need anybody telling me what to do.

Now he has Mr. McClelland's gun, which is like a gift to him. If you believe in fate, or destiny—this is not an "accident" that the gun has come into Travis's hands. And so gravely he examines it. He turns the cylinder, peering into it. He is trans-fixed, there is a strange radiant smile on his face. Despite the sallow skin and dirty, matted hair I can see that my cousin is a beautiful boy. A beautiful ruin of a boy. A young-old boy, with bruised and bloodshot eyes. I am afraid of Travis but yet, I am drawn to Travis. His eyes lifting from the gun to mine, rapidly blinking as if the sight of the gun is dazzling and he is part-blinded.

"Did you ever hear of a suicide pact? I think it would be the test of love."

It is very strange to hear the word *love* uttered in Travis's scratchy voice.

But quickly I shake my head—*no*.

Though thinking, to be found dead, in a boy's arms—this is a haunting thought.

There was a couple in the high school who'd died together. But it was believed that the boy had killed his girlfriend, driven his car into a lake, through ice, so that they'd drowned together.

Like an actor in a film Travis positions himself in front of a mirror above the fireplace mantel. To my horror he presses the muzzle of the barrel against his head. He smiles at himself in the mirror, winks; brushes a strand of ratty hair out of his eyes. Then as if he has only just thought of it he lowers the revolver, carefully shakes bullets out of the cylinder, drops them into a pocket. Slyly he looks at me, who has been standing all this while a few yards away, unable to move.

"See? The gun isn't all loaded. There is a chance."

"Travis, no. Please—put the gun away."

"'Russian roulette.' Just one bullet left. It's cool."

Fascinated by what he sees Travis continues to stare at himself in the mirror. His posture is straight as a soldier's. He seems to have forgotten me. He poses holding the muzzle of the barrel against his forehead as a dreamy look comes into his eyes. It appears that he is about to pull the trigger, then he whirls like a gunfighter in a western, with bent knees, aims the muzzle at me instead and pulls the trigger. There is a *click!*—on an empty chamber.

I am so frightened, I have wetted my underwear. My heart is pounding. Sweat breaks out in my underarms. But Travis just laughs at me.

"Try another time? Hey?"—he points the barrel at me and I crouch, shielding my head. As if this would stop a bullet.

Begging, "No please. No—please. Travis . . ."

Travis laughs. He is excited, elated. He has me powerless. I am his captive. His vassal. He is the Black Snake Avenger, about to execute a hapless captive.

"I told you, there's just one bullet in the cylinder. There's a chance."

I am too terrified to respond to my teasing cousin.

Travis says, "Kneel down."

"No, Travis. No please."

Travis rubs the muzzle of the gun against the side of my face which I try to keep hidden—the ugly red birthmark beneath my left eye. Cruelly teasing—"Hey. Want me to shoot this off?" He thrusts the barrel into my mouth. I am choking, terrified. He would not pull the trigger and murder me—would he? The muzzle strikes against my teeth, a pain so intense it registers as numbness. I am trying not to cry uncontrollably. I am trying to obey Travis so that he will pity me, and have mercy on me as he'd used to do when we were children. Telling myself he would not kill me, for he loves me. Yet, Travis is laughing meanly. That sniggering laughter of boys who have found someone weak to torment, who cannot hurt them in return.

And now Travis does something I would not believe he would do—he tears open my sweater and pushes the gun muzzle against my breasts—the puckered, terrified flesh inside my small white cotton 32-A brassiere. The gun muzzle is damp from my saliva but still cold and I am shivering and shuddering and so frightened, I have wetted myself—again. And Travis shoves the gun barrel down inside the waistband of my corduroy pants—as if he wants to "tickle" my stomach—and farther down, between my legs—and I am screaming now with pain, and squirming—Travis is grunting and laughing quick as if out of breath from running—flush-faced telling me that I will have to be punished for wetting myself for I am a dirty disgusting girl.

I am crying helplessly now. Travis has mercy on me, but it is the mercy of disgust. With his booted foot he shoves me away. He drops the gun onto the leather chair as if it has been defiled by the wetness in my underwear.

"Stop crying! Nobody has hurt you—yet. Walk—on your knees. Walk, and you can save yourself."

I am on my knees, close beside the chair. Desperately, clumsily I reach for the gun—the gun Travis has let drop—it is a miracle that I have the gun in my hand—in both hands. The gun is heavy—heavier than I would expect. The barrel is long, and hard to keep lifted—it wants to lower itself, like a dousing rod. Seeing me with the gun in my hands Travis cries, "Hey! God damn you—" as I pull the trigger—try to pull the trigger; it is not easy, and at first the trigger doesn't move—and then it moves, with a *click!* on an empty chamber. Travis is furious now swooping to snatch the gun from me and I pull the trigger again and this time there is no *click!* but a deafening explosion, and Travis is jolted back—Travis is shot in the chest—the look of fury fading from his face as he falls to the floor.

Like a terrified animal I am crawling away—trying to crawl away—on my hands and knees. I am desperate to escape Travis who (I am sure) will lay his hands on me and hurt me very badly for having disobeyed him.

The gun has fallen from my hands. The gun is too heavy to hold. The gun is on the floor, close by Travis who is lying in front of the fireplace groaning and thrashing. Though I can see blood spilling from Travis's chest none of this is real to me—I cannot believe that Travis has actually *been shot*—it is clear that Travis is teasing me, and in another moment will leap to his feet, to punish me. Yet, the gun has fired—I can feel the impact of the shot, a quivering sensation in my hands and wrists. The sound was deafening, there is a roaring in my ears so loud I can't hear, and I can't think.

Except—*It was an accident. The gun fired by itself.*

12.

It was an accident—I think. Travis had the gun and his friend tried to take it from him and—the gun went off.

I did not see his face. I did not recognize his voice. When he and Travis broke into the kitchen I knew not to look at him for I was in fear of my life.

On the floor for a long time I could not move.

There was a pressure inside my head like a balloon being blown to bursting. I knew of cerebral hemorrhage, *I had looked the words up in the dictionary and had frightened myself.*

How long it was, after Travis's friend ran out of the house, I don't know. And then, there was the doorbell ringing but so far away, I could barely hear it.

And then, the neighbor came to the back door. And saw the window had been broken and saw the bright-lit kitchen and no one in it and called Hello? Hello? Is someone here?—*and came into the hall and into the room where Travis had fallen, and I had fallen, and saw that Travis had been shot and believed that I had been shot as well where I was lying unconscious on the floor, my head just off the rug and onto the hardwood floor where it had struck hard but it appeared that I was breathing, and so he knew I was alive.*

13.

Gun Accident at Drumlin Ave. Residence

Burglary Accomplices Quarrel, Gun Fires Killing Area Teen

As if the gun had fired by itself, and the bullet had lodged in the seventeen-year-old Travis Reidl's chest totally by chance, perforating his heart. The aorta was torn, within minutes Travis bled to death. Travis Reidl whom those who'd known him since childhood would call *troubled, difficult, school dropout, suspect in recent break-ins in Beechum County.* Of whom it was said that his mother had spoken of getting an injunction from the county court to keep him away from the family home—*Not a bad boy in his heart but involved with drugs and drug dealers and it is no surprise, one of those bastards killed him.*

In the *Sparta Journal* it would be reported that the individual who'd fired the gun, the "accomplice" of Travis Reidl, had not yet been apprehended by Sparta police.

14.

It is twenty-six years later. I have been staring out the window at the dark dripping November sky. Downstairs, my mother and children are in the kitchen. A smell of fresh-baked banana bread wafts up the stairs. I am expected to join them, and I am eager to join them, except—my legs are weak, the pulses in my head are still beating.

Outside there is something urgent in the sky. The swirl of the sky of early winter. The way life is sucked into a whirlpool, spinning faster and faster, until it disappears into a point. The wind has risen, the windows are drafty. Blackbirds are flocking in the tall trees that surround my parents' house, a storm of blackbirds, so many it is astonishing—almost, it is frightening. A welter of wings against the window, broken-off cries in midair. Hundreds of black-feathered wings—thousands?—preparing to migrate south. I feel a powerful yearning, impossible to describe. *I want to go with you. Where are you going, don't leave us.*

I am thinking of how I was questioned by sympathetic Sparta police officers and by other adults who cared for me, and did not wish to upset me further. For I was dazed and mute from what had been done to me and would not recover for a long time. And would not be "normal" for a long time. The story that I would try to tell over and over was a confused and incoherent story for I had been traumatized by what had been done to me by my own cousin Travis Reidl. Chipped tooth and bleeding lips from the gun muzzle shoved into my mouth, red welts on my breasts and belly, bruises in the "genital area"—in the newspapers, these shameful details would not be revealed.

Who was your cousin's accomplice, I was asked.

And all I could say was that I had not seen his face. I had not recognized his voice.

Did he threaten you, if you told? If you identified him?

Did he say that he would come back and kill you, Hanna?

I could not speak. I could not speak aloud, the men listening and taking notes.

But whispering to the woman police officer who was so sympathetic, when he'd opened his pants to urinate in Mrs. McClelland's jade plant, because he was drunk and he was high on drugs, I had quickly shut my eyes and turned away.

What is his name, could you describe him, could you identify him, but I said that I could not for it would be a terrible thing to mistakenly involve an innocent person in the death of my cousin.

Police questioned the Drumlin Avenue neighbor who'd called 911. Police questioned other neighbors who claimed to have heard a car's doors being slammed shut, men's voices outside and a girl's scream and a single gunshot at 7:10 P.M. but no one could identify the vehicle, still less the accomplice of the slain boy.

Several times police brought twenty-two-year-old Stevie Weitzel into headquarters for questioning. They were certain that Weitzel was the person who'd accidentally shot his friend Travis Reidl in a break-in/burglary that had gone wrong but each time they'd had to release Weitzel for there was not enough evidence to arrest him.

If Weitzel had been my cousin's accomplice he would have known that he had not shot Travis and just possibly, he could have guessed who had shot Travis. But Weitzel could not have claimed that someone not himself had shot Travis for to have claimed this would be to acknowledge that he'd participated in the break-in with Travis, but had run away before anything had happened.

Instead, Weitzel claimed that he knew nothing about the break-in on Drumlin Avenue, nothing about Travis Reidl that evening. He'd last seen Travis days before, he would claim.

It was not an era in which small-city police detectives knew to secure a crime scene carefully. Fingerprints on the weapon used to shoot Travis Reidl at close range were said to be "smudged." No fingerprints were taken from me.

The gun was returned soon to Gordon McClelland, for it was Mr. McClelland's lawful property.

Those weeks, months of ninth grade when I carried myself like glass that might shatter into pieces at any moment. Treated like a convalescent by my friends, as by my teachers. Seeing pity in their eyes, and a kind of repugnance. For whatever had been done to me, they did not wish to know.

In those days there were no words like *sexual abuse, molestation. Rape* would not be uttered aloud, nor would *rape* be printed in a family newspaper like the *Sparta Journal.*

And so, no one knew exactly what had happened to me, even the doctor who examined me, and wrote his report for the police. Nor could I have been expected to explain, who lacked the vocabulary also, and who lapsed into heart-pounding panic and spells of muteness if questioned too closely.

The neighbor who'd dared to come into the McClelland house would tell of having found the bodies—the shaggy-haired boy "like a biker" shot in the chest, the girl who'd looked scarcely older than twelve or thirteen collapsed and scarcely breathing, he had thought had been shot also.

He had knelt over the girl, and tried to revive her. He saw that her clothing had been torn. Her skin was deathly white. Her eyes were rolled back up into her head like the eyes of a doll that has been shaken hard and her bleeding mouth was open and slack with saliva but—she was alive.

The following week, Gordon McClelland was discharged from the medical center in Syracuse and returned to his home but the McClellands would not live in the house on Drumlin Avenue for long. Their house had been defiled, Mrs. McClelland said. The beautiful old Colonial would be sold at below its market price to a couple moving to Sparta who knew little of the "gun accident" and did not wish to know more.

Mrs. McClelland returned to our homeroom and to teaching social studies for the remainder of the school year but was not so buoyant as she'd been. Often she seemed distracted. She did not always listen to the answers to questions she herself had asked which made us restless, and uneasy.

No longer did she take time to make up her face as she'd done before. The glamorous pageboy hairstyle had vanished, often she merely brushed her hair behind her ears, or fashioned it into a knot at the nape of her neck. No one would have said that she resembled Jeanne Crain. Though she wore many of the same clothes they were no longer so striking on her.

The McClellands would move from Sparta soon after their house was sold.

After the initial period of police questioning no one spoke to me about what had happened to me that night.

There would be the rumor, that Hanna Godden had been *hurt*. By her own, older cousin—*hurt*.

In the (unspeakable, shameful) way in which a girl can be *hurt* by a boy or a man.

Yet, this was not so. I knew that this was not so. A terrible thing happened in my presence but it did not happen to *me*.

The early 1960s was not a time in which children or adolescents who had suffered "traumas" were brought to therapists. In fact, there were few therapists in Sparta. In fact, the term "trauma" was not common usage. Like other adults of the era my parents believed that healing was a matter of *not dwelling* upon the past.

Mrs. McClelland did not blame me for anything. She understood that I had not invited my cousin Travis into the house, and that I had begged him to leave. She said to my mother, "Poor Hanna! It was my fault to entrust someone so young with such a responsibility" and my mother said, flattered, "Oh no—Hanna was happy to help out. It was an accident, the terrible thing that happened."

My mother might have thought to blame herself. Of course, she did not.

When I spoke with Mrs. McClelland I was stricken with shyness. I understood that my teacher did not like me so much any longer—she did not feel comfortable with me. And all I dared to ask her was how Sasha was?—and Mrs. McClelland said, with a sudden smile, "Sasha is well. Sasha is amazingly well-recovered, and sleeps with us now almost every night."

In all that she told people Mrs. McClelland never failed to speak of me as a very good girl, one of her best students. What a tragedy it had been, those criminal intruders had forced their way inside the house. Mrs. McClelland knew who Travis Reidl was—he'd been a student of hers several years before. She'd thought that Travis was surprisingly bright and promising for a boy from rural Beechum County but she had not trusted him. Travis was the kind of student you would not dare to turn your back on, to write on the blackboard, for fear that he would make the class laugh by gesturing comically/obscenely behind your back. Mrs. McClelland said of Travis that he was a "disaster waiting to happen."

Only when I return to Sparta, and spend some time with my mother, will it be revealed that my aunt Louise had confided in my mother that she felt "sick and guilty" about what Travis had done to me. My aunt had not denounced her son to the police or to any strangers but she told my mother that she was sorry and ashamed, how Travis had behaved. "He was so fond of Hanna, that's a fact. Hanna was his favorite cousin. He'd never have wanted to hurt her if he'd been in his right mind. I hope you know that, and Hanna knows that."

My mother had said yes, we knew. And we appreciated Louise telling us.

Startling me out of my reverie at the window comes the call—*Han-na? Where are you?*

They are waiting for me downstairs. Soon, I will join them.

My children know nothing of Travis Reidl of course. My children have only the vaguest knowledge of who their mother is, and was. For who would tell them? The adults who surround them will protect them from the harm of too much knowledge.

Visiting Sparta, only a few times in twenty-six years have I encountered or even glimpsed Steve Weitzel. Once at the mall behind Sears, another time in a 7-Eleven store. Each time the encounter was uncanny, unsettling. We did not know each other when we were young, I'm sure that Steve Weitzel hadn't known my name though he'd have learned my name after the shooting. When we see each other as adults, Steve Weitzel stops in his tracks and stares at me as if he is trying to summon back a memory of me, with the effort of one trying to drag a heavy weight out of deep, black water, that is entangled with seaweed.

This is the visit when, another time, by accident, I will encounter Steve Weitzel. With my daughter Ellen crossing the parking lot behind the bank and there is a middle-aged man staring at me. He is wearing a soiled windbreaker and soiled work pants. His face looks as if it had been roughly swabbed with a wire brush. There are broken capillaries in his eyes like tiny worms. Steve Weitzel has become a thick-bodied man with badly thinning hair, a blunt brute face, sullen eyes. The kind of man who doesn't stand aside for you if you are entering a building as he is exiting it and who doesn't allow you to go first in line, though you have arrived first. Yet, seeing me, and glancing at the eleven-year-old girl beside me, Steve Weitzel hesitates, as if he is about to speak.

But I do not want this coarse-looking man to recognize me. With the polite but fleeting smile of a woman who has been away from Sparta for much of her adult life and who is no longer certain whom she should remember—(former classmate? neighbor?)—and who is a stranger, I am about to continue walking past Steve Weitzel, gripping my daughter's hand, when he says, in a voice that sounds as if it has not been used in a while, "Hanna, hello. Thought that was you."

Equatorial

1. QUITO, ECUADOR

He'd tried to kill her. She was certain.

It was not a thought that came lightly, or casually—*My husband wants to kill me. I must protect myself.*

"Audrey! Be careful."

The husband's voice was raised in alarm, yet also in annoyance. Even in her moment of panic the wife registered this.

She'd slipped, and had almost fallen—but the husband had gripped her arm, and steadied her.

Carefully they'd been descending narrow stone steps. Nearly two hundred steps of weatherworn rock, set in a hillside. And at the top, from an ancient churchyard of an abandoned stone chapel, a spectacular view of the many hills of Quito, Ecuador, of which most were densely inhabited as the hills of nightmare.

On all sides were small multicolored stone and stucco dwellings jammed together, that baffled the eye as with a powerful vertigo. *So many people! And all unknown to us.*

And beneath her feet, as they began their climb back down, were the stone steps that were alarmingly narrow, and part-eroded, and seemed to descend forever. On the outer edge of the steps was a railing—at which the wife clutched like a frightened child.

The husband was close behind her, she'd felt his impatience during the descent, for she moved slowly, in a trance of apprehension she understood to be exaggerated in his eyes. And she felt that he was crowding her. The toes of his hiking shoes nudged her heels, as if to spur her onward—downward. When the wife balked, the husband would laugh and murmur *Sorry!*—but a moment later, he would be nudging her again.

Though the husband was nine years older than the wife, the wife was a less practiced hiker, and had little of the husband's physical confidence.

"I'm sorry! I can't go any faster . . ."

"Audrey, you're doing fine. Just don't look down."

It was the husband's way to laugh at the wife's fears, which seemed to him phantom-fears. Climbing up the narrow stone steps had required much of the wife's energy but she had not felt that she was in immediate danger of falling—somehow, climbing back down was far more strenuous.

Though she'd been short of breath on the climb she'd had time to pause and admire the vista of lush, bright green foliage amid the multicolored little houses as the husband, who was behind her, stopped frequently to take pictures with his new, complicated camera. He hadn't hurried her at all. But on the way down the husband had put away his camera. Descending was far more awkward, and arduous, than ascending—the wife had to carefully position her feet, in the hiking shoes the husband had bought for her, that strained tendons in both her calves, just above the ankle; sharp stabbing pains shot up her legs, that filled her with dismay. The picturesque stone steps were far steeper than the sort of steps to which the wife was accustomed, without realizing she was accustomed. The husband would be impatient with her, if he knew. He'd accused her more than once—laughingly, but cuttingly—of being a spoiled American tourist.

The husband would criticize her for expecting *first-world conditions* in a *third-world country*. Wasn't this just like her! So the wife dared say nothing that might be interpreted by him as a complaint.

Nor could she catch her breath. Her heart beat unpleasantly rapidly like the wings of a trapped moth. The altitude of Quito was 9,000 feet (which the husband had promised would be no problem, not a serious height, like some heights he'd hiked in his younger life—Kilimanjaro at 19,300 feet for instance; some peaks in Peru)—she was beginning to be light-headed, and there was a strange quick pulse beating behind her eyes. The husband had laughed at her fears of altitude sickness but he'd asked his doctor for medication before they'd left on the trip, and he'd given the pills to her with careful instructions: the first to be taken twenty-four hours before arrival in Ecuador, the second on the first day of arrival, and so forth. Henry had assured her that Diamox was guaranteed to prevent altitude sickness—"So long as you don't convince yourself that you're sick, darling."

It had been one of the husband's ongoing charges, or jests, from the start of their marriage, that the wife imagined much: illnesses, misfortunes, the not-always-friendly intentions of others.

The husband had insisted that the wife drink bottled water, and take ibuprofen, as he was doing, to prevent altitude sickness. And in the first, exciting hours of their arrival in the capital city in the Andes, she'd thought that she would be all right—she'd followed the husband's instructions carefully, and seemed to be adjusting well. A kind of gaiety had suffused her, a hope that the husband would not be disappointed in her as a traveling companion, as he'd been in the past.

And so, eagerly the wife had said yes, of course she wanted to climb the two hundred stone steps set so beautifully in a hillside, that led to a famous chapel at the top; the husband wanted to take pictures, and did not want to make the climb alone.

Rarely was the wife able to withstand the husband's wishes. The husband was so enthusiastic, so strong-willed, and so energetic! It was a surprise to all to learn that Henry Wheeling was fifty-nine—he might have been a decade younger. Often he was impatient with others for their inability to keep up with him mentally or physically; often he was impatient with the wife. If he made a request of her, like asking her to join him on a steep climb, and if, apologetically, she declined, he would simply ask her again, and again, with increasing irascibility, until she gave in. She could not withstand him in the smallest things, and certainly not in the largest. And so she would think naively—*This will please him! He will smile, and love me again.*

How long this descent! The tendons in the wife's calves throbbed with fiery pain.

Yet, the end was in sight. The wife hardly dared look—a glance down made her feel dizzy.

Then, something happened. As she'd feared, she lost her footing suddenly, or her balance. Desperately she clutched at the railing which, to her horror, turned out not to be secure—she might almost have broken off a section of it, in her hand.

"Oh! Help me . . ."

She screamed. She was certain that she would fall, she could not regain her balance.

Of course, the husband was close behind her, on a step above her, and gripped her upper arm, and held her still.

"Darling, there's no danger! Not if you just stay calm. Hang on to the railing . . ."

"The railing isn't secure . . ."

"Hang on to me, then. Try to breathe calmly. You've been on a steeper climb than this, remember?—all those stone steps down to the shore, in Capri?"

The wife could not reply coherently, she was too upset. The wife was sure that the husband had been pressing her to go faster, nudging the backs of her hiking shoes.

The wife stammered: "I'm so sorry. I'm so sorry, Henry."

She'd come close to slipping, and falling—she was certain. If she'd fallen down these stone steps, very likely she'd have struck her head and fractured her skull, or broken her neck, or her back . . .

When they'd planned the trip, the wife had had a vision of some sort of accident, or illness; she had the dread of the non-traveler for something going wrong, in a foreign, unfamiliar place.

She understood that she imagined too much, as Henry pointed out to her. If she could only *relax and enjoy herself.*

She adored, in the husband, this air of self-assurance, confidence. Henry was the person to whom others naturally turned, and whom others trusted.

Of course the husband was likely to be dismayed by her wariness, and disappointed. But there were times when he quite seemed to like her dependence upon him—in financial matters, especially. And he was her protector. He would not want anything to happen to her, surely?

Now that she'd been stricken with panic, the wife continued the descent with painstaking slowness. She was trying to calm her breathing, that threatened to become hyperventilation.

They had been in Quito less than six hours: already it seemed to the wife that they'd been here much longer.

The couple was en route to the Galapagos Islands, and would spend two nights in Quito before flying to the islands. This was the wife's first visit to South America. In the foothills of the Andes, near the equator, it was a mild, overcast day, nor nearly so warm as the wife had anticipated; when clouds obscured the bright sun she shivered, as a thin, stinging wind came to insinuate itself through her lightweight clothing.

"Just a few more steps, darling. Careful!"

The husband was both steadying the wife as if she were a precious child, and expressing his impatience with her. His fingers, that gripped her upper arm tight, contained a sort of fury, that could send her helpless and screaming down the steps if he wished, for the husband was surprisingly strong.

She'd seen him chide their dog—*his* dog—when the Labrador retriever eagerly trotted into the kitchen of their home with muddy paws—*Damn you! Somebody should murder you.*

Of course, this was a joke. This was not a serious remark. Yet, it was a remark Henry sometimes made, with an exasperated laugh, which the wife had heard numerous times.

At last, the wife reached the bottom of the steps. Solid ground, steady earth! She was enormously relieved. Through a fissure in the clouds overheard a fiery white sun emerged, causing the wife's eyes to narrow in pain.

The husband was saying that there hadn't been any real danger, and that the wife had done very well, to come down the steps so carefully. Now that the danger was past, the wife was feeling giddy.

The husband observed that the wife needed to have more confidence in herself—"Some of the tours in the Galapagos will have some 'difficult' terrain."

Quickly the wife said yes, yes she knew.

Wanting to assure the husband *Don't lose faith in me! I will try to be a better wife.*

Back at the hotel, the wife's headache beat harder. The husband gave her another of the yellow capsules, which she took eagerly.

Altitude sickness had seized her, like a giant claw. She felt as if she'd been physically assaulted. The husband seemed now to allow that she was quite ill, genuinely so—she could not even bear his touching her, in an effort to give comfort. The wife could do nothing but lie down weakly, fully clothed, in the beautifully furnished if rather dark hotel room, her heart beating strangely and her head wracked with pain.

"I'll cancel our dinner reservation"—like one hoping to be challenged the husband spoke in a wistful voice.

The wife weakly protested no, he must not cancel. The wife knew that the husband had been looking forward to dinner in one of the highly regarded Spanish restaurants in the Old Quarter, for the husband took meals very seriously.

The husband insisted yes, he would cancel; he didn't want to go out alone, and leave her if she was feeling so ill.

"Henry, it's just altitude sickness. It isn't a real illness." She could speak only in a whisper. Her head was throbbing violently.

Their hotel, which had once been a private mansion, of pale blue-gray stone, with a mahogany interior, a high vaulted ceiling and an interior courtyard alit with bright, darting little birds, was at the edge of the historic Old Quarter of Quito. There were several Americans staying at the hotel, also en route to the Galapagos, who were colleagues of Henry Wheeling at the distinguished research institute in Princeton, New Jersey, for which he was director.

The wife was aware of these people only marginally. She didn't know their names. She supposed, since the trip to the Galapagos was quite expensive, that they were senior researchers at the Institute. When she'd asked Henry who was coming with them on the complicated trip which involved a flight from Quito to the coastal city of Guayaquil, and another flight westward into the islands, the husband had seemed evasive—"I've told you, Audrey. I'm not sure. You don't know these people, in any case."

It was curious to the wife that no matter how many times she asked the husband who his colleagues on the trip would be, he'd never seemed to know exactly. And so she'd thought—*She is a new, young love. He is paying her way.*

And then again she thought—*But Henry would not. He is a gentleman, he would not want to embarrass his wife.*

Stricken with a raging headache the wife could not think coherently. She lay helpless on her bed, flat on her back, head positioned on pillows as she had to guard herself against the slightest movement, which would cause sharp pain.

The husband was saying that he had better stay in the room with the wife, who was looking deathly pale. He would order a room service meal. "Do you think you'll be able to eat, darling? Anything? No?"

Even in her misery the wife was touched that the husband who was so exacting about food and wine was willing to stay in the room with her; this would be an enormous disappointment to him. The wife said, "Please go without me, Henry. I don't want you to stay here."

"I wouldn't feel right, Audrey. I'd better stay with you."

The husband reached for the wife's hand. Her fingers were small, vague, and chill, caught in the warm clasp of the husband's fist.

At such moments, when the wife presented no resistance to the husband, and the husband could protect or comfort her, their emotional rapport was considerable. The wife felt a deep love for the husband, and she believed that the husband loved her. It was when the wife opposed the husband, in any way large or small, that the husband's disdain for her, that wounded her greatly, was evident.

For they were not equals—of course. Henry Wheeling had a distinguished career. Audrey had scarcely had a career at all.

Here was a fact the wife hadn't wished to acknowledge: the husband hadn't seemed to want her to accompany him to Ecuador. Since she'd first met him approximately eight years ago he'd been speaking of taking a trip to the Galapagos, and at that time he'd certainly wanted her to come with him; he'd been newly in love with her, and very attentive. But more recently, while planning the complicated trip, the husband had been far less insistent, and had not shared much information with the wife. He'd purchased books on the Galapagos which he'd read without passing on to her; he'd studied maps. He had warned her that the Galapagos hikes were on "difficult" terrain—rock-strewn volcanic islands, steep hills. They would be taken from island to island in dinghies, and they would disembark sometimes in a rocky surf, not directly onto dry land. The dinghies, which were open, outboard motorboats, were sometimes swamped with water. *Darling, you've said you get seasickness easily. Well—the Galapagos Islands are surrounded by the sea!*

The husband had a new, younger woman in his life, possibly. His secret was, he was *in love* with someone else.

The more Audrey thought of it, the more self-evident this seemed. For she was the husband's third wife. He was a man who had used up women, you might be led to think.

There was something debasing in this, the wife hadn't wanted to acknowledge when they'd first met. She had fallen in love with Henry Wheeling—naively.

Marriage to Henry Wheeling had seemed to the wife like stepping into a large shiny vehicle, the husband's possession. It was not jointly owned, it was *his*. As she had stepped trustingly into a stranger's life, but he had not stepped into hers, she felt more or less constantly disoriented.

Eight years before, the wife had been the new, younger woman in Henry Wheeler's life; his wife of the time had seemed truly *old*. Now, there was little difference between her (she was almost fifty-one) and the predecessor-wife whom she could recall only vaguely like a figure in a film seen long ago.

In fact, at the time of the divorce the predecessor-wife had been younger than Audrey was now. She'd felt guilt for supplanting the woman with whom (she'd thought) she might have been friends . . . But the husband had insisted—*The marriage is over, dead. It has been for years. I'm deeply in love with you, darling.*

Henry had seemed so sincere, even anxious that she return his feeling for her! The effect on Audrey had been dazzling and disorienting as if a blinding light had been shone into her eyes, that had become adjusted to semidarkness.

She had been married before, as a tremulous young woman in her twenties. She had loved her composer-husband very much and had been devastated when he'd died of a quick-acting pancreatic cancer, at the age of thirty-one. She had not married again and had ceased to think of herself as marriageable. In time, it would seem astonishing to her that her (deceased, much mourned) husband had ever loved her.

Fortunately, she'd been able to lose herself in satisfying work—helping to manage the philanthropic affairs of her large, affluent family, who lived in residences in New York City and upstate New York, Maine, Florida, and St. Bart's, and had established a foundation. It was through her work with the Clarendon Foundation that she'd met Henry Wheeling—unless it was Henry Wheeling who'd met her.

She was an "heiress"—(the term was awkwardly nineteenth-century, suggestive of spinsterhood)—for her grandparents had pitied her as a young, childless widow, and had provided generously for her even before their deaths. She'd had no suspicion that Henry Wheeling might be interested in her for her money—at least, not exclusively for her money—for at the outset he'd seemed to love her, and to be delighted by her, very much.

She'd reminded him of Audrey Hepburn, he'd said. The very name "Audrey" was fortuitous.

As the husband's third wife, she had learned belatedly that there was a clear pattern in her husband's marriages. Liaisons with young(er) women overlapped with deteriorating marriages; as a liaison evolved into a marriage, eventually a new liaison was formed, overlapping with the new deteriorating marriage. So far as Audrey could determine her husband had remained married to his first wife for eighteen years, and to his second wife for eleven years. With each wife the difference in ages was increasing as well. But the third wife, married in her midforties, had to concede that the wives of earlier eras had been younger than she, of course, as Henry had been younger. In his mid- and late fifties Henry Wheeling had lost interest in women his own age, who were invisible to him as objects of sexual attraction; Audrey had been "young" to him then, and her delicate-boned pale-haired beauty, or what remained of that beauty, had continued to captivate his interest, to a degree.

Buffeted by headache pain the wife lay very still in the darkened bedroom. In an adjoining sitting room, a phone rang. The wife could hear the husband pick up the receiver and speak quietly, and then the husband was standing over the wife, explaining that one of his colleagues from the Institute had called, and asked him to join a group for dinner. "But I won't go, if you'd rather I didn't. I'm happy to have room service here in the room, with you."

The wife felt a swirl of nausea. The wife could not have tolerated the smell of food in close quarters; it was all she could do to keep from leaning over the edge of the bed and helplessly vomiting onto the floor, for she was too weak to make her way to the bathroom.

The wife insisted no, the husband must not stay with her, but must go out to dinner.

"Are you sure, Audrey?"—the husband stood over her, brooding.

She was too weak now to open her eyes, to observe him. She could barely respond to whatever it was he was saying. And after a while, when she could open her eyes, she saw that he was gone—the bedroom was empty.

She did not want to think—*He's with her now. This has all been planned. Why did I not see this, am I so blind?*

She had no memory of a steep hill in Capri. Or any visit to Capri at all. That must have been another, earlier wife.

A spike in her forehead. Between her eyes.

He was pounding the spike into the bone of her skull, with a mallet.

Don't be ridiculous, darling. Of course I love you.

How could there be anyone else in my life—except you?

He was laughing at her. Not openly but with a kind of pity.

She tried to push him away. She clutched at her own head, as if to lessen the throbbing.

She was feeling ever more nauseated. Naively she thought—*If I am sick, maybe this nightmare will end. The poison will be purged.*

With apologies, the husband had left the hotel. You could see that Henry Wheeling was a gentleman, and very solicitous of his wife. She supposed that he was with colleagues at the Spanish restaurant in the Old Quarter. She wondered if there was a young, female employee with them—one of the research scientists.

Eighteen years, the first marriage. Eleven years, the second.

How humiliating, the third marriage might end abruptly, after so many fewer years . . .

She was haunted by the memory of her fear on the stone steps: her husband's impatience, the way he'd nudged the backs of her shoes. The way he'd laughed at her (silly, baseless) fears. The way he'd finally gripped her upper arm as if he'd had to restrain himself from throwing her down . . .

There had been other occasions, more frequent in the past year, when it was difficult for the wife, a woman of above-average intelligence, not to suspect that the husband no longer loved her. There'd been a singular incident about six weeks ago—of which, at the present time, she didn't want to think.

Her family, relatives, friends had all seemed to like Henry Wheeling, for it was very easy to like Henry Wheeling. Yet, they'd suggested that Audrey and her husband-to-be might draw up a prenuptial agreement.

And one of her cousins had murmured *You might want to look into his background, Audrey. Just to be sure.*

She'd resented such suggestions. She had not dared bring up the possibility of a prenuptial agreement, for fear that Henry would be insulted, and not want to marry her; it was something of an affront, and Henry Wheeling himself earned a high salary at his Institute. Impulsively she broke off relations with some of her family members, as with some of her oldest friends who'd known her young husband many years before. What did they know of Henry Wheeling! He'd been a professor (neurobiology), a research scientist, a consultant, and now he was the director of one of the most prestigious research institutes in the country. They were jealous, envious. They did not wish her well. She'd been thrilled at the prospect of remarrying after so long and of being again loved, like a person who has been misdiagnosed as permanently paralyzed, told now that she can walk after all . . .

I love you very much, Audrey.

. . . deeply in love with you.

Now she had to wonder: did the husband want to kill her, or—did he simply hope that she might die?

There was a profound difference, she thought. Tried to think.

If the second, she was not in immediate danger. If the first, she was in immediate danger.

In her will most of her estate would go to the husband, whose will was more complicated since Henry had children by previous wives, and wanted to provide for them as for other family members. So far as Audrey knew, she might not even be in Henry's will.

Because Audrey had always been relatively well-to-do, finances had never been a problem for her. But she could understand how, for Henry Wheeling, who had, as he frequently said, made his way solely by his own effort, first in the academic world and then in the research/corporate world, the issue of money was not so simple.

Audrey had only the vaguest idea how much her estate was worth, in its entirety. She could not have guessed within—several million dollars? More?

She wondered if Henry thought of this. If Henry actually knew, more than she did, what her estate was worth.

What a blunder it had been, to come to this remote foreign place with Henry! When he hadn't really wanted her with him, and had been honest enough to hint at his feelings, which she'd managed to ignore.

Can't you realize, my dear wife, that I am in love with someone else? Haven't you noticed that I have not made love to you, I have scarcely glanced at you, in a very long time?

She could think of nothing else. Lying suffused with pain, her head positioned on the pillows like an explosive liquid that must not be jolted, she was mesmerized by the situation in which, in this foreign country below the equator, she found herself.

At the Institute there were a number of young women scientists. Some were very young—post-docs. Henry Wheeling was proud of the Institute's efforts at hiring *women and minorities* as he called it. He'd been involved personally, as he often said, in interviewing prospective candidates . . .

He was a very charismatic man, the husband. She had fallen in love with him within an hour of meeting him—which had seemed romantic at the time, but now less so.

She could not risk being sick to her stomach in their elegant bedroom, still less in their bed, and so shakily she made her way into the bathroom, just in time to vomit helplessly into the toilet, gasping and sobbing; the violent heaves shook her slender body, as a giant hand might have shaken her; within seconds, her mouth stung with acid. She flushed the toilet, and flushed it again. She was very warm, and still her headache raged. Another spasm of vomiting, though very little remained inside her. She was being punished for her vanity—was she? Imagining that a man of the stature of Henry Wheeling would have wished to marry *her*?

So sick! This was her punishment.

The vomiting had not seemed to help, as ordinary vomiting might have. She located the husband's toiletry bag, and fumbled inside for his medications. Barely able to see for the tears in her eyes, she found the little plastic bottle of Diamox, but when she managed to open it she saw to her surprise that the medication wasn't in yellow capsules but in chunky white pills.

For a moment she couldn't understand. Then, she realized that Henry must have substituted another medication for the altitude sickness preventative, when he'd given her the capsules.

But why would Henry have done that? Such an act of cruelty, and duplicity . . .

In another plastic bottle in the husband's bag she found the yellow capsules. These were non-prescription "lutein" vitamins.

He wants me to be sick. Deathly sick.

. . . wants me to die.

She was stunned, she could not believe this. Henry must have made a mistake with the pills . . . In her physical distress she could not think clearly.

With water, she took one of the authentic Diamox pills. Then, she took a second.

Desperately too she took two sleeping pills, ten-milligram Ambien, out of her own toiletry bag. She must sleep! She could not bear to remain conscious any longer.

She staggered back to the bed and lapsed into a tortuous nightmare-sleep and did not wake until late morning of the following day when above her, as above an opened grave, a figure stood haloed in bright sunshine and a male voice came as if from a distance uplifted, concerned—*Audrey? Darling? Please open your eyes, I'm very worried about you.*

2. GALAPAGOS

"We don't help animals here."

It was a flat blunt statement. It was not meant to sound cruel or provocative but only matter-of-fact. *Help* was such a friendly word, in the human/social world the wife inhabited, that *help* might be spoken with a kind of disdain was startling to her.

The sixteen passengers in the wave-buffeted dinghy, each wearing a bright orange safety vest, and most in shorts and hiking sandals, stared. The straight-backed Ecuadoran guide Eduardo in his National Parks khaki uniform, a dark-skinned individual of about fifty, of Indian descent, was pointing to the skeletal remains of a pelican trapped in prickly underbrush only a few yards away, at eye level, as the open boat passed. The exotic bird's wings were widespread as if it had struggled terribly and its distinctive hooked bill was open as in a desperate appeal. *Help me! Help me!*

The unlucky pelican, the guide explained, had probably been a juvenile, unaccustomed to flying, that had fallen into the underbrush and failed to free itself. It had "thrashed and thrashed" before growing exhausted and giving up.

Some of the passengers took photographs. The several children in the boat stared glumly. They had not yet seen a live pelican—but here was a pelican corpse!

In lightly accented English the guide continued, as if rebuking objections he'd heard many times in the past:

"It is not our role in the Galapagos Park to 'help'—to interfere with the animals. We never touch them, we never feed or protect them. We allow the animals to live as naturally as they would live if human beings had never existed—that is the mandate of the park."

Slowly the dinghy passed by the pelican remains. The husband was frowning into his camera. The wife shivered, and looked away from the mummified bird.

She thought—*But if Eduardo required help, he would be very grateful for whatever he could get. All of us, desperately grateful.*

Since their arrival in the Galapagos the point had been made repeatedly that no one must interfere with the animal or plant species in their pristine habitat, neither to hinder nor to help. How hostile its overseers were to notions of mercy! The previous evening, in a session on the cruise ship intended to prepare visitors for their first full day in the islands, they'd heard a lecture on a history of the Galapagos and watched a PBS documentary that dealt, in part, with the phenomenon of mass starvation of Galapagos creatures on an average of every four to seven years.

As many as 60 percent of the animals died at these times. But the 40 percent that survived "strengthened" their species—it was the Darwinian principle of *survival of the fittest by natural selection*.

Why this happened, no one seemed to know. Ordinarily this part of the Pacific Ocean constituted the richest, most nutrient-saturated waters on earth, but there was a cycle of some indeterminate kind that brought mass starvation and death.

The more familiar you were with deaths en masse, and rocky shores strewn with the decaying carcasses of sea lions, fur seals, sea turtles, shorebirds, iguanas and every sort of lizard, the more "natural" it was, the wife supposed; of course she understood that trying to alleviate conditions on such a scale was futile. Even if you wanted to help the animals survive, you could not. Yet, human famine in Africa and other devastated regions of the world was meant to be confronted, and combated; we are not supposed to give up on our fellow man, even in the interests of *natural selection*.

"It's very painful to see so much death"—in the ship's lounge the wife had spoken hesitantly. Often her remarks, though seemingly objective to her, only just statements of fact, were interpreted by the husband as *whining, complaining*.

"Well, darling—there is death literally everywhere. Each creature that is born, each plant—has to die. Isn't that self-evident?"

It was! Of course.

Since the wife's terrible illness in Quito, the husband had been kindly with her. He had not been impatient even when she'd had a bout of faintness walking slowly through the airport at Guayiquil, to the small plane that took them to Baltra Island in the Galapagos, approximately seven hundred miles from the Ecuadoran coast. He'd carried one of her bags, and had not tried to hurry her.

It had been a miracle, how the wife's altitude sickness had vanished as soon as they'd left Quito. The coastal city of Guayiquil was at sea level; once there the wife could breathe deeply again, and the raging headache subsided.

Her hours of misery in Quito had begun to blur in her memory. The husband had scheduled two days in the capital city, for there were many sights he'd wanted to see including a rain forest two hours' drive from the city, as well as local shrines and markets, to which he went (the wife assumed) with some of his colleagues; the wife had been too ill to accompany him, and had stayed behind in the hotel room with the shades drawn, near-comatose with pain and nausea. She had been able to eat virtually nothing, and must have lost nearly ten pounds. But the illness had ended, it was better now to forget.

A misunderstanding. My mistake.

He hadn't wanted me to come with him, and I'd insisted . . .

Now they were in the Galapagos National Park, staying on a one-hundred-passenger cruise ship that traveled slowly through the islands just south of the equator. The *Floreana* resembled a floating hotel, dazzling-white in sunshine, large enough not to roll with the waves, or anyway not to roll very much; the wife had taken seasickness pills, and so far she had not been ill—a relief! In fact, the wife was usually in a very good mood, thinking of how she'd escaped Quito.

"Never again! Never nine thousand feet."

It had been *nine thousand feet* that was the evil, that had made her sick.

What had happened at nine thousand feet had been her fault almost entirely, she thought. She'd been naïve about altitude sickness, thinking it much less severe than it was, hardly more than shortness of breath and fatigue, a little nausea. Henry had warned her—had tried to warn her—and she hadn't understood. So badly had she wanted to come with her husband on this romantic voyage to Ecuador . . .

When we are alone, it will be a second honeymoon.

Maybe there is no other woman . . .

In the bright, intense equatorial sunshine, the wife was beginning to feel a new enthusiasm. Her strength had returned, or nearly. Her hope for her marriage. Back home in New Jersey it was winter, and very cold. She was determined to survive!

From the *Floreana* twice a day small groups of passengers were taken in dinghies to the islands. They were divided into groups, as in summer camp: Boobies, Dolphins, Cormorants, Penguins, Frigates, Albatrosses. Most of the passengers were Americans, and Caucasians; those in the Wheelings' group (Albatrosses) included doctors, a dental surgeon, university professors (geology, psychology), a high school principal and her businessman-husband, and several young somber-browed children. All were equipped for hiking on the islands with proper shoes, sun hats and clothing. Sometimes they were able to step off the dinghy onto the rocky shore, and sometimes they had to make "wet landings," disembarking into the rocky surf, for which a kind of rubberized hiking sandal was required. The guide and his young native assistant, who operated the outboard motor, helped passengers into and out of the boat with practiced ease; the hope was to avert both panic and actual falls. The wife was grateful for such help though the husband irritably indicated that he didn't require it—"*Gracias!* But I'm perfectly capable of stepping out of a dinghy by myself."

Still, it was something of a feat, to step from the metal stairs of the cruise ship and into the bobbing dinghy, without falling into the sea.

The husband who was in excellent physical condition with strong, muscled legs and a lean, lanky body didn't see himself as an older man, the wife knew. But he was silvery-haired, and his handsome face finely wrinkled, and so surely he appeared *older* in the eyes of others in the boat, younger than himself.

The wife was determined to enjoy the Galapagos. She wouldn't be able to keep pace with the husband who hiked ahead, conversing with the guide, much of the time.

The first island they visited had been formed out of molten lava millennia ago. Virtually no vegetation, only a few primitive animal species. It was a volcanic landscape of astonishing fissures and shapes, like a great head of Medusa. And near-invisible in the island's cooled lava dreadlocks, hundreds—thousands?—of marine iguanas.

So closely did the iguanas mimic the hue and texture of the lava rocks, they were virtually indistinguishable from the rocks—primitive ugly creatures like basilisks come to life. Yet they were barely living, sensate—the wife shuddered, observing them. So many! So ugly! They appeared to be warming themselves on rocks unmindful that other, smaller lizards and crabs scuttled over them without their noticing.

It was the beginning of mating season, Eduardo explained. That was why some of the (male) iguanas were shaking their dragonlike heads and making a chuffing sound. The (smaller, female) iguanas scarcely seemed to notice. (This was amusing. Eduardo's listeners laughed.) "The female can exercise some choice of a mate, but she can't not choose to mate."

Some choice. But no choice.

Dutifully, the wife took pictures on her iPhone, like the others. She would delete most of the pictures afterward, for one iguana looks very much like another iguana; and a hillside of iguanas is too many iguanas.

Care had to be taken not to twist an ankle, walking on the lava coils, that resembled large, stony intestines. And care had to be taken not to step on an iguana.

When the strangely bright sun emerged, the wife's eyes throbbed; when the sun disappeared behind clouds the air was wetly cool. Where was this place? Why was she here, where no one had asked her to come?

Also, eerily, large spiderlike crabs of the color of boiled crabs scuttled about the lava formations, over the impassive hides of the iguanas, constantly in motion. There was something particularly repulsive about these.

By this time the husband had climbed to the highest peak of the trail, with several of the younger hikers. These were the "adventurers" among the Albatrosses—their physical stamina and agility set them off from the others.

The wife squinted at the husband, at a little distance from her. He and the other hikers were nearly out of earshot, if the guide were to call to them.

If he lost his footing? If—something happened?

"Here. Observe."

Visitors were not to approach the animals of course. But to demonstrate the iguanas' indifference to human life, Eduardo squatted beside one of the large males and very gently moved its tail along the ground; almost comically, the iguana did not seem to see or smell him, and did not shift its tail back into its original position. The stark staring eyes remained unblinking, unaware as if the creature were blind.

"The animals seem 'tame' to us, but that's a misconception. They are not 'tame.' They just have no genetic memory of human beings as predators."

Someone asked if human beings were to settle on the island, would the iguanas begin to fear them instinctively, and Eduardo said, "Eventually, yes. But not for a very long time, by which time the iguanas might have outlived the *Homo sapiens* intruders."

How interesting this was, to the wife! She wondered if there are human beings born fatally lacking a "genetic memory" for predators; if they inevitably pass away, and fail to reproduce themselves.

Eduardo added that the only predators the Galapagos animals instinctively feared were hawks, that swooped down to devour their babies.

The wife recalled a ghastly PBS documentary of baby sea turtles hatching out of eggs in a place like the Galapagos, desperately trying to make their way into the water on their short, stiff legs as predator birds rushed upon them. How cruel it had seemed, like a brutal game devised by sadistic young boys. She'd had to stop watching.

It was something of a ridiculous notion—*survival of the fittest.* Maybe it was a rule of thumb for vast numbers of creatures but not for individuals. You could be very fit but trapped behind a multitude rushing to escape a burning building. You could be very fit but stricken by a virulent disease you could not afford to have treated because you were poor and uninsured. And of course, you could die sheerly by accident—through another's carelessness.

Yet, if you perished, it was because you were *unfit*. History would not care for you in the slightest—history would not even record you.

They were left to explore on their own, though cautioned not to step off the clearly designated trails. The husband strode ahead with the most energetic of the others, climbing rocks like a man half his age.

How resilient Henry was! *He* had scarcely been slowed down by the virulent altitude sickness, that had left the wife weak as if anemic.

The wife tried not to feel lonely. She hated to be alone with her thoughts, that assailed her with the rapacity of piranha fish. She was trying not to think of the husband's new woman, if there was a new woman and not rather a woman he'd been seeing for some time, though certainly a young and beautiful woman, a stranger to the wife. An intellectual, probably—beautiful, young, and brainy.

She supposed that Henry had been discreet enough to have made sure that the new, young woman, if traveling with them in the Galapagos, would never encounter the wife. Henry would have made certain that the woman wasn't assigned to his table on the *Floreana,* or in the dinghy.

This primitive, bleak island! Though lush with its own sort of minimal life, it was very depressing. A place to contemplate suicide except—*In such a place, isn't suicide redundant?*

The wife laughed. The wife wiped at her eyes, inside the dark-tinted lenses of her glasses.

After what seemed like a long time but was probably no more than an hour, Eduardo summoned them all back to the dinghy.

What relief! The wife was one of the first to come aboard, along with the youngest children; the husband was one of the last.

He doesn't even know if I'm in the boat. He has not noticed.

This was unfair of course: Henry had seen her. He'd even smiled at her, with the gallantry with which he'd smiled at strangers. But he'd made no effort to sit beside her as the little boat filled up.

One of the remarks Eduardo had made on the lava island made a powerful impression on the wife: the rigors of survival in this place were such that but a single species, on the average of each 26,000 years, could manage to "establish" itself and live.

"It's hopeless, then!"—one of the group had said, meaning to be witty. "Might as well give up."

And all of the Albatrosses had laughed, secure in the knowledge that, as affluent white-skinned American tourists, they had managed very well to survive until now, against enormous odds.

On a circuitous route back to the cruise ship the dinghy stopped at a second island, larger and more habitable than the lava island. Here was a more familiar fecundity, less the stark brute brainless reptilian life that set the human soul to shivering: penguins, pelicans, blue-footed boobies, frigates and cormorants whose wings could no longer lift their bodies into the air.

So many wild shorebirds! Suddenly, much beauty.

Everyone was eager to take pictures of the penguins. The human eye perceives uncanny something in the penguin that resembles the *human*, and so is drawn to it.

After some minutes amid the so-strangely "tame" birds, Eduardo led the Albatrosses along a strenuous rocky trail to an inlet of sea lions, many with babies. Here were hundreds of the sleek, glistening, strangely stunted creatures with large moistly winking dark eyes and brittle whiskers. Many were braying, moaning. Except those who lay sprawled asleep in the coarse sand as if comatose, the sea lions were in constant, antic motion, as if they were performing for the visitors; nor did they register alarm at the human visitors within a dozen or so feet of their babies.

There was a subtle rapport of some kind between the species—sea lions, human beings. The wife thought so. Though no human beings ever fed the sea lions, as they did in other parts of the world, yet these sea lions seemed quite "friendly"—you would have that impression.

"Mammals have personalities. Reptiles don't. Is that so?"—the wife attempted her idea of an intelligent question, to which the Ecuadoran guide responded politely:

"All the animals have 'personalities.' They are distinctive to one another, and can be recognized by one another, in ways we don't always understand."

Earlier, the husband had engaged the guide in an exchange about the youthful Charles Darwin's visit to the island when the *Beagle* had first anchored here in 1835; it was clear to the guide that the husband knew a good deal about Darwin, Darwin in the Galapagos, and evolutionary theory, and so he spoke to Henry with particular respect. But the husband was drifting off now, with his camera.

Eduardo was a handsome, compact man of about the wife's height of five foot seven with a shaved head, a thin mustache and a resolutely calm demeanor—his background wasn't only Indian but Hispanic, German, and Norwegian. Of the half-dozen Galapagos Park guides assigned to the *Floreana*, Eduardo appeared to be the leader.

The wife worried that the husband was taking too strenuous a trail, up from the shore. He was keeping up with two of the younger men—maybe that was it. Those who stayed close to the guide were the less physically fit or adventurous of the men, and most of the women and children.

If the husband's new, younger woman were with him here— how would she behave? No doubt she was an accomplished hiker who'd have followed the husband up into the rocks . . .

No doubt, she was physically dexterous, as the wife had never quite been. Sexually daring, adventurous . . .

"Too close! Get back, please."

The guide was reprimanding one of the children who'd pushed too close to a mother sea lion and her cub. Rebuked, the boy returned quickly to his mother's side.

With sympathetic eyes the wife watched mother and son: the way the mother consoled the son, without allowing him to think that he'd been mistreated by the guide. It was subtle, and it was good mothering.

The wife wondered what kind of mother she'd have been. It seemed wrong, "unnatural"—she had lost her husband before they'd had time to have a child.

And she'd remarried too late. She'd been in mourning for most of her adult life. As if premature death were not commonplace in nature!—this was the lesson of the Galapagos, unmistakably.

She had always believed that her young husband would have wanted her to remarry, even if she couldn't have fallen in love with another man as she'd fallen in love with him, yet she'd kept herself at a distance from the life of the emotions. She'd hidden away in her work, and in the shackles of family responsibilities. Like an animal grown defenseless for lack of predators she'd been very easily approached by a skilled predator.

Her family had thought that that was what Henry Wheeling was—a predator. And she, the too-willing heiress-victim.

But I love him. That is a fact I can't alter.

The wife glanced about seeking the husband—where? He'd managed to climb to the top of a rocky trail, and was almost out of sight.

It was a windy, sun-jangling day. A day of great joy—the wife was so very happy *not to be trapped inside her raging head in Quito.*

The husband had been very sympathetic with the wife, in Quito. He had not been able to change their plane tickets to bring them to the coast earlier (he had explained), but he'd been attentive to his sick wife, and brought her medications to help her sleep, and bottles of water to prevent dehydration.

As nearby sea lions slept, brayed, frolicked and cavorted and slid into the water like animated figures in a film, the guide continued to lecture to his circle of faithful and attentive listeners. His subject was the necessity for the Galapagos National Park to control—"that is, eradicate"—those "introduced" species that had overbred on certain of the islands, and had threatened the original species with extinction by devouring their food supply. These were goats, cats, and rats brought by sailors as early as the seventeenth century and left behind on the islands to flourish in the absence of predators. Sea turtles, giant tortoises, and many bird species had come near to extinction, as a result.

Over a period of approximately a decade the Galapagos Park rangers had slaughtered the "unwanted" species almost entirely. Hunters, snipers, and carefully administered poisons had devastated goats, cats, rats in great numbers—as many as five hundred thousand goats, for instance, at a cost of—had it been $50 million?

Eduardo spoke with particular zeal of how ingeniously the eradication team had conscripted "Judas goats" to help them with the project—these were goats selected out from the original slaughter, marked with yellow crosses and "freed" into the wilderness so that, unwittingly, wanting only to rejoin their own kind, they led the death team back into the hills to find those goats that had escaped the general slaughter. "After the Judas goats fulfilled their purpose, they too were killed."

There was a moment's silence. The several children, who ordinarily listened to the guide with respectful interest, had disengaged from this account; unmistakably, they did not want to hear Eduardo speak of slaughtering goats or other animals.

The wife said she'd thought it was their policy not to "help" animals—"Not to feed them, or to protect them. Didn't you tell us that?"

"Yes. But in this case, we are not 'helping' the animals directly. We are restoring the environment to its original state, before human beings interfered with introduced species."

"Couldn't you have sterilized the goats, for instance? Or moved them somewhere else?"

"The project was a very careful one, over a period of years. Sterilization was not practical, and moving the goats to a sanctuary would have cost more than sixty million."

These answers had the air of being well rehearsed. The wife understood that Eduardo was accustomed to being questioned, and knew exactly how to reply.

The guide could sense, however, that his American tourist visitors were not so comfortable, hearing of the slaughter of animals, even in the service of maintaining a pristine environment.

"You see, the original species could not compete. The introduced species had no natural predators, and were overrunning the islands."

"But I don't understand—why are 'introduced' species of less value than 'original' species? Aren't all species 'introduced' —originally?"

Stiffly the guide said, as if reciting prepared words, "The Galapagos Park is mandated to preserve species natural to the region, before human beings arrived."

"But human beings are animals, too! If they have introduced new species to the islands, isn't that part of evolution? The way birds bring in seeds from outside, or animals . . ."

Politely the guide said, "Of course, *señora*. What you say is correct. But human beings are not natural to the islands."

Señora. The wife felt this as an insult, subtle and devastating.

Though some of the others were probably sympathetic with the wife's argument, they did not support her. In any case, such a sentimental argument was hopeless, as the wife knew. Any scientist, like the husband, would side with the Galapagos Park strategy— you did not come to the Galapagos without understanding the nature of the environment, how fragile it was, and how it had to be maintained against invasions from the outside world.

"Well—thank you! I understand a little more now. The Galapagos wouldn't *exist*, except if time is made to stand still."

Shortly after, it was time for the dinghy to depart, as it was time for another dinghy to arrive. Like clockwork the Galapagos was organized; you could see how coordinated the staff was, and how crucial that no one interfere with the precise schedule.

The wife was about to take her place in the boat when she heard cries a short distance away. Those several individuals who'd gamely hiked to the top of the rock-strewn trail were returning, and one of them seemed to have fallen—the wife stared in dismay, for the fallen person was her husband.

In that instant the wife thought—*No! God please no—don't let him be hurt.*

Desperately she made her way to Henry, to help him. It was horror to her, that her husband might be injured, and she'd been nowhere near him! Even as others were helping him rise to his feet the wife came to him—"Henry! Oh, Henry . . ."

Fleet-footed as a boy, Eduardo had gotten to the fallen man before her. "Can you stand, *señor?* Did you turn your ankle? Lean on me, please." The guide was gracious, gentlemanly—if Eduardo was alarmed that one of his Albatross charges had fallen, he knew to disguise such alarm.

The husband was smiling ruefully. A strained, stricken smile of acute surprise, and embarrassment.

Both the wife and Eduardo were helping Henry stand. He seemed to have turned his right ankle, or to have banged his leg hard—he swayed, and panted, and for a moment seemed unable or unwilling to ease his weight onto his right leg. Then, the guide's young assistant came running with a walking stick which the husband had no choice but to accept with gratitude.

Quickly the wife slipped her arm around the husband's waist, the first time in their years together she'd ever done such a thing—a gesture of sudden, and now public, intimacy. But Henry didn't want her assistance, at least not in the presence of others. Still smiling, and still wincing, he nudged her away.

"I said, I'm fine. *Gracias.*"

Familiar with the self-deceptions of his affluent American charges, Eduardo knew to stand discreetly aside even as he kept a sharp eye on the hobbling man, who was in his fifties, or older: silvery-haired, distinguished-looking, very articulate, self-assured—a professor or a scientist—Eduardo knew the type, and knew that such a man must be treated with dignity, or he would punish his native guide with a complaint to the Galapagos Park authorities.

"The rocks are very slippery here"—the wife offered the limping man this remark, to placate him; she knew how humiliated he was to have fallen in such a way, before witnesses.

Slowly, using the walking stick, the husband made his way back down the treacherous trail. In nearby rocks sea lions cavorted and brayed as if in mockery of human clumsiness.

The wife was close beside the husband, prepared to help him if he slipped again. The husband cast her a sidelong look of—was it fury?—hatred? That she had witnessed his humbling, before strangers?

The strangers he didn't hate, for he didn't know them. And the canny Eduardo knew to be respectful of the husband, and to call him *señor.*

Only the wife was vulnerable to his dislike, his hatred. She who saw the man too intimately, she who was always *there.*

This had been the fatal deficiency in the previous wives, she supposed. This wifely intimacy, that could not be borne.

"Henry, I love you. Please don't be angry with me."

So softly the wife pleaded, into the husband's reddened ear, it was not inevitable that he'd heard her. But he relented, and squeezed her hand. "Darling! Of course I'm not angry with *you.*"

In the dinghy, the husband was more reasonable. He'd had a shock, and he was in pain, but he would be stoic, uncomplaining.

He would make a joke of it, to a degree—talking and laughing with fellow passengers who commiserated with him claiming to have had mishaps on the excursions themselves. The wife was surprised, and the wife was vastly relieved. Her senses were dazed by the bright heaving waves, the equatorial sun, the physical proximity of strangers, and the disturbing proximity of the man who was *the husband*.

She did not know if she could trust him, but she knew that he could trust her. She did not know if he loved her, but she knew that she loved him. That would have to be enough.

On the island she'd had some sort of—was it a revelation? The kind of certitude that came with extreme anxiety, and exhaustion; and the sudden release and reversal of these, as if she'd been suffused with the strength required to take care of another person, fully dependent upon *her*.

She thought—*There must be some meaning, that I've survived so long. I must discover that meaning.*

The wife glanced around, to see where everyone in the small rocking boat was looking—a hundred yards away was the long whitely dazzling *Floreana* with its several decks and many portholes, its tall chimneys, floating on the sea like a great temple waiting to receive them

3. MOON DECK

"Darling, come out onto the deck! It's a perfect night."

He was gripping her hand with unusual eagerness. He urged her out onto the deck, which was the second-level deck, and brightly lit, and crowded, for at the prow of the ship was an open-air bar decorated as if it were a tropical café, where a trio of Ecuadoran musicians and a young woman singer were performing, and a few couples were dancing.

How festive it was! And above, scarcely visible beyond the bright lights, a sickle moon, which the wife could just manage to see.

By day, this part of the ship was much quieter. There was a "swimming pool"—(in fact, it was hardly larger than a children's pool, with bright-aqua water smelling strongly of disinfectant)—surrounded by lounge chairs on which passengers read and dozed in the sun scarcely mindful, as they were continually warned, that the equatorial sun was extremely powerful even when the sky appeared overcast.

Midway to the prow of the ship, as the music grew louder, and the deck more crowded, the husband changed his mind and pulled the wife back—"No. Wait. Let's go up to the higher deck, it will be more private there."

"But—"

"It will be more romantic there."

The wife had no choice but to obey, though she knew that the higher, third-level deck wasn't equipped for visitors, at least not as the second-level deck was; it was much smaller, with only a few scattered chairs and rattan tables.

But the wife had to obey the husband for his will had to be obeyed in all things small and large. They returned to the interior of the ship and the husband pulled the wife up a narrow stairway, to a door marked MOON DECK; but when they stepped out onto the third-level deck it was unexpectedly deserted, and very dark.

Elsewhere on the ship were bright-lighted areas for drinking, music, and socializing, but the Moon Deck was not one of these. Here too was a lighted area at the prow of the ship, but it was much smaller than the second-level area; there was no bar, only a few scattered, empty lounge chairs, and there were no musicians. You could hear the music from below but now it sounded frenetic, slightly distorted.

"I don't think passengers are wanted here. It isn't set up for . . ."

"Of course it is 'set up'—for us."

Henry wanted to turn left, away from the lighted prow, and grope along the railing, in the dark. It was like him to prefer an out-of-the-way place—a deserted place—a place that, just possibly, might be off-limits. The wife tried to protest, but feebly; she didn't want to antagonize the husband who was trying to walk normally, and not to limp. (She'd seen, at dinner, at their assigned table, how Henry had lost interest from time to time in conversations he had himself initiated with their dinner companions, his gaze moving restlessly about the crowded dining room. It was his pride that had been injured in the fall, as much as his ankle. She felt sorry for him, and a stab of hope—*Maybe he will be less impatient with me now. He will not expect so much of me.*)

But the husband seemed quite recovered from the dinnertime ennui. He had grasped the wife's hand like an ardent young lover.

Somehow, within seconds, the pale sickle moon had vanished. A heavy wall of clouds must have obscured it utterly. And now the ocean was so dark on this side of the ship, the sky so dark, you could not even see the waves though you could hear them, and you could feel the rolling power of the waves thrusting against the vessel. The wife protested, she didn't want to walk along this deck, they couldn't see anything and it was dangerous—no one else was there . . . The husband laughed scornfully: "What are you afraid of now? You can't possibly be swept overboard."

She thought—*No, but you can push me overboard. In an instant, it could happen.*

No one would see. No one would hear. The sound of revelry on the lower deck was too loud. Voices, laughter. Here on the third-level deck it was pitch-dark, and smelled of oil. Henry laughed as he slipped his arm around Audrey's waist, and tugged her to stand beside him at the railing, but she shrank away like a frightened child.

"Darling, really! I thought you liked 'romance.'"

The word *romance* was spoken with disdain, bemusement.

"No! Please, Henry—I think I'll go back down . . ."

"Don't be ridiculous. You're staying here with me. In another moment the moon will be out . . ."

It was a bizarre, awkward moment: the husband tugged at the wife, to urge her to stand beside him at the railing. The husband outweighed the wife by forty pounds or more, yet in her desperation the wife held firm. Henry laughed sharply. He was being playful, or rather—not so playful. He'd gripped her arm, and was squeezing her elbow. It was the same arm he'd gripped on the stone steps, and it was bruised and sore. The wife understood that his patience with her was wearing thin. She knew: she was a foolish, willful woman. She was a spoiled bourgeois woman, haphazardly educated, naïve. If examined closely, she could not have explained the mechanics of Darwinian evolutionary theory; probably she could do no more than stammer clichés, like a TV quiz contestant. Probably she'd forgotten much of what their Ecuadoran guide had told them that very day, in the Galapagos Islands.

"Henry, no. Please don't frighten me . . ."

She was poised to scream but—would anyone hear her? The sound of the ship's gigantic ventilators was loud here. And the frantic music from the lower deck, mingled with sounds of revelry . . .

The wife twisted away from the husband, breaking the grip of his fingers on her arm, as a panicked cat might break free of its captor.

Panting, frightened, yet exhilarated at having escaped the husband, the wife stumbled back inside the ship, and made her way back down the narrow steps, and into a crowd of revelers spilling out of the ship's lounge on the second level. How relieved she was!—she intended never to step out onto the Moon Deck again, no matter how Henry cajoled her.

That night in their oppressively air-conditioned cabin, in their double bed with a protruding rib of mattress down the middle, the wife whispered in the darkness: "I'm sorry, Henry—it was so dark out there, I just couldn't stay."

There was a pause. The husband was not asleep, but chose not to speak. Since he'd returned to the cabin, an hour after the wife, his breath smelling of liquor, he'd had little to say, though his manner was affable, indifferent; he'd read aloud to the wife from the tour program, describing the giant tortoises they were to see the next day, and as he'd undressed he caught her worried eye in the room's single mirror, and winked. Was this a signal of—forgiveness? Forbearance?

"I—I've been worrying that you don't love me as much as you did, Henry . . . I—feel—as if I am lost here, in these islands so far from home . . ." The wife's voice trailed off faintly.

The ship rolled, creaked. The ventilators hummed like fierce lungs.

The husband seemed touched by the wife's stammered words. He groped for her hand, and squeezed it in his quick, comforting way, as if he were embarrassed at having upset her, even as it was a surprise to him, that he had.

"Darling, we love each other as much as we ever did. Now please, it's late, let's drop the subject."

Soon after, the husband fell asleep.

The wife remained awake for some time. It did not seem to her possible that she would ever sleep again for each time she shut her eyes, bright shimmering waves rushed at her, blinding, with a threat of suffocation.

4. THE INTRUDER

She recalled: the singular incident that had happened several months before, that remained a mystery to her. She had ceased thinking of it, and had not dared speak of it again to the husband who considered the matter closed.

They'd had tickets for a production of Mozart's *Don Giovanni*—they had dinner beforehand with friends—but when the couples arrived at the theater, to their disappointment they were notified that the evening's performance was canceled.

When they returned to their house, in a rural-suburban residential area, the wife realized immediately that something was wrong: when she tried to open the rear door to the house, which led into the kitchen, and which was the door the Wheelings commonly used, she discovered that the door would not unlock, for it appeared to be double-bolted from inside.

"I don't understand. How can the door be *bolted*? We left by this door."

"Give me the key." The husband took the key from the wife, but failed to open the door also.

Annoyed, not yet alarmed, they went to the front of the house, and to the front door, but this door, too, appeared to be bolted from the inside. How strange this was! How unexpected . . . The wife peered through vertical windows set beside the door, into the front hall, which was in shadow. But a faint light was burning in the living room, she'd have sworn she had not left on.

By this time it might have reasonably occurred to the couple that someone had entered their house, and had bolted the doors against them. Yet still, irrationally, the predominant feeling between the wife and the husband seemed to be that there was some sort of physical impediment to their entering their house that had to be overcome by effort, or cunning. And so, as the husband turned the doorknob fruitlessly, muttering to himself—"Damn! God damn"—as if gaining entry to the house were a matter of strength, or skill—the wife made her way through a gauntlet of overgrown bushes at the side of the house, to a screened-in porch at the rear; the outer door to the porch was unlocked, and through the porch the wife had access to a door that led into a corner of the living room, beyond the fireplace; and this door, which no one had used in years, the wife succeeded in opening with her key.

In triumph the wife called to the husband: "Henry! Stay where you are, I'll let you in."

Calmly the wife was handling the emergency, as she saw it. Household matters were in her domain, rarely the husband's. Even now it did not occur to the wife that whoever had bolted the doors might still be inside, and might be dangerous.

Midway to the front door, however, the wife heard a voice from the top of the stairs—a stranger's voice—and looked up to see, to her astonishment, a young Chinese girl, slender, sleekly black-haired, with a very pale skin, and a red mouth.

"Ma'am!—hello! I am—I am so sorry—please don't call the police, ma'am—I will leave right now . . ."

Despite her agitation there was an air about the sleekly black-haired girl of poise and self-assurance; clearly, she was not a homeless person, a beggar or an ordinary intruder. She appeared to be in her mid- or late twenties. Her voice was a tremulous murmur and her accent was thoroughly American—"Ma'am, please! I am so sorry for this mistake, I am leaving right now . . . I am not taking anything . . . Please excuse me!"

Not quite steady on her feet, the girl made her way downstairs, leaning on the railing. She was audibly panting. She didn't appear to be wearing shoes—she was in (black) stocking feet, and her footsteps made no sound. The wife saw with a stab of shock that her face was young, beautiful—though contorted in a false bright placating smile of the kind a desperate, or manipulative, child might turn upon a baffled parent.

The wife stammered, weakly—"Just—leave. I won't call the police but—please just *leave*."

The wife stood out of the way, as the Chinese girl descended the stairs. The wife had no intention of interfering with the frantic fleeing girl. She saw that the girl was wearing stylishly tight-fitting jeans, a denim jacket studded with rhinestones, and a black turtleneck. In her delicate earlobes were tiny gold hoops. Her sleek black hair was disheveled, as if she'd been wakened rudely from sleep, but it was beautiful hair, straight-falling, shining. Her eyes were very black—the pupils were dilated. She was carrying an expensive-looking leather bag snatched up in haste, beneath her arm. At the front door the girl fumbled to unlock the bolt, which she must have locked not long before, and hurried outside into the darkness without a backward glance.

All this while the wife was staring after the girl in amazement—who was this person? What had happened?

In the meantime, the husband had followed the wife to the screened-in porch at the side of the house, and had entered the house through that door. In an alarmed voice he was calling, "Audrey? Where the hell are you? What's going on?" He had not seen the intruder, nor even heard her voice. When he encountered the wife in the front hall, at the front door, he saw that she stood stunned and unmoving, as if she'd suffered a great shock.

The husband glanced out the front door, and saw nothing—no one.

"Audrey? What's wrong? Was someone in the house?"

The wife tried to explain. The wife tried to recount what had happened so swiftly, and improbably. The wife stammered trying to explain to the disbelieving husband what she herself could scarcely comprehend: a stranger had appeared at the top of the stairs, guiltily acknowledging her presence—begging the wife not to call the police—insisting she hadn't taken anything—"And I said I wouldn't call the police if she would just *leave*."

The girl appeared to be Chinese, the wife said. She was tall, slender, with long sleek black hair—"Not young, not a teenager. In her twenties. She was carrying a leather bag, and she wasn't wearing shoes." After a pause the wife added, "She may have been 'high' on drugs . . . She seemed unsteady on her feet."

The husband was listening with a faint smile, as of disbelief. He had seen no intruder in the house, himself. He had heard no voice except the wife's upraised voice.

"I thought I heard you calling, Audrey—'Who's there?' But I didn't hear any reply."

"There was an intruder! She was talking to me! Her voice was soft, I could barely hear . . ." The wife spoke rapidly. Her heart was beating unnaturally hard, now the danger should have been past. The husband continued to question her, but didn't seem altogether convinced.

They were upstairs by now, in the darkened hall. The wife smelled a faint scent of hair lotion—not her own, she was sure. A single lamp burned in their bedroom and on the bed, with the look of having been dropped in haste, its screen still luminous, was the husband's iPad.

"Look, Henry—she had your iPad! She was using your iPad." The wife spoke decisively now, the husband would have to believe her.

"It's as if she knew we were going out for the evening, but not that the evening was canceled. She didn't have time to steal anything—we took her by surprise."

Henry snatched up the iPad, frowning. He was a person who didn't like surprises, and he didn't like intrusions. The wife spoke to him but the husband seemed scarcely to be listening, as if his mind were rapidly calculating.

The wife was regretting she'd allowed the girl to walk past her carrying a leather bag. The wife was regretting believing the girl when she'd insisted that she hadn't taken anything. "I was so taken by surprise, I didn't know what to do—but I didn't want to punish her, she seemed like a nice person . . ."

They saw that the girl had left a pair of knee-high leather boots behind, on the bedroom carpet. One supple, beautifully tooled dark boot stood erect, the other had toppled over. These were expensive, high-quality boots, the girl had abandoned in her flight.

The silk comforter on their bed had been dislodged, as if the girl had lain there, typing on the iPad, with the comforter gathered around her for warmth. You could see the intimate impress of her body in the bedclothes, where the fragrant scent of hair lotion was stronger.

The wife said, with a nervous laugh, "Do you believe me now, Henry, that someone was here?"—but the husband only just shook his head, frowning—"Well, something has happened, darling. That seems certain."

They examined the rest of the bedroom, checked closets and bureau drawers, but the wife was very rattled, and could not think clearly: it appeared that, in her closet, clothes on hangers had been shoved to the side, and her bureau drawers, that contained undergarments and stockings, might have been rifled-through—"But I don't know if she took anything."

The wife's jewelry was kept in a red-lacquer box with a half-dozen little drawers, that could be locked with a little key; she never troubled to lock the drawers, and so the jewelry box was vulnerable to theft—but again, peering into the little drawers in haste, blinking moisture from her eyes, she had no idea if the girl had taken anything.

She'd felt a little stab of dismay, and of embarrassment—her bathroom wasn't altogether clean, at least not so clean as she'd have liked it to be, if an intruder like the Chinese girl were to see it. The mirror above the sink wasn't clean, the sink counters weren't clean, the sink required scrubbing so that the chrome fixtures gleamed . . .

What the husband thought of his own bathroom, on the farther side of the bedroom, the wife had no idea. A cleaning woman came each Monday and stayed much of the day, vacuuming the numerous rooms of the house and restoring them to some degree of cleanliness, but it was four days since the woman had been here. Circumspectly the husband was saying that nothing of his had been taken, he was sure; he would look more closely in the morning.

The husband spoke irritably and negligently, as if the subject were too petty for his concern. But he'd taken up his iPad at once, and shut off the screen.

Where had the iPad been? the wife wondered. She'd have supposed that the husband kept it downstairs in his study, with his other electronic equipment; but when she asked the husband, the husband shrugged and said he had no idea.

No idea? How was that possible?

"I said, Audrey. I have no idea. I haven't even glanced at this iPad in weeks. Unless I travel, I don't use the damned thing, as you must know."

"But—what was the girl doing with it? Was she looking at your email? Or—sending messages of her own?"

"I don't know. My impression is, nothing."

"But—she must have been doing something."

"Really? How do you know? She might've just switched on the iPad when you surprised her."

The husband was walking away. The wife was speaking to the husband's back.

The wife was dismayed that, at this crucial time, when she and the husband should have been brought closer together, the husband kept himself at a little distance from her, aloof to the situation, annoyed and yet amused. The wife was dismayed that her emotional unease meant so little to the husband, who often remarked that he didn't like "weak"—"emotional"—"needy"—people.

The husband went downstairs. The wife lingered upstairs to look into other rooms, that were darkened—it did not seem likely that the girl had entered these. (In the morning, when she examined closets, she would discover that clothes had been pushed aside, and footwear on the floor appeared to be dislodged; a stack of framed photographs, kept in a closet, had been examined; but if anything had been taken, the wife could not identify it.)

"Audrey darling—look! Your intruder must have been thirsty."

Downstairs in the kitchen, where an overhead light was burning brightly, the husband had discovered a single carton of orange juice on a counter, opened.

How strange! The Chinese girl had taken the carton from the refrigerator, probably she'd stood in front of the opened door and drunk.

"I suppose it's possible that one of us left the carton on the counter," the husband said, and the wife protested, "Of course not! We might have had orange juice at breakfast but that was hours ago . . ." yet stubbornly the husband said, "Still it's possible, Audrey. You've been known to leave things out, and to be surprised at discovering them. And why on earth would this 'Chinese girl burglar' take time to drink orange juice?"

The wife had no idea. The wife could only stammer that she was sure neither of them had left the orange juice on the counter . . .

Since they'd returned from the unexpectedly canceled opera, the husband had been in a mood both irritable and playful. He'd been gracious to the wife in the presence of the couple with whom they'd had dinner, as often he was; but now he was rather coolly perfunctory, impatient.

"Henry, look!" On another counter, in front of the microwave oven, was a part-filled bowl of miso soup and ramen noodles. And in the sink, an opened eight-ounce container of plain white nonfat yogurt with a spoon stuck into it, partly empty.

"Our intruder must have been hungry. This solves the mystery —she broke inside a house to find something to eat."

The husband laughed, this was so absurd. But it was an explanation he would accept, in its very absurdity.

"She didn't look hungry, Henry. She didn't look *poor*."

"If she took time to eat in such circumstances, darling, she was by any definition *hungry*."

There was no reasoning with the husband in one of his moods.

The wife thought it strange, Henry was speaking ebulliently, as if expecting to be overheard. His hair was disheveled, as if he'd run his hands through it. He'd loosened his handsome silk necktie. Negligently he opened cupboard doors in the kitchen—opened and closed them, noisily. "Nothing missing? No more? Maybe the mystery intruder has left a dwarf accomplice behind, who will crawl out of hiding after we go to bed, and cut our throats."

The wife shuddered. Why was that so funny?

The wife wondered at the husband's mood, for the husband seemed both fascinated by the intruder, as she was, and eager to push all thoughts of the intruder aside as of little significance.

"We can look more thoroughly in the morning," the wife said, trying to speak practicably. "Tonight—it's a relief, nothing terrible happened."

"Virtually nothing 'happened' at all. If we were to summon the police, what on earth could we tell them? They would end up blaming *us*."

The wife was feeling the aftermath of the shock. Her heart still beat strangely, as if in reproach.

"I wonder if she was—'high'—on drugs? She behaved so strangely . . ."

"In what way, 'strangely'?"

"The way she looked at me—spoke to me—the pupils of her eyes seemed dilated . . ."

"If she were Chinese, as you say, her eyes would be dark. Very difficult for you to have discerned, at a distance of a few feet, if the pupils of her eyes were 'dilated.'" The husband spoke lightly, derisively.

This was so, the wife supposed. And yet—what other explanation for the girl's behavior?

"You know, Henry—we don't really know what she took from us. She was half-running right past me, with a large leather bag—I didn't think to ask her to show me what was inside."

This was not altogether true: the wife had thought of asking, but had not dared. Even at such a time, when a stranger had violated the privacy of her household, she'd felt too much the hostess—constrained, inhibited. Polite.

"Don't be silly, Audrey—you surprised the intruder. She didn't have time to stow things in her burglar's bag."

"Maybe she did, before I came in. How do you know?"

"True. I don't know. I didn't see the 'intruder' in fact—I've taken your word for it."

"'Taken my word'—what do you mean?"

"Just what I said. *I* didn't see any Chinese girl, only *you* saw her."

The wife wanted to protest—what of the iPad on the bed? What of the boots left behind?

The orange juice, the miso soup?

"And why do you persist in saying 'Chinese'? Could you really distinguish between Asian nationalities, darling? Korean, Thai, Japanese . . ."

At the Institute, the husband worked with many Asian and Asian-American scientists. The wife had to concede that probably she could not identify a Chinese face among the faces of other Asians—if she'd called the police, she would have hesitated so identifying the intruder.

The wife was confused by the husband's attitude. It was not unlike him, in a time of crisis, to turn the situation back upon her, if he could; the husband had a way, both jocular and cutting, of punishing the wife for upsetting herself and him. Throughout their marriage, the wife had become conditioned to keep mild crises to herself, to deflect "bad news" where she could, and never complain to the husband if she could avoid it.

Whining. Complaining. It isn't very becoming in a woman.
Please can we drop the subject.

But now the wife was thinking what a mistake she'd made entering a house that had been broken into, without knowing if the intruder or intruders were still inside. And Henry hadn't called her back—he'd seemed to be encouraging her, to find a way inside their house.

If the intruder had been a man, or men, with weapons! The wife might have been killed.

It hurt her, that Henry seemed indifferent to the danger she'd put herself in for his sake.

She thought—*But why isn't he upset? Why doesn't he care?*

As if he'd only now just thought of it, the husband went to check his study. The husband's at-home study was a large, spacious room at the rear of the house, the door to which was sometimes locked. (To keep out the wife? But the wife would never have entered the husband's study uninvited.) Tonight, the door was securely shut but not locked. And the room was darkened. The husband switched on an overhead light and glanced about, frowning—"Doesn't look as if anyone has been in here."

"Are you sure, Henry? Your desk . . ."

The husband's computer screen was dark, but the drawers of his desk were part-open. The husband usually kept the drawers uniformly shut, as he tried to keep his desk top clear and uncluttered. His success as an administrator, Henry often joked, lay in his insistence upon answering emails daily, if not as quickly as they came in.

It was possible the intruder had visited this room. The wife heard the husband curse, under his breath. But then he laughed, as if the situation were absurd—preposterous. He would not become indignant. He would not become upset. He would examine his study more thoroughly in the morning, he said. "There's no hurry now, obviously. The 'intruder' has departed."

The wife said, uncertainly, "Are you absolutely sure we shouldn't call the police, Henry? Maybe . . ."

"No. The last thing we want is police officers bumbling around our house and blaming us for leaving a door unlocked."

Locking up the house had fallen to the wife's responsibility and it was true, sometimes Audrey didn't trouble to lock a door during the daytime, if she wasn't going to be away for long. But leaving the house for an evening was a different matter. The wife was sure she'd locked the door. It had become second nature for her to make sure that the doors of the house were locked, as she took care to lock the doors of her vehicle.

Half-ironically the wife said, "What shall I do with the boots?"

"Put them outside in the morning. Not by the front door, but out by the driveway. Maybe the mysterious 'Chinese girl' will come back to get them."

It was like the husband to issue such a command, with a smile. And to add, after a beat, as if he'd only just thought of it, "*Please*."

The wife thought it was strange, and yet it felt natural—to treat an intruder with such thoughtfulness. For the Chinese girl was clearly not a burglar—not a criminal. Nor was she homeless. To have called the police to arrest her would be cruelly punitive, and the wife did not want to hurt her. Thinking—*She must be desperate, to behave the way she did.*

The wife was aware, too, that the husband was observing her, and judging her. Throughout their marriage of not quite eight years she'd been aware of the husband's observation and judgment, that had often been severe; she understood that something in her very soul was stunned, and niggardly. But she was determined now to behave as the husband wished her to behave, and to surprise him with her equanimity.

And so in the early morning, the wife set the handsome leather boots carefully outside, as the husband had instructed. The Wheelings' red-brick Edwardian house was set back in a large, wooded suburban-rural lot; from the front door, you could barely see the road at the end of the driveway. No one could see the boots set in the grass beside the front walk unless she made a point of coming onto the Wheelings' property, and looking for them. The wife thought it unlikely that the Chinese girl would come back for her boots, but she was determined to follow the husband in his suggestion.

The previous evening, the girl must have come to the Wheelings' house by chance. Very likely she'd been walking through the residential neighborhood of deep, wooded lots and tall trees, with no clear idea of where she was going. She'd bypassed other, more brightly lighted houses in favor of the Wheelings' darkened house. It was not possible to think that the girl had set out intending to break into their house, but somehow, she'd gained access to it. She'd dared to open the door, and step inside. The wife imagined her soft, clear, melodic voice—"Hello? Hello? Is anyone home?"

Beyond that, the wife couldn't imagine.

It was purely chance, her coming here.

It does not mean anything!

Through the morning, the boots remained beside the walk, untouched. When the wife glanced outside she was startled to see them—like a living being, they were, that had been stricken, and fallen into the grass.

At midday, the wife had to go away for a few hours; when she returned, the boots were still there in the front lawn, unmoving. And then she forgot about the boots, and in the early evening when the husband returned from his office at the Institute the husband went outside to check, and happily reported that the boots were gone.

The wife was astonished, for she was certain that the girl would never have dared return for the boots. How could the girl have even imagined that the Wheelings would leave the boots outside for her . . .

"Henry, are you sure? The boots are—*gone*?"

"Gone, darling. Gone."

The husband laughed, as if the little adventure had come to a fitting end. The wife tried to laugh, though she was hurt. After her kindness to the intruder, the girl hadn't thought to tell the wife that she was grateful.

She is ashamed, I suppose. She wants only to never see us again.

The husband seemed pleased with this ending. The husband kissed the wife, lightly on the lips. The husband was in a heightened mood, his skin flushed, and an alertness in his eye, and the wife could smell a faint smell of alcohol on his breath, for there'd been a lavish reception at the Institute late that afternoon.

"That was very generous of you, Audrey. You're a superior person—I've always known that. I love you."

The wife was radiant with sudden happiness. The kiss would burn forever in her heart. Extravagantly she thought—*He loves me! I will never doubt him again.*

5. THE PREDATOR'S SHADOW

Her.

It was on the third day of the Galapagos excursion that the wife saw, to her shock, the sleek-black-haired Chinese girl at the farther end of the ship's lounge standing amid a gathering of mostly men.

The wife stared, disbelieving. Her heart clamored like a bell of alarm—*No. Not here. Henry would not . . .*

The husband had gone on ahead, to have drinks with colleagues at the Institute, before dinner. The wife had remained in the cabin, fighting a headache. The day's outings had been strenuous: in the morning a "wet landing" in the rocky surf of Pitt Point, on San Cristóbal Island, and a two-hour hike to the top of a volcanic ridge; in the afternoon, another "wet landing" at Gardner Bay and a hike along a sandy beach amid colonies of sea lions, Galapagos hawks and sea turtles. Though the husband was still limping he'd managed to complete both hikes, using the walking stick; the wife too had begun walking with a stick. Quickly, she'd become dependent upon it.

Frequently the husband asked the wife if she was all right? If the excursions were not too much for her? For Henry could be kindly, solicitous. At times, the wife believed that her husband felt some measure of—could it be guilt? remorse?—looking at her with thoughtful eyes. And he'd been impressed, she thought, by how well she'd adapted to the Galapagos outings: she'd been only mildly seasick on the *Floreana*, once; even when staggering with exhaustion on a hike, she never complained. Her admiration for the stark, windswept beauty of the Galapagos Islands seemed to be sincere. She even spent time in the ship's library, reading about the history of the Galapagos so that she could talk intelligently about it with Henry and fellow passengers.

You're not sorry that you came with me, Audrey?

Not at all! I love it here . . . it's the adventure of my life.

The wife was determined to be *positive*. The wife was determined to *survive*!

Tried not to think of the awkward and frightening experience on the Moon Deck the previous night. As she tried not to think of the awkward and frightening incident on the stone steps in Quito.

In both instances, she'd overreacted—she knew. Feeling now a thrill of shame, that she'd behaved in such a childish manner.

Fortunately Henry seemed to have forgiven her about the Moon Deck, as about the stone steps in Quito. Airily he'd waved aside her embarrassed apology—"Darling, don't be silly! It was very dark on the deck, anyone would be frightened. We'll try again tomorrow night when there may be a full moon."

The wife shuddered, anticipating a return to the dreaded Moon Deck. But perhaps the husband wasn't serious.

This afternoon, the husband had gone snorkeling in the deep water of Gardner Bay. The wife had remained onshore with the rest of the Albatrosses. She'd been mildly anxious about the husband, swimming with mostly younger swimmers, but of course Henry was a practiced swimmer; he'd often gone scuba diving, he had told her. The wife was not a confident swimmer, and would never have dared swim in the ocean, near rocks, in waters so populated with sea life (including, at times, stingrays and sharks). Now, the wife recalled having been struck by a single female snorkeler in the water, slender, young—not a member of the Albatrosses but of another group. She wondered if the snorkeler had been the black-haired Chinese girl, if Henry and the girl had arranged to meet surreptitiously to swim together . . .

It is not possible! Henry would not deceive me so openly.

It is a girl who resembles the intruder. It is not her.

But there was the husband, tall, silvery-haired, with the group that included the Chinese girl, obviously his colleagues at the Institute. Indecisively the wife stood, staring.

Just inside the lounge entrance was a horseshoe-shaped bar about which customers crowded. The wife couldn't see past them clearly, and was hidden by them, should the husband glance around looking for her.

It was a festive time! Drinks, after the rigors of the day. The ship's ornate interior, after the primitive windswept exteriors of the day. Music was playing loudly, tinnily. The wife clutched at her head trying to think.

Go away. You didn't see. He hasn't seen you. Nothing has happened that is irrevocable.

Henry didn't expect her until dinner, at their usual table in the dining room on the lower level. If the black-haired girl was at dinner somewhere in the dining room, it had to be at a distant table since the wife had not seen her before.

More reasonably then she thought—*But this young woman is one of Henry's colleagues at the Institute. Not the other* . . .

The sleek-black-haired girl who'd broken into their house could not possibly be the sleek-black-haired girl with whom

Henry was speaking. The wife berated herself, for thinking this could be so.

It was like the episode on the Moon Deck. The wife had thought—*Of course, he wants to kill me.* Even as the wife thought—*That is not possible. He loves me.*

"Drink, ma'am?"—one of the Ecuadoran waiters smiled at her with a flash of friendly white teeth. In the staff's eyes she was *ma'am* and of no more interest than the small number of older, grand-motherly and white-haired women among the ship's passengers.

Surreptitiously the wife made her way forward. Her heart was beating as in the presence of a terrible danger; her eyes flooded with tears of grief and humiliation. She saw that Henry was speaking with the tall sleek-black-haired girl, among oth-ers; they were all relaxed, laughing together; clearly these were Institute colleagues of Henry's whom Audrey had not met, or hadn't recalled meeting, for there were many colleagues and the wife didn't attend all Institute events. Almost, she felt relief: if Henry were romantically involved with the girl, would they be so openly together? So blatant?

She wondered if the girl had a companion on the ship. One of the men? If so, it was hardly possible that the girl and Henry Wheeling were having an affair. It was possible, but it was unlikely.

Unlikely, and loathsome.

The sleek-black-haired girl was certainly Asian, and very at-tractive, and in her mid- or late twenties, but the individual whom the wife had seen hastily descending the stairs in her house had not been so tall, she was sure. (But was this young woman wearing high-heeled shoes?) She was wearing a tight-fitting floral-print Chinese silk dress that fitted her like a glove, worn with a vivid green silk shawl. And around her slender neck, gleaming slate-colored pearls. The intruder had had whiter skin, and a striking red mouth, while this young woman didn't seem to be wearing lipstick at all. And her hair didn't fall past her shoulders in a shining cascade but only just to the tips of her ears. Had she cut her hair? *Was* this the same person?

The wife saw the husband laughing, and the girl was laughing with him. The wife saw the husband lightly touch the girl's shoulder—adjusting the silk shawl. It was an innocent gesture, she was sure.

They were colleagues, Henry and the sleek-black-haired Asian girl. That was all.

Bravely the wife decided to come forward, to meet them. In her hand was an Ecuadoran fruit drink laced with vodka, she didn't remember taking. And she didn't remember sipping the drink, though her throat burned pleasantly.

As she approached Henry and his colleagues, the heel of her shoe caught in the carpet and the wife nearly tripped. Henry turned, and saw her, and smiled quickly. "Darling! Just in time . . . I'd like you to meet Steffi Park, one of our newest and brightest neurobiologists."

The wife was introduced to several others, whom (she supposed) she'd met before, though she couldn't recall their names. Everyone, including the Asian girl, called her "Mrs. Wheeling" and was very polite to her.

Steffi Park's handshake was forthright. Steffi Park was not at all shy. And she was not so young: in her thirties at least. Her skin was beautiful but slightly sallow, and there were fine white lines bracketing her eyes. Still, her dark eyes shone with a kind of intellectual merriment. She and Henry Wheeling were very good friends, you could see. And the fragrance of the girl's shining black hair was such, the wife felt as if she might swoon.

Henry was smiling, and Steffi Park was smiling. It was an astonishing joint performance—the husband introducing, to the wife, the very individual who'd broken into their house a few months before, whom the wife had confronted. *And they are daring me to recognize her. To accuse them.*

The wife saw the arrogant couple regarding her with bemusement, unless it was pity. She saw their mouths move—but could hear no words. She was feeling faint. A sensation of cold washed over her. On one of the islands the guide had described how the shadows of hawks, falling over even adult Galapagos creatures like the gigantic tortoises, triggered panic responses in them. She felt that now. The shadow of a predator hawk gliding over her.

Wildly she thought—*They will kill me. I can't prevent it, I am helpless.*

6. "LITTLE APPLES OF DEATH"

"Because I am Indian, I can touch the leaves. But you must not—your skin will burn."

Eduardo paused to tell his listeners of the poison apple tree beside the steeply ascending trail on the island of Santa Cruz— the "little apples of death"—which resembled a crab apple tree, with stunted, greenish-yellow fruit. Carefully Eduardo touched a leaf with his forefinger—he did not pluck the leaf, and he did not squeeze it. "The leaf may sting even me, a little. But if one of you touched it, you would develop a painful rash, and if you touched your eyes—well, you would not want to do that!"

If he were to tear the leaf, Eduardo continued, which he would not do, a "white, milky sap" would appear—"Like fire on the skin." The "little apples of death" were so virulent that just a mouthful of the fruit would start a process that destroys a person's digestive tract, and eventually brings about an excruciating death.

"Once the process begins, nothing can stop it. It can be mis-diagnosed as simple stomach trouble . . . Children, please keep your distance from the tree. And parents, please watch your children!"

Scattered on the ground, even on the trail, were some of the wizened little apples. The wife shuddered, considering these innocuous-looking fruits that more resembled misshapen pears than apples.

She would take care not to step on a poison apple, for if pulp got onto the sole of her hiking shoes it might then get onto an article of clothing in her suitcase, and so onto her hands . . .

As usual, Henry was at the head of the group of hikers, as Audrey was at the rear; like several other women, she made no effort to keep up with the faster-paced hikers. She saw with relief that Henry had gone ahead and stepped clear of the fallen fruit, following close behind Eduardo. He was in a brusque, ebullient mood—though his ankle was much better, he continued to use the walking stick. That morning he'd said, shaving, "Well—our last full day in the Galapagos! And we've survived." He'd winked at Audrey in the mirror, and she'd tried to smile brightly back.

Thinking—*If I can just get back home! I will never take such a risk again.*

In the bright sunny equatorial morning, her fears of the previous night began to seem insubstantial. And she was less certain that the sleek-black-haired Steffi Park could be the brazen intruder who'd broken into their house months before . . .

Yet still, it was probable that the husband and the sleek-black-haired "neurobiologist" were having an affair. There was an unmistakable sexual ease between the two, that dismayed the wife who had never felt such ease with Henry Wheeling even in the early, romantic days of their courtship.

Unmistakable too were glances of pity from Henry's Institute colleagues. *Poor woman! So naïve, foolish—so blind . . .*

They had no idea that her life was in danger, however. They had no idea how ruthless, calculating, cruel Henry Wheeling could be.

From a passenger whom she'd befriended in the ship's library the wife had learned the chilling fact that cruise ships in international or foreign waters did not have to comply with U.S. law. In fact, there was no "U.S. law" outside the territorial United States. The *Floreana* was registered in Ecuador. Other cruise ships with predominantly American passengers were registered in countries as remote as Liberia! Any crimes committed on the vessels could be investigated and prosecuted only by authorities in these countries, that were notoriously open to bribes. Nor was there any likelihood of successful lawsuits filed by passengers who had due cause to be unhappy or aggrieved. In horror the wife had listened as the other passenger, an American woman of her own approximate age, recounted incidents of theft, harassment, vandalism, extortion, sexual molestation and rape, assault, even murder on the "high seas"—and how rare it was for any perpetrator to be arrested.

Again the wife shuddered. How naïve she'd been, in so many ways!

She felt faint with dread. An accident could happen to her on the ship, easily . . . In the pitch-dark moonless night she might fall—she might be pushed—overboard, and her body would never be found. If she disappeared from her cabin, her husband would report her missing—he would be "inconsolable."

Her family might suspect that her husband had killed her, or had left her behind in some terrible remote place to die. They'd never trusted him, and she had not listened to them. Love had isolated her, like a disease. She'd loved her husband too much and had no one else in whom to confide.

In her imagination she'd begun letters to her older sister Imogene from whom she'd become estranged since her marriage to Henry Wheeling.

Dear Imogene—

You would not ever guess where I am! In equatorial waters, in the famous Galapagos Islands off the coast of Ecuador.

It is a very beautiful if stark & "primitive" place. Henry had not wanted me to come initially, he'd worried that I am not fit or strong enough for the strenuous hikes, but I am doing well, I think. Indeed it is the most fascinating place I have ever visited in my life.

But this was a false voice. This was the "wifely" voice, a fabrication.

Dear Imogene—

The truth is, I am so ashamed. I am afraid for my life. I am afraid of Henry. I think he is involved with another woman, a beautiful Chinese neurobiologist who must be thirty years younger than Henry, whom he has hired at the Institute. She has been in our house—she has been in our bedroom! I think Henry hopes that his wife—his present wife—will disappear from his life.

There have been near-accidents. "Accidents"—that could have been fatal.

I remember how you & others tried to warn me against Henry Wheeling. I am sick with shame, that I did not listen to you. For I fear that you are correct, & if I never see you again—I love you.

Do not let my husband inherit my estate! I beg you.

But the truth is more complicated—I love Henry. My suspicion is like a paralysis or a poison. I am anxious that this is all a mistake—my suspicions are in error—& I have misjudged an innocent man. For I believe that at any moment the husband who had loved me so much will return, & we will be happy again.

Your loving sister
Audrey

This letter, she would write quickly, as soon as she had some private time on the *Floreana* later that day, and she would leave it with the tour director—"In case something happens to me."

Now, as the others moved carefully past the poison tree, the wife stooped to tie a shoelace. No one would glance twice at her, stooping to tie a shoelace. In the deep pockets of her cargo pants she'd brought wads of tissues. Carefully she used these tissues to pick up several of the wizened little apples, and carefully she wrapped the apples in the tissues, and placed them in her pockets.

A thimble of poison. *If I bite into an apple, that will be the end.*

The wife recalled the terrifying ending of Flaubert's *Madame Bovary.* The novel was one of her favorites but she'd never quite accepted that Emma Bovary wasn't a heroine but a foolish romantic-minded victim. Unhappy in love, hopelessly in debt, poor Emma had anticipated a languid slipping-into-sleep, but in fact she'd died horribly vomiting and convulsing, having swallowed arsenic.

The wife would never behave so desperately. She would never swallow poison, she was sure. Yet—there is a melancholy consolation in having such a powerful poison close at hand . . .

She hurried to catch up with the others who were making their way downhill to a greener and marshier area of the island populated by giant tortoises. Here was the high point of the Galapagos adventure—the famous giant tortoises, the largest of all tortoise species. Seen at a little distance these prehistoric-looking creatures did not appear exceptionally large, because the human eye, or the brain, "corrected" for their size; but as you approached them, you saw that they were enormous, moving with glacial slowness and dignity like Volkswagens fashioned of thick tortoiseshell. Their legs were large, rubbery-goiterous, and scaly; their protruding heads were bald and phlegmatic; their eyes were beady and unblinking, chilling to behold.

I too am alive, like you. But I will outlive you.

"Please do not approach the tortoises. They may appear sleepy but they are keenly aware of us. Their senses are acute."

In a muddy field were several of the massive tortoises. Each weighed, by Eduardo's estimate, more than eight hundred pounds. They might be as old as a century—at least. Their hearts beat very slowly. They could hold their breath underwater for eight hours. They moved slowly and yet deliberately: it might take two months for giant tortoises to reach the sea, but they would get there, and back. They had no natural predators except, as babies just out of the shell, the Galapagos hawk.

Eduardo warned that, if you got too close to a tortoise, he would show his displeasure by making a hoarse, snuffling sound and drawing his neck, head, legs and tail back into his shell—"And then you will have only the shell to look at."

It was a strangely beautiful shell, the wife thought. In a trance the wife stared, as others took photographs.

. . . *outlive you. All of you.*

Small, foolish creatures who stand upright and want, want, want.

Sailors had slaughtered the great tortoises since the sixteenth century. Food, oil, tortoiseshell. For humankind was the most ravenous and pitiless predator. By the mid-twentieth century the creatures were headed for extinction; in the 1970s, less than three thousand remained in the Galapagos. Fortunately, the Ecuadoran government intervened with the establishment of Galapagos National Park.

Here again was the story of slaughter—nonindigenous species eradicated en masse to provide a stable environment for the tortoises. The wife understood the logic of course. But—so much bloodshed, in the service of ecology!

It was a revelation to the wife, how precarious life is. These great tortoises, that looked as if they would be invulnerable to most natural harm, were in fact highly vulnerable. Goats could overrun their islands and devour their food supplies. Within a few years, they could disappear forever from the earth. Already, entire subspecies of tortoises had vanished, to prevail in a transmogrified form in Victorian combs and the backs of looking glasses. It was a terrible thing, life devouring life. But the vanishing, the extinction—that seemed yet more terrible.

The wife was considering the precariousness of her own life. To survive, she must be very vigilant. She was not trained in vigilance, she had led a sheltered life for more than forty years, yet now she would have to make decisions.

Desperation, cunning.

Adapting to changing circumstances.

You might believe that you are relatively strong and self-sufficient and yet your (physical) survival depends upon a lucky confluence of temperature, rainfall, and food. Too much rainfall, too little—you perished. Climate too warm, or too cool—you perished. And you never lived beyond your food supply, no matter how developed your brain, or what a good person you were.

Most of the Galapagos creatures, the great reptiles, lived in a torpor of quasi-consciousness. The most primitive sort of life, of vertebrates. They had no idea how "endangered" they were.

"Here, you see the interior of a tortoiseshell. You see?—it is not a 'detachable' shell as people sometimes think, but part of the creature's spine." Eduardo had led them to a grassy area beneath an awning, where the shell of a giant tortoise was on display. This was a shocking sight—the great, beautiful shell, and no creature inside. When Eduardo lifted it, with some effort, you could see the cartilaginous remains of the creature's backbone. Eduardo invited some of the children to crawl under the shell, to be photographed by their parents.

The wife felt a kind of hurt, an insult—the giant tortoise was too noble a creature, for its shell to be photographed in this way!

"I don't think you should do that," Audrey said. "I think—it's a kind of sacrilege of the animal . . ."

Several others murmured agreement. But Eduardo did not hear, or did not acknowledge hearing. One by one the children crawled beneath the massive shell, and their parents took pictures.

The wife's eyes filled with tears. Oh, this was ridiculous! She could not reasonably feel grief for the mere carapace of a tortoise—an emptiness . . .

The husband came to stand beside her as if in commiseration. He too had been annoyed by the misappropriation of the shell, which he'd been photographing until Eduardo issued his invitation to the children.

"Are you all right, darling? Quite a trek this morning. This sun is hot."

The husband touched her wrist. The wife smiled up at him, blinded by light.

With a flood of relief thinking—*Of course this man isn't trying to kill me. He is my husband who loves me, he doesn't want me to die.*

7. MOON DECK, REVISITED

"Darling? The moon is out, finally. A fuller moon."

It was their last night on the *Floreana*. Strolling musicians entertained the passengers at dinner and all of the ship's crew and the Galapagos guides wore festive Ecuadoran costumes. Even the dignified Eduardo wore a papier-mâché hat and a colorful shirt, and posed for passengers to take pictures of him.

"Thank you, Eduardo!"—the wife, too, took a picture. Though secretly she was disappointed with Eduardo now.

At dinner the wife had had two glasses of wine where often she'd had none. The husband had arranged for some of his Institute colleagues to be seated at their table, with whom he could talk about scientific matters; the friendly strangers who'd been at the table had vanished, the wife had no idea where.

The husband often behaved in this way. Behind the scenes, he banished, discharged, "terminated"—sometimes employees, assistants, friends and acquaintances. Wives.

If the wife were to ask what had happened to their dinner companions the husband would say smilingly—"Who?"

At least, the husband had not arranged for Steffi Park to be at their table. Or perhaps Steffi Park had demurred, out of consideration for the wife.

As the wife, eight years before, had several times demurred accompanying Henry Wheeling to events, out of consideration for the Mrs. Wheeling of the time.

Much of the dinner passed in a blur for the wife. She was not accustomed to drinking and the air of frantic festivity was jarring. She could not keep from glancing about the crowded room in search of the beautiful black-haired Asian girl whom she saw, or thought she saw, in a farther corner.

Talk at dinner was of the Galapagos project of maintaining endangered species by way of the "eradication" of unwanted species. Initially the project had stirred controversy from animal rights groups, but its success had made it a model for ecological agencies worldwide.

Of course, Henry and his fellow scientists were totally in agreement with the project of slaughter in the maintenance of a privileged species. It was a scientific principle, and not really open to debate. In silence the wife listened until at last, emboldened by wine, she protested: "But the 'introduced' species have evolved too, haven't they? Wouldn't they be of interest, biologically?"

The men looked at her as if a trained creature, a parrot perhaps, had spoken in their language, almost coherently.

"Audrey, dear—the goats were of no ecological interest, they aren't a species in danger of extinction! Several Galapagos species were in danger, and have been stabilized now. If the 'introduced' species hadn't been eradicated, the Galapagos species would have vanished. There would be no 'Galapagos' now—just islands of goats." Henry spoke sympathetically, as if he were addressing a slow-witted individual whose feelings he must not hurt. The other men laughed. "The goats had overrun some of the islands and had devoured most of the vegetation, which the tortoises need to survive. And the cats were devouring the birds . . ."

"But the guide told us that they don't 'help' the animals. They don't 'interfere' with the animals. But clearly they do."

"The goal was to restore the islands to pre-human intervention. That was the goal, and it seems to have worked well."

"It just seems wrong to slaughter living things. Just— slaughter . . . A terrible bloodbath, and no one cared."

The wife spoke somewhat wildly. Wine seemed to have dampened her natural reticence. The men listened as if respectfully, and only the husband replied: "Individuals don't matter, dear. Species matter. No one slaughtered an entire species, only a subspecies on the islands. Perhaps we should change the subject now, since you seem to be emotional?"

Stubbornly the wife persisted, "But the goats, by the twentieth century, would be an established species themselves. They were 'introduced' by human beings the way species are 'introduced' by birds, or the wind, or other animals . . . Isn't that what is meant by evolution?"

"No! The goats were not among the original species."

"But—isn't that what the Nazis said about Jews and gypsies? Not Aryans—not indigenous species and so they have to be eradicated."

Now Henry was furious with her. His colleagues looked away, in embarrassment.

"I think we should change the subject, Audrey. You are out of your depth, and making a fool of yourself."

"But—I was only just defending the goats. Why weren't the Galapagos goats an interesting subspecies of *goat*? They were here three hundred years. Why didn't any biologist care about them?"

But it was hopeless. The (slaughtered, banished) goats were hopeless. As a single uplifted voice amid the theorizing of Nazis— *What about the Jews, the gypsies, the "despised" minorities, granted these non-indigenous races, granted the horror of "race mingling"*

*and "mongrelization"—would no one come to the defense of these
subspecies? No biologist? No one?*

No one.

Dessert was served. And with dessert, a sweet wine.

There was a raspberry mousse, and there was a greenish-yellow
creamy pie. There was something like a banana custard topped with
mango. Desserts on the *Floreana* were exotic, delicious. The husband
appreciated exquisite desserts like these—mousses, crème brûlée.
The wife had learned to make such desserts for him, and for dinner
parties; she was grateful for his praise, which did not come casually.

Carefully she would remove the "little apples of death" from
the tissues in which they'd been wrapped. She saw herself mash-
ing the little apples into a paste, in the privacy of her kitchen. If
she checked her larger suitcase, the apples could not be detected.
She would wrap them in layers of cloth, in underwear. She would
not touch them with her bare fingers.

She would use her blender to whip the greeny-yellow paste
into a liquid. She would add cream, and she would add a tea-
spoon of liqueur. She would serve the dessert in a special dessert
glass, which the husband particularly admired, from a set of
heirloom crystal she'd been given for their wedding.

For herself she would make a dessert that mimicked the husband's dessert. Like the marine iguanas that so closely resembled
their volcanic-rock habitat they could scarcely be distinguished
from the habitat, the wife's dessert (yogurt, banana) would mimic
the husband's (lethal) dessert.

The husband trusted the wife utterly. For she had not ever given him reason to distrust her. Unquestioning, the husband would eat the dessert, and the husband would never suspect. Even when he began to be ill, and when he began to be very ill, the husband would never suspect.

"Darling? The moon is out, finally. Come!"

Weakly the wife tried to resist with the excuse of feeling light-headed after hours that day in the equatorial sun, and several glasses of wine, but the husband said, "It's our last night on the *Floreana*. Our last night in these 'enchanted isles.' Tomorrow is—home."

Home, so intoned that it rhymed with *doom*.

The husband had seized the wife's hand as you might seize a small fluttering bird, to still it. A captive hand. The wife thought—*I didn't write to Imogene. She will never know.*

It was late: near midnight. On the second-level deck at the lighted prow of the ship revelers were laughing, dancing. Ecuadoran musicians played noisily.

"No, darling—the Moon Deck. One more flight."

The wife had no choice but to obey. She could not scream—no one would hear her. And why would she scream? There was no danger, Henry was clasping her hand protectively.

They stepped out onto the Moon Deck. It was windy here, yet smelled of oil. It was very dark. Earlier the wife had glimpsed a faint, full moon but now, so strangely the moon seemed to have vanished.

Clouds of the hue of tar covered the sky on all sides like a tent-top pegged tight to the ground. In gusts of wind, the wife could not breathe.

The wife was about to turn to the right, toward starry lights at the deserted prow of the ship, but the husband said, with a gentle tug at her elbow, "This way, Audrey"—to the left, into the deepest pitch of darkness.

Big Momma

"Damn you, Violet—you are a shameless *liar.*"

Her mother was disgusted with her, again. But how could her mother *even guess* that Violet hadn't been telling the truth? Could her mother *read her mind*?

So she'd taken a few dollars out of her mother's wallet. She hadn't taken any large-denomination bills (twenties, fifty) but only small-denomination (ones, fives) and she'd left much more than she'd taken. Her mother used credit cards anyway, rarely cash. But there was her mother fuming and fussing like she'd stolen a thousand damn dollars.

"Were you at the mall? With who? How'd you get there? Did you take the bus? Did someone give you a ride? Who? How'd you get back? Where've you been? It's after six."

It's after six. So what. Violet made a pinched little face, luckily her mother didn't see or she'd have gotten a sharp slap.

In her mother's hot-vibrating presence Violet wore her sulky face. It was an airtight mask of some material like satin or silk, which she could draw down over her actual face. Like

Hallowe'en. That morning at school she'd borrowed her friend Rita Mae's new lipstick, dark maroon, near-to-black, to apply to her mouth, that gave her a dazzling-sexy look (she thought), so after school the eyes of older guys trailed after her.

Trouble was, she'd forgotten to wipe the lipstick off when she returned home. First thing her mother said, staring at her— "You! At your age! Looking like a, a . . ." Her voice trailed off, she could not utter the word Violet flinched to hear.

Second thing, "How dare you take money from me? How much did you take?"

Inside the sulky mask Violet mumbled what sounded like *Don't know*. Or, *Didn't take anything*.

"Don't you know that the mall is *dangerous*? Hanging out there is *dangerous*?"

Inside the sulky mask Violet mumbled something totally unintelligible. Could've been *uh-huh*, or *OK*. Or *nah*.

"Don't they warn you at school? Or don't you *listen*? There've been children 'abducted' here—a two-year-old toddler taken right out of a backyard, with her mother just inside a screen door on a telephone.

"Right now there's a five-year-old girl missing for a week, her mother was buying something in JCPenney and when she turned around, *the little girl was gone*. And before we moved here, a three-year-old boy who disappeared allegedly *from inside his own house* just a few blocks from here. All of them—*vanished without a trace*."

"Jeez, Mom! Those were *little kids*."

"What do you mean, 'were'? Why do you say 'were'?"

"I mean—they're *really little kids*, that somebody could pick up and walk away with, kind of easy. Not like—"

"And you're so 'big'—*you*? You're thirteen years old, you weigh—what?—ninety pounds?"

Violet's face flamed as if her mother had slapped her. She was *short for her age* and *fat for her height*—in fact Violet weighed ninety-five pounds. And she was only four feet eleven inches—one of the shortest girls in eighth grade.

Worse yet she was growing breasts, and hips—soft, spongy flesh she *just hated*—envying the skinny girls who eyed her with disdain if not pity. Even Rita Mae who was practically her only friend pitied her.

Shamed, furious, Violet ran away upstairs. Heavy-footed on the stairs to show her mother what she thought of her—there was nothing so upsetting to Violet as her *weight*, didn't her cruel mother know?

At the foot of the stairs her mother was shouting up at her—"I know you took money and I want it back, Violet—*every penny, I want back*."

Violet slammed the door to her room. Her heart was beating crazy-hard. Her lips felt swollen as if in fact her mother had slapped her.

"Hate hate hate you. Wish I was dead." Thinking, then—"Wish *you were dead*."

* * *

225

Couldn't stop from crying, quick hot tears, for going to the mall after school with Rita Mae Clovis and Carliss LaMotte had been a dumb idea since the other girls had even less money than Violet did and had to "borrow" from her. That was why, in fact, Violet had taken the money—only seventeen damn dollars!—because Rita Mae had suggested it: "Your Mom won't know it's gone. In our house it's just Dad who has cash in his wallet but you could never get Dad's wallet from *him*." Violet had been so eager to please Rita Mae, and the other girl who was mostly Rita Mae's friend, she'd done what Rita Mae had said. Now, her mother would never trust her again.

They hadn't taken the bus to the mall after school. They'd gotten a ride with a high school senior Carliss knew, who worked at the New Liberty Mall. They'd gotten a ride back from the mall with some older guys Rita Mae claimed to know, two of the girls (Violet, Carliss) crammed into the rear of the station wagon smelling of spilt beer, stale cigarettes, dirty gym clothes, so tight that Carliss (giggling like an idiot) had to sit on the lap of one of the guys and Violet was crushed against a door, ignored. Everyone was loud-laughing and acting stupid except Violet staring out the window wishing she was anywhere else including dead because it was pretty clear, the guys were not remotely interested in *her*.

At South Valley Middle School Violet Prentiss was "new": a transfer student.

Damn she hated South Valley!—twice the size of her old school where she'd had at least three good friends, girls she'd known since kindergarten. At the new school, unless she wore Midnight Kiss lipstick and painted her nails dark maroon, faked a black rose tattoo on the inside of her arm, and "pierced" her ear with a mean-looking silver clamp the way Rita Mae Clovis showed her, Violet was totally invisible.

They'd moved to this new city just eighteen miles south of their former city because Wells Fargo had transferred Violet's mother and she'd had no choice but to move. Her mother said it was lucky she hadn't been *downsized* only just *relocated* in a branch of the bank in a faster-growing suburb than the one in which they'd been living for as long as Violet could recall.

(If Violet tried to remember further back things got blurry as in a watercolor left out in the rain. That memory of the scratchy-jawed beer-smelling funny-face man who'd been Daddy made her choke up and *snivel*.)

It was true, as Violet's mother had said, small children were *going missing* in the area. Two little girls, a little boy—just in the past six weeks—no one had any idea what had happened to them. Local and state police were "investigating all leads" but had "not yet made any arrests." Weirdly, there were also missing pets—cats, dogs, rabbits. In fact, the pets had begun to disappear at least a year ago and there were many more of these missing than children. As soon as Violet and her mother had moved into their new apartment they'd started seeing these sad posters in stores and on walls and fences—pictures of lost children, lost cats, lost dogs, lost rabbits with headlines MISSING, or HAVE YOU SEEN ME?

Some of the pictures of dogs, cats, rabbits were so *cute*, Violet wanted to cry to think they were lost. The children's pictures she didn't look at too closely.

Older people like Violet's mother said how strange it was there didn't seem to be *kidnappings* in the United States any longer, only just *abductions*. Violet asked what was the difference between a *kidnapping* and an *abduction* and her mother said, "If a child is kidnapped, the kidnappers contact the parents and ask for a 'ransom.' And the child might be returned safely. That was how it used to be in the old days! Now, the child is just—taken away . . ."

And never heard from again, Violet thought with an excited little shiver.

At South Valley Middle School the *missing children* were spoken of with the same sort of excited shivers. No one actually knew any of the missing children or their families—and it was only "little kids" who were at risk, not older children—so it was possible for the cruder boys to make jokes about the abductions. (Violet flinched to hear these jokes. Yet a few times to her shame Violet heard herself laugh with the others.)

At a school assembly the principal (a stout fussy woman named Mrs. Flanagan) addressed them in a grave voice warning them not ever to be "cajoled into" getting into a vehicle with a stranger, and not to walk home from school alone if they could avoid it. "Use your common sense, children! You're old enough to be vigilant. If you miss your school bus, report to the office immediately. Do not walk alone on the busy truck routes at any time. *Do not walk anywhere after dark alone—or even with a friend.*"

Police had a theory that the abductions were the work of out-of-state truckers who drove their enormous trailer trucks along Ajax Boulevard, which turned into state highway 103 outside the city limits. This would account for the fact that the children had vanished into thin air—it would be easy to carry captives inside a storage truck. (Especially if it had a deep freeze!—the boys joked.) Police claimed there'd been witnesses to "attempted abductions" by truckers on Ajax Boulevard but unfortunately the witnesses hadn't been able to see the truck licenses, only just to notice that, by their color, the licenses had been *out-of-state*.

(Violet would learn that Rita Mae Clovis's older brother Emile was one of the witnesses who'd reported to police what he'd seen, or almost seen—an out-of-state tractor trailer truck stopped at a red light and the driver opened his door and tried to "drag a boy into the truck" before the light changed; but the light turned green before he could get the boy inside the cab of the truck, and the driver—"Must've been six foot five, weighed two hundred fifty pounds, one of those droopy mustaches like they wear in Mexico and sort of dark-skinned," as Emile had reported—had to drive away.)

People debated whether the *missing pets* had anything to do with the *missing children*. It was not likely that the truckers—(if it was truckers who were abducting children)—would bother with mere dogs and cats and rabbits, if they could get children;

but then, could it be a coincidence that children, cats, dogs, pet rabbits were all being taken at the same time, by different people?

So far there'd been eight cats, five dogs, a dozen or more pet rabbits that had *disappeared*. Each had left behind a bereft family, including stricken children.

Talking about the *disappearances* Rita Mae said, with a shudder, "Wonder where they all *are*. Seems like the poor things would be all in the same place."

"Some kind of heaven, y'think?" Violet said.

Rita Mae giggled. "Or hell."

VALLEY GARDEN APARTMENTS was the sign in front of the apartment complex where Violet and her mother lived, that resembled a two-storey motel of stucco painted dull orange. "Garden" had to be some kind of joke—there wasn't any garden that Violet could see from their first-floor windows, only a parking lot with laser-lights that bored through the venetian blinds in her room and kept Violet awake at night. Her mother insisted the apartment was "just fine" and anyway it was "just temporary" and Violet didn't even bother to contradict her, it was too depressing.

Just temporary? Like, the rest of their lives?

Violet's mother could drop her off at school (three miles away) before work but how Violet made her way home after school was the issue. Which city bus would she take, if she missed the 3:30 P.M. school bus to which she was assigned. (Violet never "missed" the school bus except on purpose. Already during the first week of school she'd grown to fear and hate the school bus for the driver was indifferent to older boys bullying younger children and girls. The driver seemed not even to notice how Violet had been singled out by several ninth-grade boys for particular torment since she was new, and easily intimidated. *They're just teasing, can't take a joke, how'n hell are you going to survive in the real world?* Somehow it was worse, the driver was a woman.)

Violet knew better than to complain to her mother who might become hysterical over the phone making threats against the school principal, or whoever—if the damn bullies stopped, it would be just for a few days. Then they'd start again, nastier.

So when Violet "missed" the school bus she had to take a city bus which meant walking to Meridian Avenue, and taking the bus that came every twenty minutes; unless she walked to Curtiss Boulevard, where a bus came every thirty minutes. But sometimes she got confused, or frightened, and ended up taking a bus that dropped her off a quarter-mile from her home on the wrong side of a busy street. It was all so exhausting!

Her mother didn't like Violet taking the city buses, and she didn't like Violet waiting for any bus on Curtiss Boulevard which had almost as much heavy truck traffic as Ajax Boulevard. So Violet allowed her mother to think—(it wasn't like lying outright, was it?)—that most days she took the school bus home, with no problem.

When the weather got bad in the winter, Violet would be miserable, she supposed, but as it happened, something so wonderful occurred by the last week of September, she never had to worry about the damn old buses again.

She'd been walking toward Meridian Avenue when there came a call—"Vi'let! Hey! Want a ride?"—and she'd looked around to see a girl from her homeroom waving to her out the window of an SUV with mud-splattered fenders and scraped sides, that looked as if it had been in use for some time.

This was such a nice surprise! Violet could not believe her good luck. She had been noticing Rita Mae Clovis at school but had felt too shy even to smile at the tall skinny girl who wore glittery silver piercings in her ears, eyebrows, and nose, and dark maroon lipstick—in eighth grade.

Of course, Violet said *yes*. Violet ran to the SUV and climbed into the rear seat, that smelled of something delicious—yeasty-sugar doughnuts, greasy fried hamburger meat with ketchup. (On the floor were crumbled food bags.)

"Hi, 'friend of Rita Mae'—I'm Rita Mae's father, Harald Clovis."

Mr. Clovis was smiling at Violet in the rearview mirror. He was a friendly-looking man with fair, fawn-colored hair in waves that fell to his shoulders, and eyebrows so thick they reminded Violet of caterpillars in a children's picture book—something to make you smile, not shrink away.

It was strange and wonderful how, from the start, Violet didn't feel shy with the Clovises. She was smiling and laughing and just *so grateful* to be where she was and not out on windy Meridian Avenue waiting for some damn bus.

Rita Mae was much friendlier to Violet than she'd ever been at school. She told her father that Violet was "just about the smartest girl" in eighth grade which made Violet laugh, for it wasn't true, but the thought behind it was so generous, if maybe silly—Violet laughed and blushed as if Rita Mae had leaned back over her seat and tickled her. And there was Mr. Clovis regarding her in the rearview mirror, with a big smile.

"Well, I hope that Violet will become a good friend of yours, Rita Mae. Seems like you could use some smartenin'-up not dumbin'-down."

Violet would discover that all of the Clovis family talked like this, smart-snappy like TV dialogue that went on and on seemingly without any effort. You expected a laugh track with such clever talk.

Mr. Clovis asked Violet about her family, and Violet told him a few facts, in an embarrassed mumble; but Violet did not tell Mr. Clovis that nobody was waiting for her inside the Valley Garden Apartments and that her mother sometimes didn't get home until after 7:00 P.M.—some evenings, her mother didn't get home until 10:00 P.M. and when she did, her breath smelled of some evil mix of garlic, beer, and cigarette smoke. Gross!

Mr. Clovis extracted from Violet the information that her mother was a "single parent" and that Violet was an "only child." Mr. Clovis seemed to find this information valuable for he smiled and winked at Violet in the rearview mirror as if she'd given the correct answers to some tricky questions.

"Rita Mae, are there any doughnuts left?—just pass the bag back to your friend Vi'let."

Violet had vowed not to eat fattening things, delicious fattening things like cinnamon glazed doughnuts, especially between meals—but Mr. Clovis's generosity could not be rebuffed.

"Oh *thank you*, Mr. Clovis!"

"You're certainly welcome, 'friend of Rita Mae.'"

At first it had seemed like a happy coincidence—"Seren-dippity" Mr. Clovis called it—that Violet happened to be walking along the street when Mr. Clovis's SUV came along, at least twice a week; then, one day at school Rita Mae told Violet that she could have a ride home any time she needed it—"My dad really likes you, Violet. He says you're *special*." This was so utterly amazing, Violet had to wipe tears from her eyes. Rita Mae seemed embarrassed but pleased. In the SUV Mr. Clovis said, with his sunny smile, "Hey, it's no trouble, Vi'let. We're going almost that way, anyhow."

Sometimes, one or two other Clovis children were in the SUV with Rita Mae, so Violet got to know Trissie and Calvin too, who were both younger than Rita Mae; eventually she met Eve, who was older and in high school, and Emile who was the oldest, who'd dropped out of South Valley High a year or two ago.

All of the Clovis children were friendly, and all took an interest in *her*.

And suddenly Violet had friends at school also, at least Rita Mae Clovis's girlfriends with whom she could sit in the cafeteria and eat lunch, instead of huddling at a remote table by herself, hoping/dreading that someone, anyone, would join her.

Almost overnight Violet had stopped hating school. In fact, Violet had begun to look forward to school each morning.

"You're making friends, are you? I told you, you would."

Violet's mother was so damn *smug*. But Violet was too happy to mind.

Once on the way to Violet's home when there were just Violet and Rita Mae in the SUV, and Violet was sitting in front beside Rita Mae, Mr. Clovis took the girls to Edgewater Park where he bought ice cream cones for the three of them. Violet hesitated for a fraction of a second, for it threw her into despair how *damn fat* she was, compared to the girls she most admired at school, then she gave in—"Mr. Clovis, thanks!"

When Rita Mae went to use a restroom in the park Mr. Clovis said in a tender voice to Violet, "Any friend of my daughter's is a friend of mine. No questions asked!"

It near-about broke Violet's heart, these words like the words of a song. And the way Mr. Clovis lay his hand lightly on the nape of her neck, like you'd stroke a nervous cat. She'd have flinched away except—*she was so happy.*

In October it began to happen that, since Violet's mother wasn't home anyway, Violet was often invited to come home with Rita Mae to visit, or even to stay for supper.

Violet's mother was making new friends of her own, Violet had reason to believe. She'd hear her mother singing in the bathroom, and she'd smell her mother's special cologne, and began to notice her mother making up her face ever more glamorously.

Think I care? I do not care.

I hate you.

The Clovises started their evening meal early, between 5:00 P.M. and 5:30 P.M. Most days there was a whirlwind of busyness in the kitchen, until the meal was on the table. Often the family straggled in and out of the messy kitchen until early evening—nobody was in a hurry to clear away the table or wash or even rinse or soak dishes, the way Violet's mother was insistent upon Violet helping to clean up the kitchen after every meal. ("My mom says a dirty kitchen 'breeds bacteria,'" Violet told Rita Mae, expecting her friend to laugh scornfully; but Rita Mae said, frowning, "Oh *gross*. I saw on TV once, what a *kitchen sponge* looks like under a microscope. Made me want to throw up." But nobody fussed much over the sanitary conditions in the Clovis's kitchen, or anywhere in the Clovis house.)

Something or someone was missing at the Clovis house—at first, Violet couldn't think what it was. *Who*.

Unlike Violet's mother who was always muttering about "nutrition" —"organic foods"—"omega fats"—Mr. Clovis allowed the kids to eat anything they wanted, and as much of it as they wanted. *He* certainly didn't fuss—for Mr. Clovis a "gourmet meal" was fresh pizza picked up on the way home, instead of frozen pizza heated in the microwave. An "ultra-gourmet" meal was takeout from Tong Lee Chinese Kitchen, packages of leaky sugary-oily food and sticky white rice, fortune cookies in crinkling cellophane wrappers. Mr. Clovis brought hefty bags from McDonald's, Kentucky Fried Chicken, Taco Bell, Wendy's, Dunkin' Donuts to slide onto the kitchen table with a grin and the greeting—"Hey, kids! Chow time." And seeing Violet there beside Rita Mae, Mr. Clovis would wink, adding, "*And Vi'let. Did I get around to adopting you yet, sweetheart?*"

Adopting was a charged word at the Clovis house. For some of the children, Violet had reason to believe, were *adopted*; others, like Rita Mae, were *home-born*.

But where was the children's mother? Violet didn't want to ask for fear there was some sad, tragic story behind her absence. She supposed that, in time, she would be informed.

Violet was fascinated by the possibility of being *adopted*. It would explain so much, like why she and her mother just could not get along—"It's like we have two different strands of DNA. But I think I am my father's actual child."

"How'd you know that?" Rita Mae asked, staring at her with a skeptical smile.

"Just some thought I have. Just *intuition*."

"Vi'let, you are weird. But wonderful."

Weird but wonderful. Violet who'd always thought she was totally ordinary if slightly "plump" and not very pretty flushed crimson with joy.

And so, one day, the mystery was solved. Or anyway, the mystery was acknowledged.

Just as Violet's father had vanished from Violet's life when she'd been a little girl, so Rita Mae's mother had vanished from Rita Mae's life when she'd been a little girl. Violet felt how close they were in that instant, like sisters. She asked, "Do you miss your mom?" and Rita Mae said, sniffing, "I *do not*. It's, like, she walked out on *us*. Dad says."

Violet was impressed. "That's cool! My dad *walked out on us*, or anyway my mom says so."

"Don't you believe her?"

"D'you believe your dad?"

"Yes! My daddy never lies." Rita Mae spoke so vehemently, with such a fierce glare at Violet, Violet felt rebuffed and embarrassed. She hadn't meant anything by her silly question. But she was impressed with the way Rita Mae claimed her father never lied, as Rita Mae claimed that her father was *the best father there was, who'd do anything for his family*.

Violet had to consider that she didn't know if she believed her mother much of the time, or any of the time, or all of the time. She just *did not know*.

But she guessed she didn't love her mother the way Rita Mae and the other Clovis kids loved their dad. The way they looked at Harald Clovis, sort of eager and anxious, as if there was something unspoken among them that no one dared bring up.

"Don't you wonder where your mother went?" Violet couldn't resist asking Rita Mae.

"I said—*no*. Dad said she'd 'betrayed' the family by leaving us, so that's all I know. Nobody ever thinks of her any longer."

"How long has she been gone?"

Rita Mae shrugged. As if to say *Why ask me? Who cares?*

* * *

Unlike the boring residential neighborhood in which Violet lived, the Clovises lived in what Mr. Clovis called a "rural retreat." Their house was a sprawling old farmhouse at the edge of town, in an open field that had once been, Rita Mae said proudly, a "pasture."

Behind the farmhouse were decaying outbuildings—hay barn, storage barn, chicken coop, silo. There were the remains of a decaying apple orchard and at the rear of the property a straggling forest of deciduous trees. The nearest neighboring house wasn't even visible—"Lots of privacy for my brood," Mr. Clovis said, with a wink.

(*My brood*. Violet wondered what that meant! It made you think of a mother hen fussing protectively over her chicks.)

Rita Mae told Violet that she thought her father had "inherited" the property somehow and that it had once been much larger—"Acres and acres. Now there's just two acres."

Rita Mae did not seem to recall if her mother had ever lived in this house or if she'd "disappeared" before Mr. Clovis moved the family here when Rita Mae had been just about old enough to walk.

Violet thought it was cool, to live in such a big sprawling old house that you could find an actual room to be in alone, if you needed to be alone. Though most of the upstairs rooms were empty of furnishings, and were very dirty with dust balls on the floors, cobwebs everywhere, and the husks of dead insects underfoot, and a pervasive smell of grime, she much preferred the Clovis house to the cramped two-bedroom apartment at Valley

Garden Apartments. There, Violet was often alone—lonely. And even when her mother was home, Violet felt lonely.

You could see that the original farmhouse had been plain and utilitarian like a square box of two storeys; added to this were additions on both sides, like wings, that tilted just a little, as if the foundation beneath them had not been secure.

Close behind the house were rows of small nasty-smelling cages with wire mesh, which Rita Mae said were "rabbit-hutches." In all, there must have been more than a dozen of these. Violet wasn't sure if there were rabbits in these enclosures or if the enclosures were empty; or if, horribly, there were remains of rabbits inside, that had never been cleared away.

"It's OK, Vi'let," Rita Mae said, seeing Violet's nose crinkled at the smell, "—*you* don't have to clean them. You're not family—yet."

The downstairs of the Clovis house smelled of scorched and spilled food and a not-unpleasant aroma as of overripe fruit. The kitchen was pleasantly hot, even steamy. One afternoon Rita Mae's older sister Eve was preparing supper, cooking spaghetti sauce in a large pot on the stove. Mr. Clovis kept popping into the kitchen to taste the sauce, and to add "pinches" of spice—"I like my Italian sauce *hot and spicy*. Don't you, Vi'let?" Eve had emptied cans of tomato sauce into the pot, then added tomatoes, onions, red peppers, and some kind of coarse-ground meat like hamburger. (What was this meat? Violet wanted not to eat meat, she'd have liked to be a vegetarian—but it was so hard to resist! Her mouth watered at the smell.)

Of course, Violet was invited to stay for supper. Mr. Clovis insisted she should call her mother on her cell phone to ask permission—"That is the polite way, Vi'let." But Violet knew better than to call her suspicious mother who'd just say *no* out of meanness.

Discreetly Violet went into another room to call so that the Clovises could hear her bright voice—"Oh hi, Mom! Hey listen—Rita Mae's dad says I can stay for supper with them, then he'll drive me home. OK? It's real nice here, Mom—a 'rural retreat.'" Violet paused, breathing quickly. Then, "Thanks, Mom!"

When she returned Mr. Clovis said approvingly, "It is always the proper thing, dear Vi'let, *to be polite to your elders.*"

Again, Mr. Clovis winked at Violet. That wink!—Violet squirmed, and giggled, and shivered, and looked quickly away. She felt just slightly guilty about misleading Mr. Clovis, well— lying to him. But he would never know, she was sure.

Violet wished that Mr. Clovis would lay his hand on the nape of her neck as he sometimes did, to stroke her like you'd stroke a cat. But Mr. Clovis never did this except if they happened to be alone, which was not often. Too many Clovis children!

Was there something happening in the Clovis household? Violet noticed the younger children excited and giggling. And there came Emile home, sort of excited, too. Violet had been looking out a window and had seen Emile climb out of the SUV with a canvas bundle in his arms, that was bulky and awkward-sized, and looked almost as if it was moving, but later when Emile came into the kitchen he didn't have the bundle.

Emile was the oldest of the Clovis children whom Violet had met, somewhere beyond eighteen, Rita Mae believed—maybe as old as twenty-two. (To Violet and Rita Mae, both thirteen, this was *old*.) Emile had quit high school to take a job with "the county" which was where Mr. Clovis worked, too: road repair, construction, snow removal, storm and flood cleanup. He wore colorful T-shirts, jeans with deep rips, and safety boots big and clunky as a horse's hooves. He had a sexy close-shaved head that looked small on his shoulders, gold studs in both ears, tattoos scattered on both muscled arms. From the waist up Emile was normal-seeming but when he was on his feet you could see that his legs were strangely short. He was not so very much taller than Violet and Rita Mae. When Emile walked quickly he seemed to scuttle like a crab as if one leg was slightly shorter than the other. It was Emile who held the "family record" for pizza: he'd once eaten three entire medium-large pizzas without pause, as well as several sixteen-ounce Cokes. Violet blushed when Emile winked at her for it was clear that, for all his teasing of Rita Mae and Violet, he had special feelings for her.

That day, Violet saw Rita Mae whispering with Eve and Emile. And there was Mr. Clovis smiling in her direction. Rita Mae said to them, in a voice loud enough for Violet to overhear, "Hey, it's cool. Vi'let's cool."

What was it? Violet felt anxious, wondering what they were saying. Were they talking about *her*?

"Would you like to meet Big Momma, Vi'let? Before we sit down for supper?"

Violet smiled uncertainly. She glanced at Rita Mae who said, "Sure she would, Dad!"

Mr. Clovis took Violet's hand in his warm calloused hand, and led her along a corridor into the rear of the house. She'd never been in this part of the Clovis house before. Her nostrils begin to pinch at a new, strange smell.

Mr. Clovis said, "It's a little surprise. We have a special pet— we don't show just anyone. Big Momma is her name."

"What kind of pet?"—Violet's heart beat quickly.

"Not your ordinary pet."

Out of his pocket Mr. Clovis took a key to unlock an unusually heavy door, that looked as if it were reinforced with steel. When he led Violet into the room beyond, Rita Mae and the others followed close behind, and the door was shut behind them.

"Big Momma, look who's here! Vi'let, our new friend."

At first Violet couldn't make out what the thing—the creature —was on the other side of a glass barrier. Was it a *snake*? A *huge snake*? The largest snake she had ever seen, even in photographs, lay languid and unmoving on the floor inside an enclosure like a large aquarium, only about ten feet away on the other side of the scummy glass. Strange words came to her, like stuttering—*boa ricter? boa stricter?* The immense snake was thick as a big man's body, with a scaly glittering skin splotched in diamond shapes, tawny and brown like a rotted banana. The air in the windowless room was oppressively humid, like a jungle. There was a smell as of rotted fruit and a sharper, saltier smell.

Violet's heart was pounding so violently she nearly fainted.

"Oh—what is it? A s-snake?"

"Python."

"*Reticulated* python."

Proudly the Clovises told Violet of Big Momma who was some age beyond ten years, and weighed more than three hundred pounds—"That's just our estimate. Nobody's ever weighed *her*." Big Momma was as long as twenty feet when she stretched out straight which she rarely did. Mostly, Big Momma lay in *coils*.

Rita Mae said excitedly, "I knew you'd like her, Vi'let! We all think she is *way cool*. Daddy bought her from a carnival when we lived in Florida. The carnival was disbanding, so Daddy got her cheap. She wasn't so big then, I guess. A python is way, way bigger than a boa constrictor. She got her name 'Big Momma' by just *growing*."

One of the Clovises nudged Violet in the small of the back, to push her forward for a better look at the python.

Languidly the snake's eyes moved as if Violet, stepping forward, had stepped into the snake's vision. The head was so *large*! Violet stared at the hideous huge snake that was staring back calmly at her.

It was unnerving, the snake had such large eyes. Intelligent and alert eyes they seemed, the size of oranges, tawny in color, with dark slits for pupils.

And did the snake have eyelashes? Violet trembled to see that she did.

Then Violet saw, the snake's cylindrical body was distended, about five feet from the head. Something fairly large had been swallowed whole.

The Clovises were eager to speak of Big Momma in whom they clearly took much pride.

"Big Momma was fed a few days ago. She doesn't eat often—just eats *a whole lot*. Then she rests."

"Big Momma sleeps a lot, you'd think. But see, she isn't actually *sleeping*. She's *watching*."

"Big Momma doesn't have teeth like we do, to grind up food. She swallows her food whole."

"She catches her food in her coils and squeezes it so it's paralyzed but she doesn't care for dead food. She likes *live*."

"Her mouth stretches open, sort of unhinges, you wouldn't believe how wide, so she can swallow her food . . . It's awesome."

"It only looks like she's sleeping. But if you were to go inside, she'd *wake up fast*."

The Clovises laughed. The prospect of venturing inside the glass enclosure made Violet feel panicked.

There was a buzzing in Violet's head so that she had difficulty hearing the Clovises. She saw Mr. Clovis glancing at her with his warm brown eyes and friendly smile, and Rita Mae, and Emile—to see how she was taking Big Momma. Was it a test?—to see if Violet was one of them, or a coward?

Violet asked, "What—do you feed her?"

"Rabbits. Lots of rabbits."

"Sometimes mice."

"Lots and lots of mousies!"

"Lots of *rabbits*."

Doubtfully Violet said, "That doesn't look like the size of a rabbit . . ."

"Well, it could be a *jack rabbit*. They're real big."

The Clovises laughed, excited. Violet saw Emile clenching and unclenching his fists. His face shone with pride.

Now Violet noticed that there were cages along the walls of the room, the size of the outdoor rabbit hutches Fortunately these cages were all empty. In a corner was an ax, and on the floor scattered pages of newspaper soaked with dark stains.

"Where do you get the r-r-rabbits?"—Violet was trying not to stammer.

"Where do we get the rabbits, Dad?"—Emile asked, as if he couldn't recall.

"Pet supply store, son. Out Ajax Boulevard."

"D'you think Big Momma is beautiful, Vi'let?"—Rita Mae's breath was warm against Violet's cheek.

"Y-Yes. Big Momma is beautiful . . ."

Violet spoke in such a halting voice, all of the Clovises laughed. It was like teasing her, she knew.

Did that mean that they liked her, if they teased her? She thought so!

Mr. Clovis trailed his hand lightly against the nape of Violet's neck. Violet shivered, and did not shrink away.

"Next time we feed Big Momma, you can help, Vi'let—would you like that?"

Hesitantly Violet nodded *yes*.

The rest of the visit at the Clovis's house, that day, passed in a haze.

The spicy Italian tomato sauce, lavishly poured onto fresh-cooked spaghetti, was the most delicious meal Violet had ever had. After seeing Big Momma in her glass enclosure, Violet was *hungry*.

Violet was excited, and nervous, and anxious, and *hungry*. Though she hated garlic and would never have eaten garlic bread prepared by her mother, she had several pieces of garlic bread at supper.

During the meal Mr. Clovis regarded all of the faces around the table with a playful sort of scrutiny as if he had the power to read minds. This was how Mr. Clovis—the "resident pa-triarch" as he called himself—behaved at most meals Violet had attended.

She both dreaded and wished for the man's gaze moving onto her because that made her feel so *self-conscious*—but of course there was no escape: "Vi'let! You know, Big Momma is our family secret. You must never tell. Promise?"

"Oh yes, Mr. Clovis. I promise."

"But I didn't need to tell you that, did I? You already knew."

"Oh yes, Mr. Clovis. I knew."

"And you know, Vi'let, you'd be a whole lot prettier if you smiled more, and didn't frown."

Mr. Clovis leaned over, past Rita Mae who was sitting between them, to smooth Violet's forehead with his thumb. It was such a sudden gesture, Violet couldn't shrink away. She blushed to realize she'd been frowning the way her mother often frowned.

"Just remember, Vi'let: your step-daddy Clovis prefers you to *smile*. Every time you're about to frown, think: *Step-Daddy Clovis prefers me to smile.*"

Violet collapsed into a fit of giggling that got everyone giggling with her. It went on *and on*.

When Mr. Clovis and Rita Mae drove Violet home it was shockingly late—past 8:00 P.M. Luckily, Violet's mother wasn't yet home.

There was a macaroni-and-cheese casserole in the refrigerator for Violet to heat up in the microwave. Her favorite food!

Anyway, used to be her favorite food.

Violet felt sickish at the prospect of more food but heated the casserole up dutifully so that the food-smell would be in the air when her mother came home. She scraped most of the casserole into the garbage disposal. The yellowish melted cheese with splotches of brown reminded her of—something . . . She laughed nervously and pressed the chilly back of her hand against her forehead. She was feeling just slightly nauseated.

Here was a strange thing: Violet had to force herself to recall the very special thing she had seen at Rita Mae's house that day. The *reticulated python*.

The *reticulated python* kept slithering out of her consciousness like a TV screen turning dim. Violet kept swallowing, her mouth was very dry. She was feeling very sleepy.

On the sofa, with the TV on but muted, and printouts of math homework problems in her lap, Violet fell asleep and was wakened by a stranger's hand nudging her shoulder at 10:55 P.M.

"Violet? Sweetie? Are you *asleep*?"

It wasn't clear if Violet's mother was angry, or annoyed, or abashed. She'd stumbled coming into the semi-darkened room in her high-heeled shoes holding her hand over her mouth as if she didn't want Violet to smell her breath.

Violet's mother's hair was streaked blond now and her eyebrows were sharply defined in dark pencil. She was apologetic telling Violet that she hadn't meant to come home so late except something had "come up" in the office and she'd had to remain at work later than she'd planned.

"I didn't know banks were open at night, Mom." But Violet was yawning, to show that she didn't care.

"Don't be silly, banks are *not open at night*. Not to the public. But the world of finance never sleeps. If you work in the world of finance, you can never sleep. I see you ate the casserole, sweetie. All of it?"

Assiduously Violet had scraped every last scorched bit of the macaroni-and-cheese into the garbage disposal. She'd done a heroic job scouring out the casserole bowl with steel wool and had placed it in the dishwasher.

"Did you stay after school today, Violet?"

"No."

"When I called you, you didn't answer. Why was that?"

"Charge ran down, I guess." Violet yawned.

"You don't lie to your mother, sweetie, do you?"

"Do *you*?"

"Violet! I'm asking you a question."

But Violet was yawning so, her jaws stretched wide and aching, she couldn't pay attention to whatever her mother was saying.

"Sweetie, I love you. You know that, don't you?"—Violet's mother stooped over Violet to help her onto her feet, to walk her to her bedroom and to bed. It was just 11:00 P.M., hardly any time had passed.

When Violet crawled into bed, Violet's mother kissed her forehead with lipstick lips that smeared though neither Violet not her mother noticed at that moment.

"Is macaroni-and-cheese still your favorite food, Violet?"

Violet nodded *yes*.

"You know your mother loves you very very much, don't you, Violet?"

Violet nodded *yes*.

"Let's hear from Violet—'smartest girl at South Valley Middle School.'"

Violet blushed crimson. She knew that Mr. Clovis was just teasing but it was a sweet tender flirtatious kind of teasing that lit up her heart like Christmas tree bubble lights.

She'd been thinking she would not accept a ride from Mr. Clovis and Rita Mae any longer but, well—a few days after her last visit there she was on Meridian Avenue walking kind of slow and distracted in a light-falling rain, and there came the welcome cry—"Vi'let! Hey! Why didn't you wait for me after homeroom? *Want a ride home?*"

So, Violet hadn't any choice but to run to the curb, to swing up into the shiny black SUV. Thinking of her mother with a stab of satisfaction—*Don't need you. Hate you.*

At the Clovis house, she'd near-about forgotten what was kept in the locked room at the end of the corridor. Not one person spoke of B___ M___ and when Violet tried to think what or who B___ M___ was, her brain came up blank like a computer screen when there's no Internet connection.

What Violet loved about the Clovis household, next to the way they all seemed so fond of her, was how everybody *talked*, and everybody *listened*.

All sorts of serious things, they discussed. Like whether there was God, and whether animals have souls; whether there was "some special meaning" to life, and a "heaven where people would meet their loved ones." The loudest voices would prevail initially but then Mr. Clovis would tap his water glass and call *Quiet!* so that Violet could speak.

Crinkling her nose Violet said, "But what if you didn't have any 'loved ones'? Or what if you and your 'loved ones' didn't much like each other?"—and everyone around the table laughed, especially Mr. Clovis who appreciated *wit*. Violet blushed with pleasure.

"There'd always be somebody who liked *you*, Vi'let," Emile said in a voice so lowered and soft, Violet felt faint.

After supper, Rita Mae smoothed out a local newspaper onto the table, and some of the Clovises peered at a two-page spread of MISSING PETS. These dated back to autumn of the previous year, before Violet and her mother had moved into the Valley Garden Apartments. "So sad," Rita Mae said, biting at a thumbnail, "—it says here there are *nineteen pets missing* as of this last Monday."

Pictures of cats, pictures of dogs, pictures of lone-looking rabbits—these were melancholy creatures who'd seemed to know, when their pictures were being taken, that they would wind up as they had—MISSING PETS in a weekly newspaper.

"If a little kid is missing, you can blame the parents. At least the mother. But if a pet is missing, that's different—it doesn't seem like the same thing."

Rita Mae spoke thoughtfully. Violet was staring at the pictures trying to select which cat, which dog, which rabbit she would choose to save, if she had the opportunity.

Fluffy. Ivor. Big Mitts. Snowball. Scottie. Fiji. Mr. Ruff. Otto.

"I feel sorry for those families, who are still looking for their pets. Or their children."

"I don't! They have to be realistic."

"That's a harsh thing to say. Are *you* realistic?"

"Yes. I try to be. I try not to believe in the Easter bunny!"

"And if an older child disappears, someone who should know better, you can just blame *her*, or *him*."

How do you think your mother would feel, Violet?—if you 'disappeared'?"

"She wouldn't feel a thing. She'd *rejoice*."

Did Violet believe this? She wasn't sure.

That night, Mr. Clovis drove Violet home late. It was almost 10 P.M. Rita Mae almost didn't come with them, then changed her mind at the last minute. As they drove, Rita Mae squeezed Violet's hand. Was she feeling sorry for Violet, for what Violet had said about her mother? The word *rejoice* was just a—a word . . . Violet wasn't sure she'd meant it, at the time of uttering it.

At the Garden Apartments, Violet sat in the car and could hardly move. Her legs felt like lead. For she could see that the first-floor windows of her apartment were darkened which meant that her mother was "working late" that night.

"Oh Mr. Clovis—I wish I could live with *you*."

Rita Mae said, "I wish you could too, Violet. Why don't you ask your mother?"

Quickly Mr. Clovis said, in his most tender voice, "I don't think that's a wise idea, Rita Mae. You'll just get your dear friend in trouble if you put her up to such a thing. Violet's mother loves her, just as I love you and your brothers and sisters. You can't just steal away a girl from her own mother."

"I wish I could!" Rita Mae said.

Violet wiped at her eyes. She was deeply moved.

This was certain: in all of Violet Prentiss's life no one had ever talked like this about *her*.

* * *

"The way you're behaving lately around here, somebody's going to take you."

Violet's mother spoke in her shrill warning voice. It was break-fast time and Violet wasn't hungry at all for soggy sugary cereal. She was trying not to lift her eyes to her mother's eyes, that were boring at her like slits. In her denim jacket pocket was a bor-rowed Midnight Kiss lipstick from Rita Mae, and wrapped in a clean tissue were silver ear clamps and the kind of "piercing" you could clamp onto your nose or eyebrow.

"Mom, you're really confused. The way you hate me, nobody'd want *me*."

Her mother laughed, startled. She was in the midst of lighting a cigarette—(though hadn't Violet's mother stopped smoking, since before they'd moved to this new town?—wasn't that one of the points of moving, that Violet's mother could *reinvent herself and begin again*?)—and paused now to look at Violet, with a hurt expression as if Violet had slapped her.

"Honey, nooo. I don't hate you. That's not—that's not right."

"Isn't it!"

"Of course not. Just because I have to discipline you some-times, for your own good . . . It's like those math problems you bring home, Violet. There are rules for triangles, that can't be changed. An 'isos-celis' triangle . . ."

" 'Isosceles.' "

". . . is different from an 'equatorial' triangle . . ."

" 'Equilateral,' Mom! Jeez."

"Well. The point is, sometimes a parent has to discipline, for a child's own good. It does not mean that *I hate you*, for heaven's sake!"

"Hey, it's OK to hate me, Mom. 'Cause I sure do *hate you*."

Violet laughed to show that she wasn't serious. Violet's mother stared at her not knowing what to think.

"Violet, that isn't funny. Why are you saying such things?"

"I'm not 'saying such things.' I'm just—saying—the thing that I said. Not 'such things.'"

Violet wiped at her eyes, and shrank away when her mother tried to touch her. Especially, Violet did not want her mother to brush her lips against her forehead and smear lipstick on her skin. *She did not want that.*

After school Violet was walking fast in the rain on Ajax Boulevard, where she hadn't meant to walk. Was there a bus that stopped here? Somebody had told her *yes*. But there hadn't been a bus for forty minutes.

For three days she'd been avoiding Rita Mae at school. Some reason, she didn't know why . . .

But now there came the familiar mud-splattered SUV slow along the boulevard, amid heavy truck traffic. Stubbornly Violet was staring at the wet-glittering pavement, and would not look up when the call came—"Vi'let! Hey! C'mon get in, we'll take you home."

There was some reason Violet wasn't going to climb into that SUV one more time. She'd made a vow in a dream (maybe). But she'd made a vow.

But she was feeling lonely, and weak. And somehow it happened, she ran to the curb, and Rita Mae was laughing and helping her up into the cab.

"Vi'let, you're damn *wet*. We better get you home to dry off."

It was Big Momma's feeding day. Violet might have known this, but had forgotten. At the Clovis household everyone seemed excited, restless. Emile was smiling and winking at her—"Hi, Vi'let! How's it going?"

Just the second time Mr. Clovis led Violet along the corridor to the secret back room but it felt like she'd been there many more times.

Again the jungly smell, and humid air. Violet was weak-kneed, Mr. Clovis slid his warm strong arm around her waist to help her walk.

How often did the *reticulated python* feed? Big Momma was a beautiful slick-skinned snake with glittery diamond-patterns on her body that seemed to ooze along the floor, slow, but alert in every muscled inch. Twenty feet was so long, you could hardly see the tail-end of the snake if you were staring at the big hard-looking head. The thick-lashed eyes were particularly alert and alive and hungry. Violet wondered—was there nothing in that brain except, in a tiny molecule, an upside-down image of herself, as in a tiny mirror? *Did Big Momma recognize her from the other time?*

She didn't want to think that Big Momma was hardly more than a gigantic alimentary track inside that beautiful skin. She didn't want to think that nothing more came of it, than Big

Momma opening her jaws to a width of, how many feet?—three? The strong bones unhinging, and again hinging, as the squirming prey was swallowed inch by inch.

"Time for mousies. Bunnies. Lots mousies, and lots of bunnies."—Emile was joking awkwardly.

"That isn't funny, Emile. You're not funny one bit."

"Mousies and bunnies are best. I hate having to use that ax to 'dismember.'"

"Emile, *shut up*." Mr. Clovis spoke the sharpest Violet had ever heard the "resident patriarch" speak.

"The point is, Big Momma won't eat anything that isn't alive. What d'you think, Big Momma is some kind of disgusting scavenger?"

"Big Momma isn't that choosy."

"Big Momma *is*."

Mr. Clovis gave Violet one of his special-blend drinks which he'd prepared in a blender in the kitchen. Pomegranate juice, apricot juice, dollops of yogurt, blended to a froth. Maybe he'd put something else in the mixture, a grainy white powder, to "tranquilize" Violet's jumpy nerves. She hoped so!

Big Momma's enclosure was very cleverly designed, Violet saw. She'd been too nervous to notice the first time but there was an inner enclosure, which was the larger space, where the giant snake was at the present time; and there was an outer enclosure, much smaller, separated from the larger by a sliding glass partition operated by a lever. In this way you could venture inside the outer area, to leave fresh food and water for Big Momma while

Big Momma remained locked in the inner enclosure. Then, the inner partition would be opened by a lever, and Big Momma could crawl out for her meal.

Mr. Clovis was doing that now—sliding open the outer glass door. It was a totally *safe place*—so long as the inner glass remained shut. Even if the *reticulated python* was desperate with hunger, she could probably not have broken the thick plate glass, scummy from its saliva and the oily ooze of its great coils.

For such a great beast, Big Momma was a *captive*.

Mr. Clovis said, in a tender voice, "Rita Mae was right about you, dear Vi'let. You are *special*. We will not soon forget *you*."

She felt a thrill of pride. But her eyelids were heavy, it was like sprawling on the sofa with the TV on but muted. *Just. So. Hard. To. Stay. Awake.*

"It's your turn to feed Big Momma, Vi'let. Would you like that?"

"I—I don't know."

"Big Momma is very grateful when she's fed. You haven't seen that yet but it is a sight to behold."

Violet was feeling sleepy. Buzzing in her ears. Wanting to shut her eyes, and lay her head down. What was in Mr. Clovis's fizzy drink? It was creamy-smooth and sweet, delicious. But it left a chalky taste in her mouth.

Rita Mae wasn't there. Violet missed Rita Mae! She'd heard Mr. Clovis and the others say sharply to Rita Mae—*Stay away then. We don't need you.*

"Vi'let, this will be your only chance, to feed Big Momma. If you refuse, I'll have to take you home—that's that."

Weakly Violet protested. Anything but that lonely apartment!
"No! I—I can feed Big Momma."

There was a hot, humid atmosphere here, like the inside of a
gut. Just a few feet away on the far side of the splotched plate
glass Big Momma lay tense and quivering and not so languid-
seeming as she'd been at the first visit. Violet stumbled a little
as Mr. Clovis led her into the outer enclosure, and eased her
down onto the floor where she could shut her eyes. Lightly
he pressed his lips onto the nape of her neck where the little
hairs stirred.

"Say hello to Big Momma."

"H-Hello . . ."

So close by, only inches away on the other side of the glass,
Big Momma was waiting. Big Momma's eyes were sharp now,
staring right at Violet as if she recognized her after all. Violet's
eyelids were very heavy. Her vision was dimming slowly, like
encroaching dusk. She felt peaceful and not anxious and had
forgotten—whatever it was, in the first-floor apartment overlooking the parking lot.

"Good, sweetheart! Just sleep. It's nice and warm here, you
can sleep here all night." Mr. Clovis left Violet, so silently she
scarcely knew he had stepped out of the enclosure.

Violet was lying on the floor, on her side. One of her arms
was extended, limp. Her fingers moved just slightly, as if she was
grasping for something—what? She had no idea.

She could feel, without knowing how to name or identify it,
something like a vibratory hum, through the plate glass against

which she was pressed. This might have been Big Momma breathing, or quivering, or tensing up her coils . . .

This was so comforting, Violet's eyes filled with tears. But before the tears could spill over she'd curled into a snug little ball hugging herself, her knees to her chest. Within seconds in a swoon of the sweetest surrender she was asleep.

Mystery, Inc.

I am very excited! For at last, after several false starts, I have chosen the perfect setting for my bibliomystery.

It is Mystery, Inc., a beautiful old bookstore in Seabrook, New Hampshire, a town of fewer than two thousand year-round residents overlooking the Atlantic Ocean south of New Castle.

For those of you who have never visited this legendary bookstore, one of the gems of New England, it is located in the historic High Street district of Seabrook, above the harbor, in a block of elegantly renovated brownstones originally built in 1888. Here are the offices of an architect, an attorney-at-law, a dental surgeon; here are shops and boutiques—leather goods, handcrafted silver jewelry, the Tartan Shop, Ralph Lauren, Esquire Bootery. At 19 High Street a weathered old sign in black and gilt creaks in the wind above the sidewalk:

MYSTERY, INC. BOOKSELLERS
New & Antiquarian Books, Maps, Globes, Art
Since 1912

The front door, a dark-lacquered red, is not flush with the sidewalk but several steps above it; there is a broad stone stoop, and a black wrought iron railing. So that, as you stand on the sidewalk gazing at the display window, you must gaze *upward*.

Mystery, Inc. consists of four floors with bay windows on each floor that are dramatically illuminated when the store is open in the evening. On the first floor, books are displayed in the bay window with an (evident) eye for the attractiveness of their bindings: leather-bound editions of such nineteenth-century classics as Wilkie Collins's *The Moonstone* and *The Woman in White,* Charles Dickens's *Bleak House* and *The Mystery of Edwin Drood,* A. Conan Doyle's *The Adventures of Sherlock Holmes*, as well as classic twentieth-century mystery-crime fiction by Raymond Chandler, Dashiell Hammett, Cornell Woolrich, Ross Macdonald, and Patricia Highsmith and a scattering of popular American, British, and Scandinavian contemporaries. There is even a title of which I have never heard—*The Case of the Unknown Woman: The Story of One of the Most Intriguing Murder Mysteries of the 19th Century*, in what appears to be a decades-old binding.

As I step inside Mystery, Inc. I feel a pang of envy. But in the next instant this is supplanted by admiration—for envy is for small-minded persons.

The interior of Mystery, Inc. is even more beautiful than I had imagined. Walls are paneled in mahogany with built-in bookshelves floor to ceiling; the higher shelves are accessible by ladders on brass rollers, and the ladders are made of polished wood. The ceiling is comprised of squares of elegantly hammered tin; the floor is parquet, covered in small carpets. As I am a book collector myself—and a bookseller—I note how attractively books are displayed without seeming to overwhelm the customer; I see how cleverly books are positioned upright to intrigue the eye; the customer is made to feel welcome as in an old-fashioned library with leather chairs and sofas scattered casually about. Here and there against the walls are glass-fronted cabinets containing rare and first-edition books, no doubt under lock and key. I do feel a stab of envy, for of the mystery bookstores I own, in what I think of as my modest mystery-bookstore empire in New England, not one is of the class of Mystery, Inc., or anywhere near.

In addition, it is Mystery, Inc.'s online sales that present the gravest competition to a bookseller like myself, who so depends upon such sales . . .

Shrewdly I have timed my arrival at Mystery, Inc. for a half-hour before closing time, which is 7:00 P.M. on Thursdays, and hardly likely to be crowded. (I think there are only a few other customers—at least on the first floor, within my view.) In this wintry season dusk has begun as early as 5:30 P.M. The air is wetly cold, so that the lenses of my glasses are covered with a fine film of condensation; I am vigorously polishing them when a young woman salesclerk with tawny gold, shoulder-length hair approaches me to ask if I am looking for anything in particular, and I tell her that I am just browsing, thank you—"Though I would like to meet the proprietor of this beautiful store, if he's on the premises."

The courteous young woman tells me that her employer, Mr. Neuhaus, is in the store, but upstairs in his office; if I am interested in some of the special collections or antiquarian holdings, she can call him . . .

"Thank you! I am interested indeed but just for now, I think I will look around."

What a peculiar custom it is, the *openness of a store*. Mystery, Inc. might contain hundreds of thousands of dollars of precious merchandise; yet the door is unlocked, and anyone can step inside from the street into the virtually deserted store, carrying a leather attaché case in hand, and smiling pleasantly.

It helps of course that I am obviously a gentleman. And one might guess, a book collector and book-lover.

As the trusting young woman returns to her computer at the checkout counter, I am free to wander about the premises. Of course, I will avoid the other customers.

I am impressed to see that the floors are connected by spiral staircases, and not ordinary utilitarian stairs; there is a small elevator at the rear which doesn't tempt me as I suffer from mild claustrophobia. (Being locked in a dusty closet as a child by a sadistic older brother surely is the root of this phobia, which I have managed to disguise from most people who know me, including my bookstore employees who revere me, I believe, for being a frank, forthright, commonsensical sort of man free of any sort of neurotic compulsion!) The first floor of Mystery, Inc. is American books; the second floor is British and foreign-language books, and Sherlock Holmesiana (an entire rear wall);

the third floor is first editions, rare editions, and leather-bound sets; the fourth floor is maps, globes, and antiquarian artworks associated with mayhem, murder, and death.

It is here on the fourth floor, I'm sure, that Aaron Neuhaus has his office. I can imagine that his windows overlook a view of the Atlantic, at a short distance, and that the office is beautifully paneled and furnished.

I am feeling nostalgic for my old habit of *book theft*—when I'd been a penniless student decades ago, with a yearning for books. The thrill of thievery—and the particular reward, a *book*! In fact for years my most prized possessions were books stolen from Manhattan bookstores along Fourth Avenue that had no great monetary value—only just the satisfaction of being *stolen*. Ah, those days before security cameras!

Of course, there are security cameras on each floor of Mystery, Inc. If my plan is successfully executed, I will remove the tape and destroy it; if not, it will not matter that my likeness will be preserved on the tape for a few weeks, then destroyed. In fact I am *lightly disguised*—these whiskers are not mine, and the black-plastic-framed tinted glasses I am wearing are very different from my usual eyeglasses.

Just before closing time at Mystery, Inc. there are only a few customers, whom I intend to outstay. One or two on the first floor; a solitary individual on the second floor perusing shelves of Agatha Christie; a middle-aged couple on the third floor looking for a birthday present for a relative; an older man on the fourth floor perusing the art on the walls—reproductions of fifteenth-century German woodcuts titled *Death and the Maiden*, *The Dance of Death*, and *The Triumph of Death*—macabre lithographs of Picasso, Munch, Schiele, Francis Bacon—reproductions of Goya's *Saturn Devouring His Children*, *Witches' Sabbath*, and *The Dog*. (Too bad it would be imprudent of me to strike up a conversation with this gentleman, whose taste in macabre artwork is very similar to my own, judging by his absorption in Goya's Black Paintings!) I am indeed admiring—it is remarkable that Aaron Neuhaus can sell such expensive works of art in this out-of-the-way place in Seabrook, New Hampshire, in the off-season.

By the time I descend to the first floor, most of these customers have departed; the final customer is making a purchase at the checkout counter. To bide my time, I take a seat in one of the worn old leather chairs that seems almost to be fitted to my buttocks; so comfortable a chair, I could swear it was my own, and not the property of Aaron Neuhaus. Close by is a glass-fronted cabinet containing first editions of novels by Raymond Chandler—quite a treasure trove! There is a virtual *itch* to my fingers in proximity to such books.

I am trying not to feel embittered. I am trying simply to feel *competitive*—this is the American way!

But it's painfully true—not one of my half-dozen mystery bookstores is so well-stocked as Mystery, Inc., or so welcoming to visitors; at least two of the more recently acquired stores are outfitted with ugly utilitarian fluorescent lights which give me a headache, and fill me with despair. Virtually none of my customers are so affluent-appearing as the customers here in Mystery, Inc., and their taste in mystery fiction is limited primarily to predictable, formulaic bestsellers—you would not see shelves devoted to Ellery Queen in a store of mine, or an entire glass-fronted case of Raymond Chandler's first editions, or a wall of Holmesiana. My better stores carry only a few first editions and antiquarian books—certainly, no artworks! Nor do I seem able to hire attractive, courteous, intelligent employees like this young woman—perhaps because I can't afford to pay them much more than the minimum wage, and so they have no compunction about quitting abruptly.

In my comfortable chair it is gratifying to overhear the friendly conversation between this customer and the young woman clerk, whose name is Laura—for, if I acquire Mystery, Inc., I will certainly want to keep attractive young Laura on the staff as my employee; if necessary, I will pay her just slightly more than her current salary, to insure that she doesn't quit.

When Laura is free, I ask her if I might examine a first-edition copy of Raymond Chandler's *Farewell, My Lovely*. Carefully she unlocks the cabinet, and removes the book for me—its publication date is 1940, its dust jacket in good, if not perfect, condition, and the price is $1,200. My heart gives a little leap—I already have one copy of this Chandler novel, for which, years ago, I paid much less; at the present time, in one of my better stores, or online, I could possibly resell it for $1,500 . . .

"This is very attractive! Thank you! But I have a few questions, I wonder if I might speak with . . ."

"I will get Mr. Neuhaus. He will want to meet *you*."

Invariably, at independently owned bookstores, proprietors are apt to want to meet customers like *me*.

Rapidly I am calculating—how much would Aaron Neuhaus's widow ask for this property? Indeed, how much is this property worth, in Seabrook? New Hampshire has suffered from the current, long-term recession through New England, but Seabrook is an affluent coastal community whose population more than quadruples in the summer, and so the bookstore may be worth as much as $800,000 . . . Having done some research, I happen to know that Aaron Neuhaus owns the property outright, without a mortgage. He has been married, and childless, for more than three decades; presumably, his widow will inherit his estate. As I've learned from past experiences widows are notoriously vulnerable to quick sales of property; exhausted by the legal and financial responsibilities that follow a husband's death, they are eager to be free of encumbrances, especially if they know little about finances and business. Unless she has children and friends to advise her, a particularly distraught widow is capable of making some very unwise decisions.

Dreamily, I have been holding the Raymond Chandler first edition in my hands without quite seeing it. The thought has come to me—*I must have Mystery, Inc. It will be the jewel of my empire.*

"Hello?"—here is Aaron Neuhaus, standing before me.

Quickly I rise to my feet and thrust out my hand to be shaken—"Hello! I'm very happy to meet you. My name is—"

As I proffer Neuhaus my invented name I feel a wave of heat lifting into my face. Almost, I fear that Neuhaus has been observing me at a little distance, reading my most secret thoughts while I'd been unaware of him.

He knows me. But—he cannot know me.

As Aaron Neuhaus greets me warmly it seems clear that the proprietor of Mystery, Inc. is not at all suspicious of this stranger who has introduced himself as "Charles Brockden." Why would he be? There are no recent photographs of me, and no suspicious reputation has accrued to my invented name; indeed, no suspicious reputation has accrued about my actual name as the owner of a number of small mystery bookstores in New England.

Of course, I have studied photographs of Aaron Neuhaus. I am surprised that Neuhaus is so youthful, and his face so unlined, at sixty-three.

Like any enthusiastic bookseller, Neuhaus is happy to answer my questions about the Chandler first edition and his extensive Chandler holdings; from this, our conversation naturally spreads to other, related holdings in his bookstore—first editions of classic mystery-crime novels by Hammett, Woolrich, James M. Cain, John D. MacDonald, and Ross Macdonald, among others. Not boastfully but matter-of-factly Neuhaus tells me that he owns one of the two or three most complete collections of published work by the pseudonymous "Ellery Queen"—including novels published under other pseudonyms and magazines in which Ellery Queen stories first appeared. With a pretense of naïveté I ask how much such a collection would be worth—and Aaron

Neuhaus frowns and answers evasively that the worth of a collection depends upon the market and he is hesitant to state a fixed sum.

This is a reasonable answer. The fact is, any collectors' items are worth what a collector will pay for them. The market may be inflated, or the market may be deflated. All prices of all things—at least, useless beautiful things like rare books—are inherently absurd, rooted in the human imagination and in the all-too-human predilection to desperately want what others value highly, and to scorn what others fail to value. Unlike most booksellers in our financially distressed era, Aaron Neuhaus has had so profitable a business he doesn't need to sell in a deflated market but can hold on to his valuable collections—indefinitely, it may be!

These, too, the wife will inherit. So I am thinking.

The questions I put to Aaron Neuhaus are not duplicitous but sincere—if somewhat naïve-sounding—for I am very interested in the treasures of Aaron Neuhaus's bookstore, and I am always eager to extend my bibliographical knowledge.

Soon, Neuhaus is putting into my hands such titles as *A Bibliography of Crime & Mystery Fiction 1749–1990*; *Malice Domestic: Selected Works of William Roughead, 1889–1949*; *My Life in Crime: A Memoir of a London Antiquarian Bookseller (1957)*; *The Mammoth Encyclopedia of Modern Crime Fiction*, and an anthology edited by Aaron Neuhaus, *One Hundred and One Best American Noir Stories of the 20th Century*. All of these are known to me, though I have not read one of them in its entirety; Neuhaus's *One Hundred and One Best American Noir Stories* is one of the backlist bestsellers in most of my stores. To flatter Neuhaus I tell him that I want to buy his anthology, along with the Chandler first edition—"And maybe something else, beside. For I have to confess, I seem to have fallen in love with your store."

At these words a faint flush rises into Neuhaus's face. The irony is, they are quite sincere words even as they are coolly intended to manipulate the bookseller.

Neuhaus glances at his watch—not because he's hoping that it's nearing 7:00 P.M., and time to close his store, but rather because he hopes he has more time to spend with this very promising customer.

Soon, as booksellers invariably do, Aaron Neuhaus will ask his highly promising customer if he can stay awhile, past closing time; we might adjourn to his office, to speak more comfortably, and possibly have a drink.

Each time, it has worked this way. Though there have been variants, and my first attempt at each store wasn't always successful, necessitating a second visit, this has been the pattern.

Bait, bait taken.

Prey taken.

Neuhaus will send his attractive salesclerk home. The last glimpse Laura will have of her (beloved?) employer will be a pleasant one, and her recollection of the last customer of the day—(the last customer of Neuhaus's life)—will be vivid perhaps, but misleading. *A man with ginger-colored whiskers, black plastic-framed glasses, maybe forty years old—or fifty . . . Not tall, but not short . . . Very friendly.*

Not that anyone will suspect *me*. Even the brass initials on my attaché case—*CB*—have been selected to mislead.

Sometime this evening Aaron Neuhaus will be found dead in his bookstore, very likely his office, of natural causes, presumably of a heart attack—if there is an autopsy. (He will be late to arrive home: his distraught wife will call. She will drive to Mystery, Inc. to see what has happened to him and/or she will call 911 to report an emergency long after the "emergency" has expired.) There could be no reason to think that an ordinary-seeming customer who'd arrived and departed hours earlier could have had anything to do with such a death.

Though I am a wholly rational person, I count myself one of those who believe that some individuals are so personally vile, so disagreeable, and make the world so much less pleasant a place, it is almost our duty to eradicate them. (However, I have not acted upon this impulse, yet—my eradications are solely in the service of business, as I am a practical-minded person.)

Unfortunately for me, however, Aaron Neuhaus is a very congenial person, exactly the sort of person I would enjoy as a friend—if I could afford the luxury of friends. He is soft-spoken yet ardent; he knows everything about mystery-detective fiction, but isn't overbearing; he listens closely, and never interrupts; he laughs often. He is of moderate height, about five feet nine or ten, just slightly taller than I am, and not quite so heavy as I am. His clothes are of excellent quality but slightly shabby, and mismatched: a dark brown Harris tweed sport coat, a red cashmere vest over a pale beige shirt, russet-brown corduroy trousers. On his feet, loafers. On his left hand, a plain gold wedding band. He has a sweetly disarming smile that offsets, to a degree, something chilly and Nordic in his gray-green gaze, which most people (I think) would not notice. His hair is a steely gray, thinning at the crown and curly at the sides, and his face is agreeably youthful. He is rather straight-backed, a little stiff, like one who has injured his back and moves cautiously to avoid pain. (Probably no one would notice this except one like myself who is by nature sharp-eyed, and has had bouts of back pain himself.)

Of course, before embarking up the coast to Seabrook, New Hampshire, in my (ordinary-seeming, unostentatious) vehicle, attaché case on the seat beside me, and plan for the elimination of a major rival memorized in every detail, I did some minimal research into my subject who has the reputation, in bookselling and antiquarian circles, of being a person who is both friendly and social and yet values his privacy highly; it is held to be somewhat perverse that many of Neuhaus's male friends have never met his wife, who has been a public school teacher in Glastonberry, New Hampshire, for many years. (Dinner invitations to Neuhaus and his wife, from residents in Seabrook, are invariably declined "with regret.") Neuhaus's wife is said to be his high school sweetheart whom he first met in 1965 and married in 1977, in Clarksburg, North Carolina. So many years—faithful to one woman! It may be laudable in many men, or it may bespeak a failure of imagination and courage, but in Aaron Neuhaus it strikes me as exasperating, like Neuhaus's success with his bookstore, as if the man has set out to make the rest of us appear callow.

What I particularly resent is the fact that Aaron Neuhaus was born to a well-to-do North Carolina family, in 1951; having inherited large property holdings in Clarksburg County, North Carolina, as well as money held for him in trust until the age of twenty-one, he has been able to finance his bookstore(s) without the fear of bankruptcy that haunts the rest of us.

Nor was Neuhaus obliged to attend a large, sprawling, land-grant university as I did, in dreary, flat Ohio, but went instead to the prestigious, white-column'd University of Virginia, where he majored in such dilettantish subjects as classics and philosophy. After graduation Neuhaus remained at Virginia, earning a master's degree in English with a thesis titled *The Aesthetics of Deception: Ratiocination, Madness, and the Genius of Edgar Allan Poe*, which was eventually published by the University of Virginia Press. The young Neuhaus might have gone on to become a university professor, or a writer, but chose instead to apprentice himself to an uncle who was a (renowned, much-respected) antiquarian bookseller in Washington, D.C. Eventually, in 1980, having learned a good deal from his uncle, Neuhaus purchased a bookstore on Bleecker Street, New York City, which he managed to revitalize; in 1982, with the sale of this bookstore he purchased a shop in Seabrook, New Hampshire, which he renovated and refashioned as a chic, upscale, yet "historic" bookstore in the affluent seaside community. All that I have learned about Neuhaus as a businessman is that he is both "pragmatic" and "visionary"—an annoying contradiction. What I resent is that Neuhaus seems to have weathered financial crises that have sent other booksellers into despair and bankruptcy, whether as a result of shrewd business dealings or—more likely—the unfair advantage an independently well-to-do bookseller has over booksellers like myself with a thin profit margin and a fear of the future. *Though I do not hate Aaron Neuhaus, I do not approve of such an unfair advantage—it is contrary to Nature.* By now, Neuhaus might have been out of business, forced to scramble to earn a living in the aftermath of, for instance, those hurricanes of recent years that have devastated the Atlantic coastline and ruined many small businesses.

But if Mystery, Inc. suffers storm damage, or its proprietor loses money, it does not matter—there is the *unfair advantage* of the well-to-do over the rest of us.

I want to accuse Aaron Neuhaus: "How do you think you would do if our 'playing field' were level—if you couldn't bankroll your bookstore in hard times, as most of us can't? Do you think you would be selling Picasso lithographs upstairs, or first editions of Raymond Chandler; do you think you would have such beautiful floor-to-ceiling shelves, leather chairs and sofas? Do you think you would be such a naïve, gracious host, opening your store to a ginger-whiskered predator?"

It is difficult to feel indignation over Aaron Neuhaus, however, for the man is so damned *congenial.* Other rival booksellers haven't been nearly so pleasant, or, if pleasant, not nearly so well-informed and intelligent about their trade, which has made my task less of a challenge in the past.

The thought comes to me—*Maybe we could be friends? Partners? If . . .*

It is just 7:00 P.M. In the near distance a church bell tolls—unless it is the dull crashing surf of the Atlantic a quarter-mile away.

Aaron Neuhaus excuses himself, and goes to speak with his young woman clerk. Without seeming to be listening I hear him tell her that she can go home now, he will close up the store himself tonight.

Exactly as I have planned. But then, such *bait* has been dangled before.

Like any predator I am feeling excited—there is a pleasurable surge of adrenaline at the prospect of what will come next, very likely within the hour.

Timing is of the essence! All predators/hunters know this.

But I feel, too, a stab of regret. Seeing how the young blond woman smiles at Aaron Neuhaus, it is clear that she reveres her employer—perhaps loves him? Laura is in her midtwenties, possibly a college student working part-time. Though it seems clear that there is no (sexual, romantic) intimacy between them, she might admire Neuhaus as an older man, a fatherly presence in her life; it will be terribly upsetting to her if something happens to him . . . When I acquire Mystery, Inc., I will certainly want to spend time in this store. It is not far-fetched to imagine that I might take Aaron Neuhaus's place in the young woman's life.

As the new owner of Mystery, Inc., I will not be wearing these gingery-bristling whiskers. Nor these cumbersome black plastic-framed glasses. I will look younger, and more attractive. I have been told that I resemble the great film actor James Mason . . . Perhaps I will wear Harris tweeds, and red cashmere sweater vests. Perhaps I will go on a strenuous diet, jogging along the ocean each morning, and will lose fifteen pounds. I will commiserate with Laura—*I did not know your late employer but 'Aaron Neuhaus' was the most highly regarded of booksellers—and gentlemen. I am so very sorry for your loss, Laura!*

Certainly I will want to rent living quarters in Seabrook, or even purchase property in this beautiful spot. At the present time, I move from place to place—like a hermit crab that occupies the empty shells of other sea creatures with no fixed home of its own. After acquiring an old, quasi-legendary mystery bookstore in Providence, Rhode Island, a few years ago, I lived in Providence for a while overseeing the store, until I could entrust a manager to oversee it; after acquiring a similar store in Westport, Connecticut, I lived there for a time; most recently I've been living in Boston, trying to revive a formerly prestigious mystery bookstore on Beacon Street. One would think that Beacon Street would be an excellent location for a quality mystery bookstore, and so it is—in theory; in reality, there is too much competition from other bookstores in the area. And of course there is too much competition from online sales, as from the damned, unspeakable Amazon.

I would like to ask Aaron Neuhaus how he deals with book theft, the plague of my urban-area stores, but I know the answer would be dismaying—Neuhaus's affluent customers hardly need to steal.

When Aaron Neuhaus returns, having sent the young woman home, he graciously asks if I would like to see his office upstairs. And would I like a cup of cappuccino?

"As you see, we don't have a café here. People have suggested that a café would help book sales but I've resisted—I'm afraid I am just too old-fashioned. But for special customers, we do have coffee and cappuccino—and it's very good, I can guarantee."

Of course, I am delighted. My pleasurable surprise at my host's invitation is not feigned.

In life, there are predators, and prey. A predator may require *bait*, and prey may mistake *bait* for sustenance.

In my leather attaché case is an arsenal of subtle weaponry. It is a truism that the most skillful murder is one that isn't detected as *murder* but simply *natural death*.

To this end, I have cultivated toxins as the least cumbersome and showy of murder weapons, as they are, properly used, the most reliable. I am too fastidious for bloodshed, or for any sort of violence; it has always been my feeling that violence is *vulgar*. I abhor loud noises, and witnessing the death throes of an innocent person would be traumatic for me. Depending upon the toxin, I am nowhere near my prey when he (or she) is stricken by death, but miles away, and hours or even days later. There is never any apparent connection between the subject of my campaign and me—of course, I am far too shrewd to leave "clues" behind. In quasi-public places like bookstores, fingerprints are general and could never be identified or traced; but if necessary, I take time to wipe my prints with a cloth soaked in alcohol. I am certainly not obsessive or compulsive, but I am *thorough*. Since I began my (secret, surreptitious) campaign of eliminating rival booksellers in the New England area nine years ago, I have utilized poisoned hypodermic needles; poisoned candles; poisoned (Cuban) cigars; poisoned sherry, liqueur, and whiskey; poisoned macaroons; and poisoned chocolates—all with varying degrees of success.

That is, in each case my campaign was successful. But several campaigns required more than one attempt and exacted a strain on nerves already strained by economic anxieties. In one unfortunate instance, after I'd managed to dispose of the bookseller, the man's heirs refused to sell the property though I'd made them excellent offers . . . It is a sickening thing to think that one has expended so much energy in a futile project and that a wholly innocent party has died in vain; nor did I have the heart to return to that damned bookstore in Montclair, New Jersey, and take on the arrogant heirs as they deserved.

The method I have selected to dispatch the proprietor of Mystery, Inc. is one that has worked well for me in the past: chocolate truffles injected with a rare poison extracted from a Central American flowering plant bearing small red fruits like cranberries. The juice of these berries is so highly toxic, you dare not touch the outside of the berries; if the juice gets onto your skin it will burn savagely, and if it gets into your eyes—the very iris is horribly burnt away, and total blindness follows. In preparing the chocolates, which I carefully injected with a hypodermic needle, I wore not one but two pairs of surgical gloves; the operation was executed in a deep sink in a basement that could then be flooded with disinfectant and hot water. About three-quarters of the luxury chocolates have been injected with poison and the others remain untouched in their original Lindt box, in case the bearer of the luxury chocolates is obliged to sample some portion of his gift.

This particular toxin, though very potent, is said to have virtually no taste, and it has no color discernible to the naked eye. As soon as it enters the bloodstream and is taken to the brain, it begins a virulent and irrevocable assault upon the central nervous system: within minutes the subject will begin to experience tremors and mild paralysis; consciousness will fade to a comatose state; by degrees, over a period of several hours, the body's organs cease to function; at first slowly, then rapidly, the lungs collapse and the heart ceases to beat; finally, the brain is struck blank and is annihilated. If there is an observer it will appear to him—or her—as though the afflicted one has had a heart attack or stroke; the skin is slightly clammy, not fevered; and there is no expression of pain or even discomfort, for the toxin is a paralytic, and thus merciful. There are no wrenching stomach pains, hideous vomiting as in the case of cyanide or poisons that affect the gastrointestinal organs; stomach contents, if autopsied, will yield no information. The predator can observe his prey ingesting the toxin and can escape well in time to avoid witnessing even mild discomfort; it is advised that the predator take away with him his poisoned gift, so that there will be no detection. (Though this particular poison is all but undetectable by coroners and pathologists. Only a chemist who knew exactly what he was testing for could discover and identify this rare poison.) The aromatic lavender poisoned candles I'd left with my single female victim, a gratingly flirtatious bookseller in New Hope, Pennsylvania, had to work their dark magic in my absence and may have sickened, or even killed, more victims than were required . . . No extra poisoned cigars should be left behind, of course; and poisoned alcoholic drinks should be borne prudently away. Though it isn't likely that the poison would be discovered, there is no point in being careless.

My gracious host Aaron Neuhaus takes me to the fourth floor of Mystery, Inc. in a small elevator at the rear of the store that moves with the antique slowness of a European elevator; by breathing deeply, and trying not to think of the terrible darkness of that long-ago closet in which my cruel brother locked me, I am able to withstand a mild onslaught of claustrophobia. Only a thin film of perspiration on my forehead might betray my physical distress, if Aaron Neuhaus were to take particular notice; but, in his affably entertaining way, he is telling me about the history of Mystery, Inc.—"Quite a fascinating history, in fact. Someday, I must write a memoir along the lines of the classic *My Life in Crime*."

On the fourth floor Aaron Neuhaus asks me if I can guess where his office door is—and I am baffled at first, staring from one wall to another, for there is no obvious sign of a door. Only by calculating where an extra room must be, in architectural terms, can I guess correctly: between reproductions of Goya's Black Paintings, unobtrusively set in the wall, is a panel that exactly mimics the room's white walls that Aaron Neuhaus pushes inward with a boyish smile.

"Welcome to my *sanctum sanctorum*! There is another, purely utilitarian office downstairs, where the staff works. Very few visitors are invited *here*."

I feel a frisson of something like dread, and the deliciousness of dread, passing so close to Goya's icons of Hell.

But Aaron Neuhaus's office is warmly lighted and beautifully furnished, like the drawing room of an English country gentleman; there is even a small fire blazing in a fireplace. Hardwood floor, partly covered in an old, well-worn yet still elegant Chinese carpet. One wall is solid books, but very special, well-preserved antiquarian books; other walls are covered in framed artworks including an oil painting by Albert Pinkham Ryder that must have been a study for the artist's famous *The Race Track* (*Death on a Pale Horse*)—that dark-hued, ominous and yet beautiful oil painting by the most eccentric of nineteenth-century artists. A single high window overlooks, at a little distance, the rough waters of the Atlantic that appear in moonlight like shaken foil—the very view of the ocean I'd imagined Aaron Neuhaus might have.

Neuhaus's desk is made of dark, durable mahogany, with many drawers and pigeonholes; his chair is an old-fashioned swivel chair, with a well-worn crimson cushion. The desk top is comfortably cluttered with papers, letters, galleys, books; on it are a Tiffany lamp of exquisite colored glass and a life-sized carved ebony raven—no doubt a replica of Poe's Raven. (On the wall above the desk is a daguerreotype of Edgar Allan Poe looking pale-skinned and dissolute, with melancholy eyes and drooping mustache; the caption is *Edgar Allan Poe Creator of C. Auguste Dupin 1841.*)

Unsurprisingly, Neuhaus uses fountain pens, not ballpoint; he has an array of colored pencils, and an old-fashioned eraser. There is even a brass letter-opener in the shape of a dagger. On such a desk, Neuhaus's state-of-the-art console computer appears out of place as a sleek, synthetic monument in an historic graveyard.

"Please sit, Charles! I will start the cappuccino machine and hope the damned thing will work. It is very Italian—*temperamental.*"

I take a seat in a comfortable, well-worn leather chair facing Neuhaus's desk and with a view of the fireplace. I have brought my attaché case with the brass initials *CB*, to rest on my knees. Neuhaus fusses with his cappuccino machine, which is on a table behind his desk; he prefers cappuccino made with Bolivian coffee and skim milk, he says. "I have to confess to a mild addiction. There's a Starbucks in town but their cappuccino is nothing like mine."

Am I nervous? Pleasurably nervous? At the moment, I would prefer a glass of sherry to cappuccino!

My smile feels strained, though I am sure Aaron Neuhaus finds it affable, innocent. It is one of my stratagems to ply a subject with questions, to deflect any possible suspicion away from me, and Neuhaus enjoys answering my questions which are intelligent and well-informed, yet not overly intelligent and well-informed. The bookseller has not the slightest suspicion that he is dealing with an ambitious rival.

He is ruefully telling me that everyone who knew him, including an antiquarian bookseller uncle in Washington, D.C., thought it was a very naïve notion to try to sell works of art in a bookstore in New Hampshire—"But I thought I would give myself three or four years, as an experiment. And it has turned out surprisingly well, especially my online sales."

Online sales. These are the sales that particularly cut into my own. Politely, I ask Neuhaus how much of his business is now online?

Neuhaus seems surprised by my question. Is it too personal? Too—*professional*? I am hoping he will attribute such a question to the naïveté of Charles Brockden.

His reply is curious—"In useless, beautiful artworks, as in books, values wax and wane according to some unknown and unpredictable algorithm."

This is a striking if evasive remark. It is somehow familiar to me, and yet—I can't recall why. I must be smiling inanely at Aaron Neuhaus, not knowing how to reply. *Useless, beautiful . . . Algorithm . . .*

Waiting for the cappuccino to brew, Neuhaus adds another log to the fire and prods it with a poker. What a bizarre gargoyle, the handle of the poker! In tarnished brass, a peevish grinning imp. Neuhaus shows it to me with a smile—"I picked this up at an estate sale in Blue Hill, Maine, a few summers ago. Curious, isn't it?"

"Indeed, yes."

I am wondering why Aaron Neuhaus has shown this demonic little face to *me*.

Such envy I've been feeling in this cozy yet so beautifully furnished *sanctum sanctorum*! It is painful to recall my own business offices, such as they are, utilitarian and drab, with nothing sacred about them. Outdated computers, ubiquitous fluorescent lights, charmless furniture inherited from bygone tenants. Often in a bookstore of mine the business office is also a storage room crammed with filing cabinets, packing crates, even brooms and mops, plastic buckets and stepladders, and a lavatory in a corner. Everywhere, stacks of books rising from the floor like stalagmites. How ashamed I would be if Aaron Neuhaus were to see one of those!

I am thinking—*I will change nothing in this beautiful place. The very fountain pens on his desk will be mine. I will simply move in.*

Seeing that he has a very admiring and very curious visitor, Aaron Neuhaus is happy to chat about his possessions. The bookseller's pride in the privileged circumstances of his life is almost without ego—as one might take pleasure in any natural setting, like the ocean outside his window. Beside the large, stark daguerreotype of Poe are smaller photographs by the surrealist photographer Man Ray, of nude female figures in odd, awkward poses. Some of them are nude torsos lacking heads—very pale, marmoreal as sculpted forms. The viewer wonders uneasily: are these human beings, or mannequins? Are they human female *corpses*? Neuhaus tells me that the Man Ray photographs are taken from the photographer's *Tresor interdite* series of the 1930s—"Most of the work is inaccessible, in private collections, and never lent to museums." Beside the elegantly sinister Man Ray photographs, and very different from them, are crudely sensational crime photographs by the American photographer Weegee, taken in the 1930s and 1940s: stark portraits of men and women in the crises of their lives, beaten, bleeding, arrested and handcuffed, shot down in the street to lie sprawled, like one well-dressed mobster, facedown in their own blood.

"Weegee is the crudest of artists, but he is an artist. What is notable in such 'journalistic' art is the absence of the photographer from his work. You can't comprehend what, if anything, the photographer is thinking about these doomed people . . ."

Man Ray, yes. Weegee, no. I detest crudeness, in art as in life; but of course I don't indicate this to Aaron Neuhaus, whom I don't want to offend. The man is so boyishly enthusiastic, showing off his treasures to a potential customer.

Prominent in one of Neuhaus's glass-fronted cabinets is a complete set of the many volumes of the famous British criminologist William Roughead—"Each volume signed by Roughead"; also bound copies of the American detective pulps *Dime Detective, Black Mask,* and a copy of *The Black Lizard Big Book of Pulps.*

These were magazines in which such greats as Dashiell Hammett and Raymond Chandler published stories, Neuhaus tells me, as if I didn't know.

In fact, I am more interested in Neuhaus's collection of great works of the "Golden Era of Mystery"—signed first editions by John Dickson Carr, Agatha Christie, and S. S. Van Dine, among others. (Some of these must be worth more than $5,000 apiece, I would think.) Neuhaus confesses that he would be very reluctant to sell his 1888 first edition of *A Study in Scarlet* in its original paper covers (priced at $100,000), or a signed first edition of *The Return of Sherlock Holmes* (priced at $35,000); more reluctantly, his first edition of *The Hound of the Baskervilles*, inscribed and signed, with handsome illustrations of Holmes and Watson (priced at $65,000). He shows me one of his "priceless" possessions—a bound copy of the February 1827 issue of *Blackwood's Magazine* containing Thomas de Quincey's infamous essay, "On Murder Considered as One of the Fine Arts." Yet more impressively, he has the complete four volumes of the first edition (1794) of *Mysteries of Udolpho* (priced at $10,000). But the jewel of his collection, which he will never sell, he says, unless he is absolutely desperate for money, is the 1853 first edition, in original cloth with "sepia cabinet photograph of author" of Charles Dickens's *Bleak House* (priced at $75,000), signed by Dickens in his strong, assured hand, in ink that has scarcely faded!

"But this is something that would particularly interest you, 'Charles Brockden'"—Neuhaus chuckles, carefully taking from a shelf a very old book, encased in plastic, with a loose, faded binding and badly yellowed pages—Charles Brockden Brown's *Wieland; or The Transformation: An American Tale*, 1798.

This is extraordinary! One would expect to see such a rare book under lock and key in the special collections of a great university library, like Harvard.

For a moment I can't think how to reply. Neuhaus seems almost to be teasing me. It was a careless choice of a name, I suppose—"Charles Brockden." If I'd thought about it, of course I would have realized that a bookseller would be reminded of Charles Brockden Brown.

To disguise my confusion, I ask Aaron Neuhaus how much he is asking for this rare book, and Neuhaus says, "'Asking'—? I am not 'asking' any sum at all. It is not for sale."

Again, I'm not sure how to reply. Is Neuhaus laughing at me? Has he seen through my fictitious name, as through my disguise? I don't think that this is so, for his demeanor is good-natured; but the way in which he smiles at me, as if we are sharing a joke, makes me uneasy.

It's a relief when Neuhaus returns the book to its shelf, and locks up the glass-fronted cabinets. At last, the cappuccino is ready!

All this while, the fire has been making me warm—over-warm.

The ginger-colored whiskers that cover my jaws have begun to itch.

The heavy black plastic glasses, so much more cumbersome than my preferred wire-rim glasses, are leaving red marks on the bridge of my nose. Ah, I am looking forward to tearing both whiskers and glasses from my face with a cry of relief and victory in an hour—or ninety minutes—when I am departing Seabrook in my vehicle, south along the ocean road . . .

"Charles! Take care, it's very hot."

Not in a small cappuccino cup but in a hearty coffee mug, Aaron Neuhaus serves me the pungent brewed coffee, with its delightful frothed milk. The liquid is rich, very dark, scalding-hot as he has warned. I am wondering if I should take out of my attaché case the box of Lindt chocolates to share with my host, or whether it is just slightly too soon—I don't want to arouse his suspicion. If—when—Aaron Neuhaus eats one of these potent chocolates I will want to depart soon after, and our ebullient hour together will come to an abrupt conclusion. It is foolish of me perhaps, but I am almost thinking—well, it is not very realistic, but indeed, I am thinking—*Why could we not be partners? If I introduce myself as a serious book collector, one with unerring taste (if not unlimited resources, as he seems to have)—would not Aaron Neuhaus be impressed with me? Does he not, already, like me—and trust me?*

At the same time, my brain is pragmatically pursuing the more probable course of events: if I wait until Aaron Neuhaus lapses into a coma, I could take away with me a select few of his treasures, instead of having to wait until I can purchase Mystery, Inc. Though I am not a *common thief*, it has been exciting to see such rare items on display; almost, in a sense, dangled before me, by my clueless prey. Several of the less-rare items would be all that I could dare, for it would be a needless risk to take away, for instance, the Dickens first edition valued at $75,000—just the sort of greedy error that could entrap me.

"Are you often in these parts, Charles? I don't think that I have seen you in my store before."

"No, not often. In the summer, sometimes . . ." My voice trails off uncertainly. Is it likely that a bookstore proprietor would see, and take note, of every customer who comes into his store? Or am I interpreting Aaron Neuhaus too literally?

"My former wife and I sometimes drove to Boothbay, Maine. I believe we passed through this beautiful town, but did not stop." My voice is somewhat halting, but certainly sincere. Blindly I continue, "I am not married now—unfortunately. My wife had been my high school sweetheart but she did not share my predilection for precious old books, I'm afraid."

Is any of this true? I am hoping only that such words have the ring of plausibility.

"I've long been a lover of mysteries—in books and in life. It's wonderful to discover a fellow enthusiast, and in such a beautiful store . . ."

"It is! Always a wonderful discovery. I, too, am a lover of mysteries, of course—in life as in books."

Aaron Neuhaus laughs expansively. He has been blowing on his mug of cappuccino, for it is still steaming. I am intrigued by the subtle distinction of his remark, but would require some time to ponder it—if indeed it is a significant remark, and not just casual banter.

Thoughtfully, Neuhaus continues: "It is out of the profound mystery of life that 'mystery books' arise. And, in turn, 'mystery books' allow us to see the mystery of life more clearly, from perspectives not our own.'"

On a shelf behind the affable bookseller's desk are photographs that I have been trying to see more clearly. One, in an antique oval frame, is of an extraordinarily beautiful, young, black-haired woman—could this be Mrs. Neuhaus? I think it must be, for in another photograph she and a youthful Aaron Neuhaus are together, in wedding finery—a most attractive couple.

There is something profoundly demoralizing about this sight—such a beautiful woman, married to this man not so very different from myself! Of course—(I am rapidly calculating, cantilevering to a new, objective perspective)—the young bride is no longer young, and would be, like her husband, in her early sixties. No doubt Mrs. Neuhaus is still quite beautiful. It is not impossible to think that, in the devastated aftermath of losing her husband, the widow might not be adverse, in time, to remarriage with an individual who shares so much of her late husband's interests, and has taken over Mystery, Inc. . . . Other photographs, surely family photos, are less interesting, though suggesting that Neuhaus is a "family man" to some degree. (If we had more time, I would ask about these personal photos; but I suppose I will find out eventually who Neuhaus's relatives are.)

Also on the shelf behind Neuhaus's desk is what appears to be a homemade artwork—a bonsai-sized tree (fashioned from a coat hanger?)—upon which small items have been hung: a man's signet ring, a man's wristwatch, a brass belt buckle, a pocket watch with a gold chain. If I didn't know that Neuhaus had no children, I would presume that this amateurish "art" has found a place amid the man's treasures which its artistry doesn't seem to merit.

At last, the cappuccino is not so scalding. It is still hot, but very delicious. Now I am wishing badly that I'd prepared a box of macaroons, more appropriate here than chocolate truffles.

As if I have only just now recalled it, I remove the Lindt box from my attaché case. An unopened box, I suggest to Aaron Neuhaus—freshly purchased and not a chocolate missing.

(It is true, I am reluctant to hurry our fascinating conversation, but—there is a duty here that must be done.)

In a display of playful horror Neuhaus half-hides his eyes— "Chocolate truffles—my favorite chocolates—and my favorite truffles! Thank you, Charles, but—I should not. My dear wife will expect me to be reasonably hungry for dinner." The bookseller's voice wavers, as if he is hoping to be encouraged.

"Just one chocolate won't make any difference, Aaron. And your dear wife will never know, if you don't tell her."

Neuhaus is very amusing as he takes one of the chocolate truffles—(from the first, poisoned row)—with an expression both boyishly greedy and guilty. He sniffs it with delight and seems about to bite into it—then lays it on his desk top as if temporarily, in a show of virtue. He winks at me as at a fellow conspirator—"You are quite right, my dear wife needn't know. There is much in marriage that might be kept from a spouse, for her own good. Though possibly, I should bring my wife one of these also—if you could spare another, Charles?"

"Why of course—but—take more than one . . . Please help yourself—of course."

This is disconcerting. But there is no way for me to avoid offering Neuhaus the box again, this time somewhat awkwardly, turning it so that he is led to choose a chocolate truffle out of a row of nonpoisoned truffles. And I will eat one with much appetite, so that Neuhaus is tempted to eat his.

How warm I am! And these damned whiskers itching!

As if he has only just thought of it, Aaron Neuhaus excuses himself to call his wife—on an old-fashioned black dial phone, talisman of another era. He lowers his voice out of courtesy, not because he doesn't want his visitor to overhear. "Darling? Just to alert you, I will be a little late tonight. A most fascinating customer has dropped by—whom I don't want to shortchange." *Most fascinating.* I am flattered by this, though saddened.

So tenderly does Neuhaus speak to his wife, I feel an almost overwhelming wave of pity for him, and for her; yet, more powerfully, a wave of envy, and anger. *Why does this man deserve that beautiful woman and her love, while I have no one—no love—at all?*

It is unjust, and it is unfair. It is intolerable.

Neuhaus tells his wife he will be home, he believes, by at least 8:30 P.M. Again it is flattering to me, that Neuhaus thinks so well of me; he doesn't plan to send me away for another hour. Another wife might be annoyed by such a call, but the beautiful (and mysterious) Mrs. Neuhaus does not object. "Yes! Soon. I love you too, darling." Neuhaus unabashedly murmurs these intimate words, like one who isn't afraid to acknowledge emotion.

The chocolate truffle, like the cappuccino, is indeed delicious. My mouth waters even as I eat it. I am hoping that Neuhaus will devour his, as he clearly wants to; but he has left both truffles untouched for the moment, while he sips the cappuccino. There is something touchingly childlike in this procrastination—putting off a treat, if but for a moment. I will not allow myself to think of the awful possibility that Neuhaus will eat the unpoisoned truffle and bring the poisoned truffle home to his wife.

To avoid this, I may offer Neuhaus the entire box to take home to his wife. In that way, both the owner of Mystery, Inc. and the individual who would inherit it upon his death will depart this earth. Purchasing the store from another, less personally involved heir might be, in fact, an easier stratagem.

I have asked Aaron Neuhaus who his customers are in this out-of-the-way place, and he tells me that he has a number of "surprisingly faithful, stubbornly loyal" customers who come to his store from as far away as Boston, even New York City, in good weather at least. There are local regulars, and there are the summertime customers—"Mystery, Inc. is one of the most popular shops in town, second only to Starbucks." Still, most of his sales in the past twenty-five years have been mail-order and online; the online orders are more or less continuous, emails that come in through the night from his "considerable overseas clientele."

This is a cruel blow! I'm sure that I have *no overseas clientele* at all.

Yet it isn't possible to take offense, for Aaron Neuhaus is not boasting so much as speaking matter-of-factly. Ruefully I am thinking—*The man can't help being superior. It is ironic, he must be punished for something that is not his fault.*

Like my brother, I suppose. Who had to be punished for something that wasn't his fault: a mean-spirited soul, envious and malicious regarding *me*. Though I will regret Aaron Neuhaus's fate, I will never regret my brother's fate.

Still, Aaron Neuhaus has put off eating his chocolate truffle with admirable restraint! By this time I have had a second, and Neuhaus is preparing two more cups of cappuccino. The caffeine is having a bracing effect upon my blood. Like an admiring interviewer I am asking my host where his interest in mystery derives, and Neuhaus replies that he fell under the spell of mystery as a young child, if not an infant—"I think it had to do with my astonishment at peering out of my crib and seeing faces peering at me. Who were they? My mother whom I did not yet know was my mother—my father whom I did not yet know was my father? These individuals must have seemed like giants to me—mythic figures—as in the *Odyssey*." He pauses, with a look of nostalgia. "Our lives are odysseys, obviously—continuous, ever-unexpected adventures. Except we are not journeying home, like Odysseus, but journeying away from home inexorably, like the Hubble universe."

What is this?—"Hubble universe"? I'm not sure that I fully understand what Aaron Neuhaus is saying, but there is no doubt that my companion is speaking from the heart.

As a boy he fell under the spell of mystery fiction—boys' adventure, Sherlock Holmes, Ellery Queen, Mark Twain's *Pudd'nhead Wilson*—and by the age of thirteen he'd begun reading true crime writers (like the esteemed Roughead) of the kind most readers don't discover until adulthood. Though he has a deep and enduring love for American hard-boiled fiction, his long-abiding love is for Wilkie Collins and Charles Dickens— "Writers not afraid of the role coincidence plays in our lives, and not afraid of over-the-top melodrama."

This is true. Coincidence plays far more of a role in our lives than we (who believe in free will) wish to concede. And lurid, over-the-top melodrama, perhaps a rarity in most lives, is but inescapable at one time or another.

Next, I ask Aaron Neuhaus how he came to purchase his bookstore, and he tells me with a nostalgic smile that indeed it was an accident—a "marvelous coincidence"—that one day when he was driving along the coast to visit relatives in Maine, he happened to stop in Seabrook—"And there was this gem of a bookstore, right on High Street, in a row of beautiful old brownstones. The store wasn't quite as it is now, slightly run-down, and neglected, yet with an intriguing sign out front—*Mystery, Inc.: M. Rackham Books*. Within minutes I saw the potential of the store and the location, and I fell in love with something indefinable in the very air of Seabrook, New Hampshire."

At this time, in 1982, Aaron Neuhaus owned a small bookstore that specialized in mystery, detective, and crime fiction in the West Village, on Bleecker Street; though he worked in the store as many as one hundred hours a week, with two assistants, he was chafing under the burden of circumscribed space, high rent and high taxes, relentless book-theft, and a clientele that included homeless derelicts and junkies who wandered into the store looking for public lavatories or for a place to sleep. His wife yearned to move out of New York City and into the country—she had an education degree and was qualified to teach school, but did not want to teach in the New York City public school system, nor did Neuhaus want her to. And so Neuhaus made a decision almost immediately to acquire the Seabrook bookstore—"If it were humanly possible."

It was an utterly impulsive decision, Neuhaus said. He had not even consulted with his dear wife. Yet, it was unmistakable—"Like falling in love at first sight."

The row of brownstones on High Street was impressive, but *Mystery, Inc: M. Rackham Books* was not so impressive. In the first-floor bay window were displayed the predictable bestsellers one would see in any bookstore window of the time, but here amid a scattering of dead flies; inside, most of the books were trade paperbacks with lurid covers and little literary distinction. The beautiful floor-to-ceiling mahogany bookshelves—carpentry which would cost a fortune in 1982—were in place, the hammered-tin ceiling, hardwood floors. But so far as the young bookseller could see the store offered no first editions, rare or unusual books, or artworks; the second floor was used for storage, and the upper two floors were rented out. Still, the store was ideally situated on Seabrook's main street overlooking the harbor, and it seemed likely that the residents of Seabrook were generally affluent, well-educated and discerning.

Not so exciting, perhaps, as a store on Bleecker Street in the West Village—yet, it may be that excitement is an overrated experience if you are a serious bookseller.

"After I'd been in the store for a few minutes, however, I could feel—something . . . An atmosphere of tension like the air preceding a storm. The place was virtually deserted on a balmy spring day. There were loud voices at the rear. There came then—in a hurry—the proprietor to speak eagerly with me, like a man who is dying of loneliness. When I introduced myself as a fellow bookseller, from New York City, Milton Rackham all but seized my hand. He was a large, soft-bodied, melancholic older gentleman whose adult son worked with him, or for him. At first Rackham talked enthusiastically of books—his favorites, which included, not surprisingly, the great works of Wilkie Collins, Dickens, and Conan Doyle. Then he began to speak with more emotion of how he'd been a young professor of classics at Harvard who, with his young wife who'd shared his love for books and bookstores, decided to quit the 'sterile, self-absorbed' academic world to fulfill a life's dream of buying a bookstore in a small town and making it into a 'very special place.' Unfortunately his beloved wife had died after only a few years, and his unmarried son worked with him now in the store; in recent years, the son had become 'inward, troubled, unpredictable, strange—a *brooding personality*.'"

It was surprising to Neuhaus, and somewhat embarrassing, that the older bookseller should speak so openly to a stranger of these personal and painful matters. And the poor man spoke disjointedly, unhappily, lowering his voice so that his heavyset, ponytailed son (whom Neuhaus glimpsed shelving books at the rear of the store with a particular sort of vehemence, as if he were throwing livestock into vats of steaming scalding water) might not hear. In a hoarse whisper Rackham indicated to Neuhaus that the store would soon be for sale—"To the proper buyer."

"Now, I was truly shocked. But also . . . excited. For I'd already fallen in love with the beautiful old brownstone, and here was its proprietor, declaring that it was for sale."

Neuhaus smiles with a look of bittersweet nostalgia. It is enviable that a man can glance back over his life, and present the crucial episodes in his life, not with pain or regret but with—nostalgia!

Next, the young visitor invited Milton Rackham to speak in private with him, in his office—"Not here: Rackham's office was on the first floor, a cubbyhole of a room containing one large, solid piece of furniture, this very mahogany desk, amid a chaos of books, galleys, boxes, unpaid bills and invoices, dust balls, and desperation"—about the bookstore, what it might cost with or without a mortgage; when it would be placed on the market, and how soon the new owner could take possession. Rackham brandished a bottle of whiskey, and poured drinks for them in "clouded" glasses; he searched for, and eventually found, a cellophane package of stale sourballs, which he offered to his guest. It was painful to see how Rackham's hands shook. And alarming to see how the older man's mood swerved from embittered to elated, from anxious to exhilarated, as he spoke excitedly to his young visitor, often interrupting himself with laughter, like one who has not spoken with anyone in a long time. He confided in Neuhaus that he didn't trust his son—'Not with our finances, not with book orders, not with maintaining the store, and not with my life.' He'd once been very close to the boy, as he called him, but their relationship had altered significantly since his son's fortieth birthday, for no clear reason. Unfortunately, he had no other recourse than to keep his son on at the store as he couldn't afford to pay an employee a competitive wage, and the boy, who'd dropped out of Williams College midway through his freshman year, for 'mental' reasons, would have no other employment—'It is a tragic trap, fatherhood! And my wife and I had been so happy in our innocence, long ago.'" Neuhaus shudders, recalling.

"As Rackham spoke in his lowered voice I had a sudden fantasy of the son rushing into the office swinging a hand ax at us . . . I felt absolutely chilled—terrified . . . I swear, I could see that ax . . . It was as if the bookstore were haunted by something that had not yet happened."

Haunted by something that had not yet happened. Despite the heat from the fireplace, I am feeling chilled too. I glance over my shoulder to see that the door, or rather the moving panel, is shut. No one will rush in upon us here in Aaron Neuhaus's *sanctum sanctorum*, wielding an ax . . .

Nervously, I have been sipping my cappuccino, which has cooled somewhat. I am finding it just slightly hard to swallow—my mouth is oddly dry, perhaps because of nerves. The taste of the cappuccino is extraordinary: rich, dark, delicious. It is the frothy milk that makes the coffee so special. Neuhaus remarks that it isn't ordinary milk but goat's milk, for a sharper flavor.

Neuhaus continues—"It was from Milton Rackham that I acquired the complete set of William Roughead which, for some eccentric reason, he'd been keeping in a cabinet at the back of the store under lock and key. I asked him why this wonderful set of books was hidden away, why it wasn't prominently displayed and for sale, and Rackham said coldly, with an air of reproach, 'Not all things in a bookseller's life are for sale, sir.' Suddenly, with no warning, the old gentleman seemed to be hostile to me. I was shocked by his tone."

Neuhaus pauses, as if he is still shocked, to a degree.

"Eventually, Rackham would reveal to me that he was hoarding other valuable first editions—some of these I have shown you, the 'Golden Age' items, which I acquired as part of the store's stock. And the first-edition *Mysteries of Udolpho*—which in his desperation to sell he practically gave away to me. And a collection of antique maps and globes, in an uncatalogued jumble on the second floor—a collection he'd inherited, he said, from the previous bookseller. Why on earth would anyone hoard these valuable items—I couldn't resist asking—and Rackham told me, again in a hostile voice, 'We gentlemen don't wear our hearts on our sleeves, do we? Do *you*?'"

It is uncanny, when Neuhaus mimics his predecessor's voice, I seem—almost—to be hearing the voice of another.

"Such a strange man! And yet, in a way—a way I have never quite articulated to anyone, before now—Milton Rackham has come to seem to me a kind of *paternal figure* in my life. He'd looked upon me as a kind of son, or rescuer—seeing that his own son had turned against him."

Neuhaus is looking pensive, as if remembering something unpleasant. And I am feeling anxious, wishing that my companion would devour the damned chocolate truffle as he clearly wishes to do.

"Charles, it's a poor storyteller who leaps ahead of his story—but—I have to tell you, before going on, that my vision of Rackham's 'brooding' son murdering him with an ax turned out to be prophetic—that is, true. It would happen exactly three weeks to the day after I'd first stepped into the bookstore—at a time when Rackham and I were negotiating the sale of the property, mostly by phone. I was nowhere near Seabrook, and received an astounding call . . ." Neuhaus passes his hand over his eyes, shaking his head.

This is a surprising revelation! For some reason, I am quite taken aback. That a bookseller was murdered in this building, even if not in this very room, and by his own son—this is a bit of a shock.

"And so—in some way—Mystery, Inc. is haunted?"—my question is uncertain.

Neuhaus laughs, somewhat scornfully—"Haunted—now? Of course not. Mystery, Inc. is a very successful, even legendary bookstore of its kind in New England. *You* would not know that, Charles, since you are not in the trade."

These words aren't so harsh as they might seem, for Neuhaus is smiling at me as one might smile at a foolish or uninformed individual for whom one feels some affection, and is quick to forgive. And I am eager to agree—I am not in *the trade*.

"The story is even more awful, for the murderer—the deranged 'boy'—managed to kill himself also, in the cellar of the store—a very dark, dank, dungeon-like space even today, which I try to avoid as much as possible. (Talk of 'haunted'! That is the likely place, not the bookstore itself.) The hand ax was too dull for the task, it seems, so the 'boy' cut his throat with a box cutter—one of those razor-sharp objects no bookstore is without." Casually Neuhaus reaches out to pick up a box cutter, that has been hidden from my view by a stack of bound galleys on his desk; as if, for one not in the "trade," a box cutter would need to be identified. (Though I am quite familiar with box cutters it is somewhat disconcerting to see one in this elegantly furnished office—lying on Aaron Neuhaus's desk!) "Following this double tragedy the property fell into the possession of a mortgage company, for it had been heavily mortgaged. I was able to complete the sale within a few weeks, for a quite reasonable price since no one else seemed to want it." Neuhaus chuckles grimly.

"As I'd said, I have leapt ahead of my story, a bit. There is more to tell about poor Milton Rackham that is of interest. I asked him how he'd happened to learn of the bookstore here in Seabrook and he told me of how 'purely by chance' he'd discovered the store in the fall of 1957—he'd been driving along the coast on his way to Maine and stopped in Seabrook, on High Street, and happened to see the bookstore—Slater's Mystery Books & Stationers it was called—'It was such a vision!—the bay windows gleaming in the sun, and the entire block of brownstones so attractive.' A good part of Slater's merchandise was stationery, quite high-quality stationery, and other supplies of that sort, but there was an excellent collection of books as well, hardcover and paperback; not just the usual popular books but somewhat esoteric titles as well, by Robert W. Chambers, Bram Stoker, M. R. James, Edgar Wallace, Oscar Wilde (*Salome*), H. P. Lovecraft. Slater seemed to have been a particular admirer of Erle Stanley Gardner, Rex Stout, Josephine Tey, and Dorothy L. Sayers, writers whom Milton Rackham admired also. The floor-to-ceiling mahogany bookshelves were in place—cabinetry that would cost a fortune at the time, as Rackham remarked again. And there were odd, interesting things stocked in the store like antique maps, globes—'A kind of treasure trove, as in an older relative's attic in which you might spend long rainy afternoons under a spell.' Rackham told me that he wandered through the store with 'mounting excitement'—feeling that it was already known to him, in a way; through a window, he looked out toward the Atlantic Ocean, and felt the 'thrill of its great beauty.' Indeed, Milton Rackham would tell me that it had been 'love at first sight'—as soon as he'd glimpsed the bookstore.

"As it turned out, Amos Slater had been contemplating sell-ing the store, which had been a family inheritance; though, as he said, he continued to 'love books and bookselling' it was no longer with the passion of youth, and so he hoped to soon re-tire. Young Milton Rackham was stunned by this good fortune. Three weeks later, with his wife's enthusiastic support, he made an offer to Amos Slater for the property, and the offer was ac-cepted almost immediately."

Neuhaus speaks wonderingly, like a man who is recounting a somewhat fantastical tale he hopes his listeners will believe, for it is important for them to believe it.

"'My wife had a faint premonition'—this is Milton Rackham speaking—'that something might be wrong, but I paid no atten-tion. I was heedless then, in love with my sweet young wife, and excited by the prospect of walking away from pious Harvard—(where it didn't look promising that I would get tenure)—and taking up a purer life, as I thought it, in the booksellers' trade. And so, Mildred and I arranged for a thirty-year mortgage, and made our initial payment through the Realtor, and on our first visit to the store as the new owners—when Amos Slater pre-sented us with the keys to the building—it happened that my wife innocently asked Amos Slater how he'd come to own the store, and Amos told her a most disturbing tale, like one eager to get something off his chest . . .

"'Slater's Books'—this is Amos Slater speaking, as reported by Milton Rackham to me—'had been established by his grandfa-ther Barnabas in 1912. Slater's grandfather was a lover of books, rather than humankind'—though one of his literary friends was Ambrose Bierce who'd allegedly encouraged Barnabas's writing of fiction. Slater told Rackham a bizarre tale that at the age of eleven he'd had a 'powerful vision'—dropping by his grandfather's bookstore one day after school, he'd found the store empty—'No customers, no salesclerks, and no Grandfather, or so I thought. But then, looking for Grandfather, I went into the cellar—I turned on a light and—there was Grandfather hanging from a beam, his body strangely straight, and very still; and his face turned mercifully from me, though there was no doubt who it was. For a long moment I stood paralyzed—I could not believe what I was seeing. I could not even scream, I was so frightened . . . My grandfather Barnabas and I had not been close. Grandfather had hardly seemed to take notice of me except sneeringly—"Is it a little boy, or a little girl? *What is it?*" Grandfather Slater was a strange man, as people said—short-tempered yet also rather cold and detached—passionate about some things, but indifferent about most things—determined to make his book and stationery store a success but contemptuous with most customers, and very cynical about human nature. It appeared that he had dragged a stepladder beneath the beam in the cellar, tied a hemp noose around his neck, climbed up the ladder and kicked the ladder away beneath him—he must have died a horrible, strangulated death, gasping for breath and kicking and writhing for many minutes . . . Seeing the hanged body of my grandfather was one of the terrible shocks of my life. I don't know quite what happened . . . I fainted, I think—then forced myself to crawl to the steps, and made my way upstairs—ran for help . . . I remember screaming on High Street . . . People hurried to help me, I brought them back into the store and down into the cellar, but there was no one there—no rope hanging from the beam, and no overturned stepladder. Again, it was one of the shocks of my life—I was only eleven, and could not comprehend what was happening . . . Eventually, Grandfather was discovered a few doors away at the Bell, Book & Candle Pub, calmly drinking port and eating a late lunch of pigs' knuckles and sauerkraut. He'd spent most of the day doing inventory, he said, on the second floor of the store, and hadn't heard any commotion.

"Poor Amos Slater never entirely recovered from the trauma of seeing his grandfather's hanged body in the cellar of the bookstore, or rather the vision of the hanged body—so everyone who knew him believed . . .

"As Milton Rackham reported to me, he'd learned from Amos Slater that the grandfather Barnabas had been a 'devious' person who defrauded business partners, seduced and betrayed naïve, virginal Seabrook women, and, it was charged more than once, 'pilfered' their savings; he'd amassed a collection of first editions and rare books, including a copy of Charles Brockden Brown's *Wieland*—such treasures he claimed to have bought at estate auctions and sales, but some observers believed he had taken advantage of distraught widows and grief-stricken heirs, or possibly he'd stolen outright. Barnabas had married a well-to-do local woman several years his senior to whom he was cruel and coercive, who'd died at the age of fifty-two of 'suspicious' causes. Nothing was *proven*—so Amos Slater had been told. 'Growing up, I had to see how my father was intimidated by my grandfather Barnabas, who mocked him as "less than a man" for not standing up to him. "Where is the son and heir whom I deserve? Who are these weaklings who surround me?"—the old man would rage. Grandfather Barnabas was one to play practical jokes on friends and enemies alike; he had a particularly nasty trick of giving people sweet treats laced with laxatives . . . Once, our minister at the Episcopal church here in Seabrook was stricken with terrible diarrhea during Sunday services, as a consequence of plum tarts Barnabas had given him and his family; another time, my mother, who was Grandfather's daughter-in-law, became deathly sick after drinking apple cider laced with insecticide my grandfather had put in the cider—or so it was suspected. (Eventually, Grandfather admitted to putting "just a few drops" of DDT into the cider his daughter-in-law would be drinking; he hadn't known it was DDT, he claimed, but had thought it was a liquid laxative. "In any case, I didn't mean it to be *fatal*." And he spread his fingers, and laughed—it was blood-chilling to hear him.)' Yet, Barnabas Slater had an 'obsessive love' of books—mystery-detective books, crime books—and had actually tried to write fiction himself, in the mode of Edgar Allan Poe, it was said.

"Amos Slater told Rackham that he'd wanted to flee Seabrook and the ghastly legacy of Barnabas Slater but—somehow—he'd had no choice about taking over his grandfather's bookstore—

'When Grandfather died, I was designated his heir in his will. My father was ill by that time, and would not long survive. I felt resigned, and accepted my inheritance, though I knew at the time such an inheritance was like a tombstone—if the tombstone toppled over, and you were not able to climb out of the grave in which you'd been prematurely buried, like one of those victims in Poe . . . Another cruel thing my grandfather boasted of doing—(who knows if the wicked old man was telling the truth, or merely hoping to upset his listeners)—was experimentation with exotic toxins: extracting venom from poisonous frogs that was a colorless, tasteless, odorless milky liquid that could be added to liquids like hot chocolate and hot coffee without being detected . . . The frogs are known as poison dart frogs, found in the United States in the Florida Everglades, it is said . . .

""The poison dart frog's venom is so rare, no coroner or pathologist could identify it even if there were any suspicion of foul play—which there wasn't likely to be. A victim's symptoms did not arouse suspicion. Within minutes (as Grandfather boasted) the venom begins to attack the central nervous system—the afflicted one shivers, and shudders, and can't seem to swallow, for his mouth is very dry; soon, hallucinations begin; and paralysis and coma; within eight to ten hours, the body's organs begin to break down, slowly at first and then rapidly, by which time the victim is unconscious and unaware of what is happening to him. Liver, kidneys, lungs, heart, brain—all collapse from within. If observed, the victim seems to be suffering some sort of attack—heart attack, stroke—'fainting'—there are no gastrointestinal symptoms, no horrible attacks of vomiting. If the stomach is pumped, there is nothing—no "food poisoning." The victim simply fades away . . . it is a merciful death, as deaths go.'" Aaron Neuhaus pauses as if the words he is recounting, with seeming precision, from memories of long ago, are almost too much for him to absorb.

"Then, Milton Rackham continued—'The irony is, as Slater told it, after a long and surprisingly successful life as a small-town bookseller of quality books, Barnabas Slater did hang himself, it was surmised out of boredom and self-disgust at the age of seventy-two—in the cellar of Slater's Books exactly as his grandson Amos had envisioned. Scattered below his hanging body were carefully typed, heavily edited manuscript pages of what appeared to be several mystery-detective novels—no one ever made the effort of collating the pages and reading them. It was a family decision to inter the unpublished manuscripts with Grandfather.'

"Isn't this tale amazing? Have you ever heard anything so bizarre, Charles? I mean—in actual life? In utter solemnity poor Milton Rackham recounted it to me, as he'd heard it from Amos Slater. I could sympathize that Rackham was a nervous wreck—he was concerned that his son might do violence against him, and he had to contend with being the proprietor of a store in which a previous proprietor had hanged himself! He went on to say, as Slater had told him, that it had been the consensus in Seabrook that no one knew if Barnabas had actually poisoned anyone fatally—he'd played his little pranks with laxatives and insecticide—but the 'poison dart frog venom' was less evident. Though people did die of somewhat mysterious 'natural causes,' in the Slater family, from time to time. Several persons who knew Barnabas well said that the old man had often said that there are some human beings so vile, they don't deserve to live; but he'd also said, with a puckish wink, that he 'eradicated' people for no particular reason, at times. 'Good, not-so-good, evil'—the classic murderer does not discriminate. Barnabas particularly admired the De Quincey essay 'On Murder Considered As One of the Fine Arts' that makes the point that no reason is required for murder, in fact to have a reason is to be rather vulgar—so Barnabas believed also. Excuse me, Charles? Is something wrong?"

"Why, I—I am—utterly confused . . ."

"Have you lost your way? My predecessor was Milton Rackham, from whom I bought this property; his predecessor was Amos Slater, from whom he, Rackham, bought the property; and *his predecessor* was a gentleman named Barnabas Slater who seems to have hanged himself in the cellar here—for which reason, as I'd mentioned a few minutes ago, I try to avoid the damned place, as much as possible. (I send my employees down, instead! They don't mind.) I think you were reacting to Barnabas Slater's philosophy, that no reason is required for murder, especially for murder as an 'art form.'"

"But—why would anyone kill for no reason?"

"Why would anyone kill *for a reason*?" Neuhaus smiles, eloquently. "It seems to me that Slater's grandfather Barnabas may have extracted the essence of 'mystery' from life, as he was said to have extracted venom from the venomous frog. The act of killing is complete in itself, and requires no reason—like any work of art. Yet, if one is looking for a reason, one is likely to kill to protect oneself—one's territory. Our ancestors were fearful and distrustful of enemies, strangers—they were 'xenophobic'—'paranoid.' If a stranger comes into your territory, and behaves with sinister intent, or even behaves without sinister intent, you are probably better off dispatching him than trying to comprehend him, and possibly making a fatal mistake. In the distant past, before God was love, such mistakes could lead to the extinction of an entire species—so it is that *Homo sapiens*, the preemptive species, prefers to err by over-caution, not under-caution."

I am utterly confounded by these words, spoken by my affable companion in a matter-of-fact voice. And that smile!—it is so boyish, and magnanimous. Almost, I can't speak, but stutter feebly.

"That is a—a—surprising thing to say, for you . . . Aaron. That is a somewhat cynical thing to say, I think . . ."

Aaron Neuhaus smiles as if, another time, I am a very foolish person whom he must humor. "Not at all 'cynical,' Charles— why would you think so? If you are an aficionado of mystery-detective-crime fiction, you know that someone, in fact many people, and many of them 'innocent,' must die for the sake of the art—for *mystery's sake*. That is the bedrock of our business: Mystery, Inc. Some of us are booksellers, and some of us are consumers, or are consumed. But all of us have our place in the noble trade."

There is a ringing in my ears. My mouth is so very dry, it is virtually impossible to swallow. My teeth are chattering for I am very cold. Except for its frothy remains my second cup of cappuccino is empty—I have set it on Neuhaus's desk, but so shakily that it nearly falls over.

Neuhaus regards me closely with concerned eyes. On his desk, the carved ebony raven is regarding me as well. Eyes very sharp! I am shivering—despite the heat from the fire. I am very cold—except the whiskers on my jaws feel very hot. I am thinking that I must protect myself—the box of Lindt's chocolate truffles is my weapon, but I am not sure how to employ it. Several of the chocolate truffles are gone, but the box is otherwise full; many remain yet to be eaten.

I know that I have been dismissed. I must leave—it is time.

I am on my feet. But I am feeling weak, unreal. The bookseller escorts me out of his office, graciously murmuring, "You are leaving, Charles? Yes, it is getting late. You might come by at another time, and we can see about these purchases of yours. And bring a check—please. Take care on the stairs!—a spiral staircase can be treacherous." My companion has been very kind even in dismissing me, and has put the attaché case into my hands.

How eager I am to leave this hellish, airless place! I am gripping the railing of the spiral staircase, but having difficulty descending. Like a dark rose a vertigo is opening in my brain. My mouth is very dry and also very cold and numb—my tongue feels as if it is swollen, and without sensation. My breath comes ever more quickly, yet without bringing oxygen to my brain. In the semidarkness my legs seem to buckle and I fall—I am falling, helpless as a rag doll—down the remainder of the metal stairs, wincing with pain.

Above me, two flights up, a man is calling with what sounds like genuine concern—"Charles? Are you all right? Do you need help?"

"No! No thank you—*I do not* . . ."

My voice is hoarse, my words are hardly audible.

Outside, I am temporarily revived by cold, fresh wind from the ocean. There is the smell and taste of the ocean. Thank God! I will be all right now, I think. I am safe now, I will escape . . . I've left the Lindt chocolates behind, so perhaps—(the predator's thoughts come frantically now)—the poison will have its effect, whether I am able to benefit from it or not.

In the freezing air of my vehicle, with numbed fingers I am jamming a misshapen key into the slot of the ignition that appears to be too small for it. How can this be? I don't understand.

Yet, eventually, as in a dream of dogged persistence, the key goes into the slot, and the engine comes reluctantly to life.

Alongside the moonstruck Atlantic I am driving on a two-lane highway. If I am driving, I must be all right. My hands grip the steering wheel that seems to be moving—wonderfully—of its own volition. A strange, fierce, icy-cold paralysis is blooming in my brain, in my spinal cord, in all the nerves of my body, that is so fascinating to me, my eyes begin to close, to savor it.

Am I asleep? Am I sleeping while driving? Have I never left the place in which I dwell and have I dreamt my visit to Mystery, Inc. in Seabrook, New Hampshire? I have plotted my assault upon the legendary Aaron Neuhaus of Mystery, Inc. Books—I have injected the chocolate truffles with the care of a malevolent surgeon—how is it possible that I might fail? *I cannot fail.*

But now I realize—to my horror—I have no idea in which direction I am driving. I should be headed south, I think—the Atlantic should be on my left. But cold moon-glittering waters lap dangerously high on both sides of the highway. Churning waves have begun to rush across the road, into which I have no choice but to drive.

Acknowledgments

"The Doll-Master" originally appeared in *The Doll Collection*, ed. Ellen Datlow (Tor Books, 2015).

"Soldier" originally appeared in the *Idaho Review* (2015).

"Gun Accident" originally appeared in *Ellery Queen* (2015).

"Equatorial" originally appeared in *Ellery Queen* (2014).

"Big Momma" originally appeared in *Ellery Queen* (2016).

"Mystery, Inc." originally appeared in The Mysterious Bookshop's *Bibliomystery* series (2015).